Copyright @ 2024 by Anthony Grace.

The right of Anthony Grace to be identified as the author of this work has been asserted in accordance with the Copyright, Design and Patents Act 1988.

All rights reserved.

This book, or any portion thereof, may not be reproduced or used in any manner whatsoever without the express, written permission of the author, except for the use of brief quotations in a book review.

The characters in this book are entirely fictitious. Any resemblance to actual persons living or dead is entirely coincidental.

CHAPTER ONE
THE FINAL FAREWELL

Cole Burroughs was the last man standing.

The funeral had ended abruptly, a sudden downpour triggering a rapidly departing procession. Coats had been fastened, umbrellas raised, excuses made. Walk, don't run. Show some respect because this wouldn't last forever. No offence to all those who had sadly departed, but a funeral was just an inconvenient interruption in the daily routines of those still living. Sad, yes, sometimes tragically so, but the sorrow would soon pass. Tears would dry, the grief would subside and life would get back to normal. One hour, two tops, before something else swooped in and occupied their thoughts. Better still, stick it on social media and let the entire world offer their condolences. An emoji-fest of broken hearts and glum faces. A week would fly by and, as if by magic, the funeral would be nothing but a distant memory. Painfully bleak, but easy to ignore when bogged down by the mundanity of everyday life.

And yet everyday life was no longer something that Cole Burroughs would ever experience again.

Lifting a hand, he wiped the rain away from his eyes. Held his ground by the graveside. Not through stubbornness, but obligation. Besides, it wasn't as if he had anywhere else to go. No warm welcome waiting for him at home. Not even a cross word or slamming door.

Just silence. And the constant menace of his own thoughts lurking just beneath the surface. The thoughts that ate away at him like greedy woodworm in a rotting door frame. They had their own agenda, of course. His thoughts, not the woodworm. They pleaded with him not to mourn. Don't wallow in self-pity, but fight back. Seek some kind of retribution. It wasn't as if it was out of his comfort zone, after all. Violence came naturally. He would barely bat an eyelid.

A hand on Cole's shoulder was enough to send his thoughts scattering for cover. Firm but friendly, he half-imagined that he could just ignore it and it would go away. No chance of that happening, though. By the feel of things, the hand was there to stay. And with it came a voice. Like the hand, it was firm but friendly.

'How you holding up?'

Cole heard the words, recognised each individual syllable, but didn't fully process the sentence.

'You'll freeze to death out here. Bloody weather. Always pissing it down in Stainmouth. Can't even get outside to mow the lawn at the moment. Garden's like a ruddy jungle. Venture too deep and you'd struggle to find your way back to the house …'

The words petered out, only to be followed by a sigh. A long, weary sigh that turned into an even longer, lingering silence.

'I don't know what to say.' The voice was back, but the words were clumsily delivered. 'I'm ... you know ... sorry. Truly, I am. I can't imagine what you're feeling. But I want you to know that ... well, I'm here for you, aren't I? I'll always be here for you. Have you thought anymore about my offer? About you coming to live with us?'

The question just hung there, unanswered, until the voice spoke again.

'No pressure. It's your choice. And the offer won't go away. I'm your brother. I'll do anything I can to help.'

Cole stirred. Focussed on one word in particular. 'Anything?'

'Anything. That's a promise. There's nothing I won't do for you.'

'Thank you,' said Cole. 'I'll bear that in mind.'

A period of shuffling feet and incessant fidgeting followed before the voice returned.

'I'm going to have to make a move. Everybody's coming back to ours and Nat will hit the roof if I'm late. It's nothing special. Sandwiches. Sausage rolls. A few drinks. Listen, you don't have to come if you don't want to. It's up to you. I just ... worry. Worry about you ... on your own ... rattling around that big house.' A pause. 'You won't do anything silly, will you?'

'Silly?' repeated Cole.

'No, not silly. Worse than that. You won't ... harm yourself?'

Cole gently shook his head. That wasn't his intention. Not

yet.

'Good. I mean ... not good, but ... right, I've really gotta' go. Take care of yourself. If I don't see you back at ours, well, I'll call you later. See how you're doing. And I ... erm ... love you. Okay?'

The hand moved.

The rain quickened.

But Cole Burroughs barely noticed. His thoughts were sparking into life as a plan began to take shape. No, he wouldn't do anything silly. He was better than that. Stronger. Smarter. Sharper. He had skills he could call upon. Years of training to an elite level.

By the time this was all over, he would have blood on his hands. The blood of his enemy.

By the time this was over, he, too, would be dead.

CHAPTER TWO
ONE MONTH LATER

Rose Carrington-Finch shuffled about in a futile attempt to get comfortable.

The wooden bench she currently occupied took in much of Shallowbeak Lake and its surrounding paths and trails. The bench was slightly damp, despite the unseasonably dry weather. November was about to roll into December, but the days were mild and the nights were frost free. Dark, yes, with the same impending hint of menace in the air, but at least you wouldn't be shivering whilst you got your purse stolen. Or head stamped on. Or maybe just leered and sneered at. Mental, not physical abuse. A Stainmouth speciality. A little harsh perhaps, but then Stainmouth did little to argue its case. If anything, it had accepted its fate a long time ago. As had the poor folk who lived there.

It was a shithole. Like it or lump it. There was always a third option, of course. Pack your bags and piss off somewhere else. If only it were that easy.

An increasingly anxious Rose put all that to the back of her

mind whilst she waited patiently, if not comfortably, for ... for
...

What was he, exactly? A friend? If she was being honest, they barely knew each other. A casual acquaintance then? No, like Rose on the damp bench, that didn't quite sit right. Her date? Rose stopped shuffling. Felt her stomach flutter. Is that what this was? Had the two of them started going out now? Were they a ... couple?

Without thinking, Rose removed a tissue from her pocket and blew her nose. It was an unnecessary action designed to both settle her nerves and occupy her mind. Pass a few seconds when it was a few minutes that actually needed passing. She was early. In this case, twenty minutes for a midday meeting. Ten minutes gone, ten to go. It was *his* idea to meet here, on the middle bench of three. He had purred over the view, waxed lyrical about how the light danced upon the shimmering water and the trees swayed in the late autumnal breeze. Poetic, yet possibly deluded.

Rose cursed herself. She wasn't usually so cynical. Maybe it was the result of spending too much time with the other men in her life. Tommy O'Strife and Lucas Thorne. Not family nor friends; just members of the same club. She had a horrible feeling that the pair of them were beginning to affect her personality. In the past, she would've turned to the third and final member, Mercy Mee, for advice, but then Mercy was no longer around to keep her on the right path. Not around as in missing, not dead. That was the general assumption, anyway.

That she was a grown woman. That she could take care of herself. It was nice to have a confidante, though. A shoulder, if not to cry on, then to take the strain. Which probably explained why Rose had turned to Rupert.

Because that was his name. The man she was meeting. Her new friend. Her casual acquaintance. Her date.

She had met him in the library, purely by accident. No, if anything it was more of a head-on collision. He had turned a corner and run straight into her. Not hard enough to knock her off balance, but enough to make him blush before he apologised profusely. Was she okay? Did she need to sit down? How could he make it up to her? He suggested a coffee and Rose, against her better judgement, had said yes. That turned out to be the right answer, as the following two hours were as enjoyable as any she could recall. The conversation had flowed, albeit a little clumsily and largely one-sided. Rose had secrets to keep, after all. They had seen each other two more times after that – just for coffee, always during the day – and now this. Rupert was at work, but did she fancy a walk during his lunch hour?

She had answered with a question of her own. Did he really need to ask?

Rose was about to reach for the tissue for a second time when she saw him. He was approaching from her right, less than twenty feet away. Striding purposefully, hands behind his back. A slim frame wrapped in jeans and a dark jacket. Smart casual. Nothing too flashy. Wavy hair and a slightly crooked nose. Oh, and he was smiling. That was nice. She couldn't remember the last time someone had smiled at her. Smiled *because* of her.

Rose smiled back at him.

'You came,' said Rupert, drawing to a halt beside the bench.

'So it seems,' replied Rose.

There was a brief, awkward silence. Limited eye contact. Furious hand rubbing.

Rupert cracked first. 'I wasn't sure you would. Come, I mean.'

'Why not?'

'I don't know ... I thought ... it doesn't matter ...' Rupert removed his hands from behind his back. He was carrying a bunch of flowers. 'These are for you. Roses for Rose.' He winced. 'Sorry. That was painfully cheesy. And it's not as if they're even roses. They're something else. I can't remember what. Sorry ... again.'

'I'll forgive you,' said Rose, as she accepted the bunch with both hands. 'Thank you. You shouldn't have. They're beautiful.'

'Beautiful flowers for a beautiful lady.' Rupert visibly cringed. 'Wow! This is going from bad to worse. I don't know what's come over me.' He gestured towards the bench. 'May I?'

'Of course.' Rose shuffled to one side so he could sit down. Not exactly right beside her, but close enough.

Rupert took a moment to rearrange his glasses. 'I tried the contacts this morning, but I still can't get to grips with them. I always think they're going to disappear behind my eyeball. I'm daft, aren't I? That's probably never happened in the history of contact lenses.'

Rose giggled. And then stopped just as suddenly, in case it was no laughing matter.

'Sorry. I'm waffling on,' said Rupert. 'It's probably just nerves.'

'You don't have to keep on apologising. And why would you be nervous?'

'It's hard to explain,' Rupert began, 'but something strange comes over me when we're together. A *good* strange, but I can't seem to get my words out, and when I do talk, it's absolute nonsense. I hope that makes sense, because if it doesn't—'

'It does,' insisted Rose.

'I'm also nervous that there might be a huge wet patch on my bum from sitting on this bench,' frowned Rupert. 'I'd hate for you to think I'd lost control of my bladder. How about we go for a walk so my jeans can dry off?'

Rose stood up immediately. Waited for Rupert to lead the way.

'The view's rubbish, by the way,' he said, the two of them side-by-side as they looked out across the lake.

'I hadn't noticed,' lied Rose.

'Nothing like the view when I'm gazing at you.' Rupert had barely finished his sentence before he slammed his palm against his forehead. 'That was the worst yet. Sorry. No, not sorry. Must stop apologising. Oh, somebody put me out of my misery once and for all.'

Don't, thought Rose. She didn't want *this* to end. Not now.

Not ever. True, Rupert was a mumbling, stumbling mess. But he was her mumbling, stumbling mess. And she didn't want him to change for anything.

She reached out, ready to take his hand, hold it tight, when a curious tingling sensation swept over her. It was enough to make her stop without warning. Glance over her shoulder.

'Something the matter?' asked Rupert.

Rose shook her head, hiding the truth for fear of the repercussions. There *was* something the matter. It wasn't her imagination. She was sure of it.

There was somebody watching them.

They were being followed.

CHAPTER THREE

'Ah, bugger me backwards! I think she's clocked me.'

Tommy O'Strife almost dropped his phone as he ducked out of sight behind a concrete block of public lavatories. Too slow, amigo. He knew it, and now Lucas Thorne knew it, too.

'You let her see you?' Lucas, his own phone to ear, was on the opposite side of the lake. 'That was clever.'

'No, I didn't let her see me – she just saw me. Big difference, dickhead.'

'There's really not. You were told to keep your distance. Not dribble down the back of her neck.'

'I'm nowhere near her sodding neck. I'm miles away. Still feels weird, though. Spying on women without them knowing. Proper pervy if you ask me. No wonder you get a kick out of it. Didn't need to drag me along too, though, did you? If you're so bothered about Rose's new boyfriend—'

'I'm not,' butted-in Lucas. 'I couldn't care less who she spends her time with. That's her business. It's Agatha who's worried.'

Agatha being Agatha Pleasant. Head honcho of the Nearly

Dearly Departed Club. Her name, no discussion necessary. A legend in her field, even if most people had no idea which field that actually was, or how to find it. If anything, the field had been sold for redevelopment. Turned into a car park. And Agatha was less of a legend and more of a disruption these days, especially to her superiors. Which made her a disruption in a car park. Catchy. Who wouldn't want that written on their headstone?

'Fine,' sighed Tommy. 'If *Agatha's* so bothered about Rose's new boyfriend, then why isn't she here sneaking about in broad daylight?'

'This is grunt work,' said Lucas. 'Agatha doesn't do grunt work. She just hovers above us like some kind of omniscient being.'

'Yeah, like I'm gonna' know what that means,' muttered Tommy under his breath. 'Still, she'd better not hover above me when I'm tucked up in bed at night. She'd see things that'd make her eyeballs pop out.'

'Lovely image.' Lucas dropped his speed from a stomp to a stroll. 'I'm just coming into view now,' he told Tommy. 'Where are you?'

'Hanging around the toilets. I'm trying to build up the courage to take another look.'

Lucas made a *clucking* sound.

'Dream on, pal,' said Tommy. 'I'm as tough as old boots.'

'Or as limp as a flip-flop.'

'I'll flip-flop all over you if you carry on.'

'I don't know what that means.' Lucas paused. 'Just take a look, will you? Find out where they are?'

'I will.'

'When?'

'Now.'

'Now as in, *right* now? This second?'

'Yeah, now,' insisted Tommy. 'Now-ish. Soon. Ah, fuck it ...' He snatched a breath and poked his head out from behind the concrete block. His imagination had conjured up an image of Rose's mousy little face close-up. She'd be angry, but she wouldn't show it. Sometimes that was worse.

He stopped imagining things when he realised she wasn't there. 'Bollocks!'

Stepping out into the open, Tommy scanned his surroundings. If he stared for long enough and tried not to blink, he could just about make out Rose and her new fella in the distance.

'They're back on the move,' he said, speaking into his phone as he started to walk. 'Just give me a second. I need to catch them up.'

'They must be heading my way,' said Lucas. 'I'll hang back.'

Yeah, you do that, thought Tommy. Leave this to the professionals.

He stuck his phone in his pocket as he followed the path that Rose had taken. If he wasn't careful, he'd lose them. That'd be embarrassing. Letting a couple of nobodies outsmart him without them even knowing. With that in mind, he broke into a steady jog. He was blowing by the time he turned the corner. The sight that greeted him, however, was enough to make him hold his breath as he veered to his right and concealed himself behind a tree.

There they were. Rose and her fella. Less than a stone's throw away. Stood with their backs to him, they had joined the queue for an ice-cream van. That was lover boy's first mistake, Tommy decided. Rose was frosty enough already without making things worse. Stick your hand up her jumper now and you'd be fondling icicles.

Tommy kept on the move. Swapped the tree for a battered black Transit. Was about to take another look when a voice disturbed him.

'What are they doing now?'

That was Lucas. Not up close, but in Tommy's pocket. Loud enough for all to hear.

Tommy removed his phone. 'Keep it down, gobby. They're … um … buying ice-creams by the look of it.'

'Ice-creams? It's almost December?'

'Maybe they're both getting hot under the collar and need to cool off,' Tommy laughed. 'I don't know why, but every time I see Rose's face, she seems to be smiling.'

'It must be love.'

'He's not that handsome. He's a lot like Rose, if I'm being honest. You know, underwhelming. Blink and you'll miss him. He has got a massive mole, though. Not a pet. On his face. It practically covers his whole cheek.'

Lucas nodded to himself. 'So, aside from the mole, there's nothing to report back to Agatha then? Nothing dodgy going on?'

'Not that I'm aware of.' Tommy came to a snap decision. 'I'm moving in for a closer look. See if I can hear what they're saying. Don't try to talk me out of it.'

'I won't. I mean, it's bound to go wrong. It always does when you're involved—'

'Thanks for the vote of confidence.' Swerving around the transit, Tommy moved quickly to secure himself a position behind the ice-cream van. The next time he spoke, his voice had dropped to a whisper. 'I'm close now. Maybe too close. I'm starting to regret it, actually.'

'Where are they?'

'Fuck knows. I think they're still in the queue, but I can't see them anymore. Hold on ... if I just take a little ... shit!'

The expletive was reserved for Rose. Not only had Tommy walked straight into her, but he had knocked the ice-cream clean out of her grasp.

'Whoops.' He held up his hands. He had been spotted. No coming back from that. Better just to front it out. 'Oh, hello, Rosemary.'

'Tommy!' A stunned Rose stared at him in disbelief. 'What are you doing here?'

Tommy pretended to look around before deciding that, yes, she was definitely talking to him. 'I was hoping to get an ice-cream. Great minds think alike, eh? I wouldn't drop mine, though. Joke.'

Rose shook her head. She wasn't buying it. Not in the slightest. 'Why here? You're a long way from home. Were you following me?'

'Following you?' Tommy's mouth fell open in mock horror. 'Why would you ask such a thing? I mean, maybe *you* were following *me*?'

Rose glared at him. 'Why would I be following you?'

'You tell me,' said Tommy, feigning outrage. 'Or not. See if I care. What flavour was it, anyway? The ice-cream?'

It took Rose a moment to pick the question out of the rest of his ramblings. 'Bubblegum,' she muttered, glancing down at the mess by her feet. 'It *was* bubblegum.'

'Bubblegum?' Tommy screwed up his face. 'That sounds fuckin' horrendous.'

'I like it,' insisted Rose. 'We both do. And we were enjoying it a lot more before you decided to disturb us.'

Tommy pressed a hand against his heart. 'Oh, pardon me for walking down the street and then stumbling upon the same ice-cream van as my favourite female. Miracles do happen, you know.'

'That's not a miracle – it's suspicious,' said Rose. 'You're not welcome here.'

'Okay, this is getting kind of awkward.' A wary Rupert stepped between them. 'I'm guessing you two know each other.'

'Unfortunately so,' said Rose.

'We live together,' announced Tommy.

Rose flinched. 'Not like that … we're not … I would never … he's not my—'

'Alright, don't stick the boot in.' Tommy turned to Rupert. Held out his hand. 'I'm Tommy. Me and Rose are housemates. No bedroom antics involved. Friends without the benefits. Rose must've mentioned me.'

'Not that I can remember,' mumbled Rupert. He took Tommy's hand and shook it. 'Maybe I've forgotten—'

'You haven't,' insisted Rose.

'Oh, it seems like I haven't,' shrugged Rupert. 'Sorry.'

'Don't be,' said Rose. She glared at Tommy. 'Can I have a word, please? In private?'

Tommy glanced over his shoulder. 'With me?'

'Yes, of course with you.' Rose grabbed him by the elbow and led him to one side. 'What is this?'

'What's what?'

Rose shook her head. 'Don't do this. It's not fair.' She stopped. Looked around. 'Where is he? Lucas? If you're here, then he must be—'

'Elsewhere,' finished Tommy. 'Honestly. Listen, I'm starting to feel bad and that's not normal for me. Maybe I'll just leave you both to it. You can eat your ice-creams in peace. Well, the one you've not dropped at least.' Side-stepping Rose, he caught Rupert's eye and waved. 'See you later, mate. Preferably when Rose isn't quite so … frosty.'

Rupert returned the gesture. That was the cue for Tommy to head back the way he had come.

'I thought you were getting an ice-cream yourself,' called out Rose. 'That's what you said. That's why you're here.'

'Yeah, I ... um ... was, wasn't I?' Tommy wrapped his arms around his body. 'I've changed my mind. Not really ice-cream weather, is it?' He waited for a reply that thankfully never came. Then he was off. Scurrying away as fast as his feet would take him.

Once he was out of sight, he grabbed his phone from his pocket. 'Did you hear that?'

'Most of it,' replied Lucas. 'The rest I could see for myself.'

Tommy looked up and saw him emerge from behind the concrete block of public lavatories. 'What kind of weirdo would hide there?'

'The same kind who's very good at lying,' replied Lucas.

'Yeah, well, I was sparing Rose's feelings, wasn't I?'

'Of course you were.' Without another word, the two of them started to walk in the opposite direction. 'So, what did you make of Rupert?' asked Lucas.

'Not a lot,' shrugged Tommy. 'I was pretty much bang on the money. He's bland. Instantly forgettable.'

'I suppose that's a good thing,' nodded Lucas. 'Agatha will be pleased. Even if Rose isn't.'

'We'll find out soon enough,' said Tommy, practically skipping along the pavement. 'Rose will be home before long. Let's hope we don't see a side of her we've never seen before.'

CHAPTER FOUR

Agatha Pleasant walked into the Sanctuary of Serenity and inhaled the perfumed air.

It was a health spa for Stainmouth's more refined clientele. All clean lines and white walls, with the occasional yucca plant thrown in for good measure. Minimalistic to the point of being empty. Very stylish, thought Agatha, as she swept through the lobby unnoticed. She kept on moving along the corridor. Past several closed doors, before stopping at one door in particular.

The Massage Room.

Lowering the handle, she walked in without knocking. The element of surprise was everything in her line of work. Better to burst in like a battering ram than announce your arrival.

Not that Clifford Goose seemed to mind.

At that very moment, the Chief Constable of Stainmouth police force was laid face down on a massage table, his top half naked, his bottom half covered by the smallest of towels.

Agatha cleared her throat.

'Ah, it's you,' said Goose, lifting his head off the pillow. 'What a ... *pleasant* surprise.'

Agatha sighed. 'Lovely play on words. Very clever.'

'Oh, somebody's feeling a little grouchy today. Let me introduce you to the solution.' Goose tilted his head towards the man mountain stood over him. Dressed all in white, the man had similarly coloured hair and eyebrows, a huge chest and incredibly large hands. 'This is Gunther,' continued Goose. 'He knows how to get into all your nooks and crevices. He's done wonders with my back. He doesn't speak English either, which is always a bonus. No tiresome small talk. Listen, I'm sure he'll give you a discount if you ask politely. Not that I'd know. Never paid a penny in my life. One of the perks of the job. Isn't that right, Gunther?'

The masseur smiled at the sound of his own name. His teeth, much like his hair, were unnaturally white.

'What a glowing recommendation,' said Agatha, struggling to conceal her frustration. 'I'll be sure to grab a price list on my way out. Now, what is it that you actually want? You said it was urgent—'

'Patience, my dear,' said Goose. 'Good things come to those who ... ooh! That's the spot, Gunther. Right there. I can't decide if it's pleasure or pain. But I like it.'

Agatha turned towards the door. 'Goodbye, Clifford. We'll talk again when you're not quite so aroused—'

'Hold your horses, woman!' Goose rolled onto his side. 'Gunther, can you give us a minute?'

The masseur stared at him, confused.

'Jog on,' said Goose, shooing him away. 'We can resume

this later without interruptions. Three's a crowd and all that nonsense ...'

Despite the language barrier, Gunther seemed to finally get the message and left the room.

'You might want to avert your eyes,' suggested Goose. 'I've got a lifetime's worth of experience hidden under this tiny towel.'

Agatha took the opportunity to examine the floor. Listened to ten seconds of grunting and groaning.

'I'm decent,' said Goose eventually.

Agatha lifted her head, slightly distressed to see that, although Goose had sat up, there was still too much flesh on show.

'All paid for,' he remarked, reading her mind.

'Unlike your massage,' said Agatha.

'Unlike my massage,' repeated Goose proudly. 'Back in the day, a man used to be respected for the size of his belly. It was a sign of wealth ... power. Now it's all six-packs and protein shakes. World's gone mad. Everyone needs a bit of timber around their middle and stodge in their diet. Keeps you warm in winter ... are you looking at my nipples?'

Agatha grimaced. Thought about lying, but quickly decided against it. 'They're very hairy, aren't they?'

'Nature's way,' shrugged Goose. 'I would move my towel, but there'll be consequences. If it wasn't my nipples on show, it would be my balls. Take your pick. I'm not shy. Seriously, if you don't like the view, you could always look the other way.'

'I'm not standing in the corner of the room like a naughty child,' frowned Agatha. 'Just hurry up and tell me what you want me to do. The less time I'm in here, the easier it'll be for me to erase this image from my mind.'

'I'm not that bad,' muttered Goose, sticking out his bottom lip. 'I'm in pretty good shape for my age.'

'Please, Clifford. There are places I need to—'

'I've got a problem.'

Agatha sighed. 'So I can see. I thought this was work-related—'

'It bloody is,' insisted Goose. 'It's a work-related problem. And guess which lucky lady is about to provide the solution?'

CHAPTER FIVE

Lucas and Tommy were the first to arrive back home.

Home being Cockleshell Farm. The actual home of Proud Mary, their elderly landlady who ruled the roost with a stern temper and iron fist. She was nowhere to be seen, however, which was either a good thing if you were afraid of her, but not so good if you were absolutely famished. Unfortunately for the male half of the Nearly Dearly Departed Club, they were most definitely in the latter camp. Stomachs were rumbling as they bounded into the kitchen and snatched at the first things on offer. In this instance, a slice of cold toast that had been left on the side since morning, and a lump of cheese that had clearly been intended for the bin. That would do for starters.

The main course was interrupted by the arrival of Rose.

Without acknowledging the pair of them, she wandered into the sitting room and sat down in the armchair, avoiding eye contact at all times.

It was Tommy who broke the silence. 'You're back early. Where's lover boy?'

Rose's initial reaction was to jump up from her chair. 'I'm

going to my room—'

'Whoa!' Lucas rushed through from the kitchen. 'I'm sorry, Rose. I was there, too. This afternoon. At the lake. We shouldn't have followed you. We didn't want to. It was Agatha's idea. She was ...concerned.'

'Concerned?' Rose stopped in the doorway and spun around. 'Why would she be concerned?'

'Why do you think?' blurted out Tommy. 'You've got a boyfriend. *You*. If that's not concerning, then I don't know what is.'

Rose glared at him. 'He's not my boyfriend. He's a ... a ... friend.'

'Who just happens to be a boy,' smirked Tommy. 'Same difference if you ask me.'

The glare intensified. 'But nobody was asking you, were they? They never do, but you still tell them what you're thinking.'

'It's better to be out-spoken than never speak at all.'

Rose ignored that. 'Go on then. Tell me. Why do you think it's so strange that somebody would want to spend time with me? Why do you *both* think that?'

Lucas held up his hands. 'Leave me out of this. I don't think there's anything strange—'

'Well, I do,' insisted Tommy. 'I mean, no offence, Rose, but you make being stuck in traffic seem interesting. Granted, you're not bad looking in the right light, but ... where are you going now?'

Rose had already disappeared from view before she replied.

'Anywhere that you're not.'

'Rose ... wait.' Lucas called out to her, but it was too little, too late. She was already up the stairs and along the landing. She didn't slam the door to her room, but then she never did. That wasn't her style.

'Bye then,' said Tommy, rolling his eyes. 'Was it something I said?'

'Not something – *everything*,' sighed Lucas. 'You need to learn to think before you speak.'

Tommy waved it away. 'She'll get over it.'

'She'll have to,' agreed Lucas, as he headed back towards the kitchen. 'The Nearly Dearly Departed Club is already down to a three-piece. I doubt Agatha will let the two of us go running around town as a double act any time soon.'

'We could be Stainmouth's answer to Batman and Robin,' said Tommy, rubbing his hands together.

'More like Del Boy and Rodney,' groaned Lucas.

'Speak for yourself,' said Tommy, as he wandered into the sitting room and collapsed onto the sofa. 'I'm practically a super hero these days. It's just the rest of the world hasn't realised it yet. They will, though. Given time.'

'Course they will.' Lucas gazed up at the ceiling in despair. 'What's your superpower?'

'Compassion,' replied Tommy, without missing a beat. 'My caring nature. You wait and see. This time next year they'll be making a film about me. I'll probably star in it. Give me something to do when I'm not saving mankind.'

'Ah, give me strength,' sighed Lucas, joining him in the sitting room. 'Where was your compassion when you were talking to Rose?'

'Rose?' Tommy stretched out on the sofa and yawned. 'It's only a superpower, mate – I'm not a fuckin' miracle worker!'

CHAPTER SIX

Agatha had one stipulation.

If they were going to talk, then the Chief Constable would have to get dressed. It was only fair, after all. Those hairy nipples were just far too distracting.

The Sanctuary of Serenity had a bar. The twenty-first century version. All organic fruits and green vegetables. Freshly squeezed and lovingly blended. Not an alcoholic beverage in sight. That was where Agatha met a fully clothed Clifford Goose. She ordered a mineral water for herself and then stepped back and enjoyed the look of pure confusion that passed across Goose's face as he struggled to decipher what was on offer.

'Is this it?' he asked, squinting at the price list above the counter. 'Where are the ... you know ... normal drinks?'

'They *are* the normal drinks,' said the young, fresh-faced, impressively perky female attendant serving him. 'Here at the Sanctuary of Serenity we pride ourselves on our wide range of vegan-friendly, organically grown, sustainable—'

'Yeah, yeah, you're preaching to the perverted, sweetheart,' butted-in Goose. 'Just get us a coffee, eh?'

'Please,' added Agatha.

'Of course,' smiled the attendant. 'What kind would you like, sir? Americano? Latte? Cappuccino? Espresso? Macchiato? Mocha? There's more on the menu.'

'Jesus wept!' groaned Goose. 'Coffee's coffee.'

'No, it's really not, sir,' argued the attendant.

'Well, give us a tea then,' said Goose smugly.

The attendant nodded, not fazed in the slightest. 'Certainly, sir. Would that be green tea? Peppermint? Chamomile? Ginger? There's more on the menu.'

Goose rubbed his forehead. 'Forget the tea. I'll have the same as her,' he said, pointing rudely at Agatha.

'A mineral water?'

'Yeah, a mineral water,' repeated Goose. 'Without the minerals, though. Just get it out of the tap. I've seen your chuffin' prices. It'd leave me without a pot to piss in.'

'Fine. One mineral water and another mineral water without the minerals. I'll bring them over,' said the attendant, trying not to smile as she turned away from the counter.

'That was hard work,' muttered Goose, as he joined Agatha at the only free table. 'When did life get so complicated?'

'We just got older,' replied Agatha.

Goose greeted that with a snort. 'Not me. I'm as fit as a ferret. Could run a marathon if I wanted to. *Two* marathons. Don't, of course. I mean, I've got better things to do, haven't I? Protecting Stainmouth for a start—'

Agatha coughed. 'That problem you mentioned …'

'Ah, the problem.' Goose waited whilst the attendant put down their drinks. Took a sip of his tap water and pulled a face. 'A man's come up on our radar,' he began. 'A good man gone slightly ... erratic. His name is Cole Burroughs. Ex-special forces. Retired now. It was his own choice to leave. He suffered a great loss not so long ago and it seems to have left him teetering on the edge. Like a human volcano about to erupt.'

Agatha moved the ice-cubes around her glass. 'And where do I come in exactly? Surely you don't expect me and my team to stop a man like that—'

'You're not listening!' barked Goose. 'Burroughs *could* blow at any moment – I'm not saying he will do. No, what I want from you is purely observational. A watching brief. Twenty-four hours a day surveillance, if that's not too much of a stretch. Log his movements and report back anything suspicious. Chances are it'll all be for nothing—'

'And if it isn't?' wondered Agatha.

'You'll be ready to react accordingly. Worst-case scenario, Burroughs goes ballistic and you call it in. Armed police can be there in a matter of minutes. It's that simple.' Goose smiled. 'I mean, we wouldn't want you getting any blood on your pretty blouse now, would we?'

'I won't be close enough for that,' said Agatha. 'I tend to let my team get their hands dirty. Which brings about a problem of its own. One of my number has gone walkabout. Mercy Mee. She's the chief suspect in a murder enquiry—'

'Keep your voice down.' Goose peered around the bar,

relieved that nobody was earwigging in on their conversation. 'I've got a reputation to uphold,' he whispered. 'I didn't know you frequented with murderers.'

Agatha shook her head. 'I don't. Largely because she didn't do it. That's not so easy to prove, though, is it? Not with our legal system.'

Goose's brow furrowed. 'I don't like where this is heading ...'

'And I don't like to ask, Clifford, but I'm going to, anyway. If you want me to do this surveillance job, then I'll need my full quota. Four, not three. Two on, two off. Day shift and night shift. It's the only way it works.'

'Can't you just get another body?'

'No. Not at short notice. And not one I'd trust.'

Goose stared into the middle distance, deep in thought. 'I don't know who you think I am. It won't be easy.'

'I never said it would be.'

'You're basically asking me to wipe her very existence off the face of the earth.'

'Yes, I am, aren't I?'

Goose muttered something unintelligible under his breath. 'Ah, the things I do for you ...' Leaning over, he spat in the palm of his hand before holding it out to be shaken. 'Deal. I'll call off the dogs and you can have your woman back. In return, you'll start tonight. There's an empty house you can use. It's on Haversham Way, directly opposite Cole Burroughs's own humble abode. I'll provide the equipment. Get it all set up this afternoon. Binoculars. Cameras. Tripods. You name it. All that techy stuff.' Goose nodded towards his hand. 'Don't you want to shake and seal the deal?'

'Not particularly.' Agatha pushed back her chair. 'I'll let you take care of the bill—'

'You're leaving?' Goose almost sounded disappointed. 'At least finish your drink. That'll set me back about five notes in a joint like this.'

'You have it,' insisted Agatha, as she stood up. 'Treat yourself. Besides, there's somewhere I've got to be. It's time I tracked down my woman, as you called her. I don't know if you've heard, but she's in the clear. And it's all thanks to our wonderful Chief Constable.'

Goose failed to recognise the irony. 'Sounds like one helluva' guy,' he said, grinning from ear to ear.

'Yes, something like that.' Agatha turned away from the table. 'So long, Clifford. We'll meet again when this is over.'

CHAPTER SEVEN

Laid flat on her back, Rose admired the long crack that ran from one end of her bedroom ceiling to the other.

Had it been that pronounced when she had first *moved* in? When Miles had dropped the four of them off and basically left them to fend for themselves in a strange house in an unknown town? She had noticed the crack before, but this was next level. It had grown. Expanded its reach. Taken ownership of the situation and grasped it with both hands.

Which made Rose wonder if it was the crack she was talking about at all. Maybe it was something – no, someone – closer to home.

Rose had never had a boyfriend before. Not a serious one. Long-term. Steady. She'd been out with boys in the past, but it was only ever casual. Never a man. A real man. Not muscles and scars and blinkered bravado, but kind, caring and trustworthy. A gentle soul who had no intention of pressurising her. Who wanted things to be special. To build slowly until their hearts melted and they were both truly ... madly ... deeply in love.

Rose felt her pulse quicken. She had got carried away. Again.

She had a habit of doing that. Dreaming big. And yet only when it concerned Rupert. The rest of her life she had largely given up on. She had no control over that. Not whilst Agatha Pleasant pulled her strings. And now the same Agatha Pleasant had gone a step too far. She had asked Lucas and Tommy to follow her. No, it was worse than that. *Spy* was a more appropriate word. And why? In case...what? Rupert threatened to take her away? Split up the team? Agatha didn't even know him. How dare she be so judgmental?

Mercy certainly wouldn't have stood for it.

Past tense. Because Mercy had been gone for over two weeks now. Nobody knew where she was, but everybody secretly doubted that she would ever return. Why would she? Where was the incentive? There wasn't any. All four of them who made up Agatha Pleasant's Nearly Dearly Departed Club basically worked for free for the privilege of being dragged back from the point of death. Any sense of joy or relief or gratitude had long since subsided. Deep down, if she was being honest, she couldn't really blame Mercy for going.

And yet she did.

Because Mercy hadn't just gone; she had run out on her. Left her in the lurch. You don't do that to a friend, if that's what they were.

Rolling over, Rose pulled her knees up to her chest and closed her eyes. She decided to leave Mercy and Lucas and Tommy and anybody else for that matter up on the ceiling with the twisted crack for company, and switched her thoughts, instead, to the only person who made her happy.

One day, Rupert might just be her route out of there. Her salvation. Her reason to get up in the morning and not feel so defeated.

For Rose, that day couldn't come quick enough.

CHAPTER EIGHT

Rose was wrong.

Somebody *did* know where Mercy was. But then that same somebody had always known. From day one. The moment she had disappeared from Cockleshell Farm. Gone underground for fear of being accused of murder. And that somebody had kept Agatha in the loop at all times. Of course they had. It didn't pay to keep secrets from the boss. But that was the last of it. Agatha had processed the information and then drawn a line in the sand. Never mentioned it again.

Until now.

The somebody was sat beside Agatha in the back of her Audi A8. Olaf, her driver, had parked up outside Rocketway Heights, an industrial block of flats to the north of Stainmouth. Unsurprisingly, the Rocketway had somewhat of a reputation. Not for the faint-hearted, you needed eyes in the back of your head and an iron constitution before you dared to even enter. Get on the wrong side of many of the locals and the best you could hope for was to escape with your tail between your legs. The worst was to leave in a body bag.

The somebody knew this, too. But then the somebody was Miles, Agatha's number two, and he tended to know most things.

'This is where we'll find Mercy,' he said, pointing up at the tower block. 'She's been hiding out in there for almost two weeks now.'

'There must be three hundred flats in the Rocketway,' frowned Agatha. 'Can't you narrow it down a bit?'

Miles shook his head. 'Unfortunately not. Her signal seems to get weaker the higher she goes.' He paused. 'I don't really fancy going door-to-door.'

'Me neither.' With that, Agatha climbed out of the Audi. As soon as she did, she was greeted by a chorus of sneers and jeers from a gang of youths loitering close by. Throw in the occasional wolf whistle and Agatha couldn't decide if she was offended or flattered.

'Someone's popular,' grinned Miles, as he joined her outside the car. 'I think you might have pulled.'

'I'm old enough to be their grandma,' muttered Agatha, setting off across the car park. She had barely moved when one of the youths approached on a bike, skidding to a halt in front of her. A boy. Twelve or thirteen at most. Riding a BMX that was at least three sizes too small for him.

'Nice wheels,' he said, practically drooling over the Audi.

'Thank you.' Agatha tried to keep walking, but the youth had other ideas. Swerving the bike from side to side, he didn't exactly block her, but still managed to slow her step.

'I'm Super,' the boy said. 'It's nice to see new faces visiting the Rocketway. Freshens things up a bit.'

'Why do they call you Super?' asked Miles, rising to the bait as he tried to physically manoeuvre the boy and his bike to one side.

Super held his ground. Pulled a face as he steadied the BMX. 'It's my name, dummy. Thought that would've been obvious. My mum and dad clearly knew I was going places.'

'True. Who wouldn't be proud of a son who rides around the estate on a tiny bike whilst harassing people?' muttered Miles under his breath.

Super let that go. He had his own agenda, after all. 'How about you give me twenty quid and I promise to look after her?' he said, winking at Agatha.

Agatha hesitated. 'Her?'

'Your motor,' said Super. 'Twenty quid, and I'll protect her from the others. There are some right animals living round here. No respect for other people's property.'

'And if we don't?' scowled Miles.

'Who knows?' shrugged Super. 'But ask yourself this. Is that a risk you're prepared to take?'

The answer to that particular question seemed to be *no*, as Agatha reached into her handbag.

'Please tell me you're not going to give him any money,' grumbled Miles. 'He's just a jumped-up little shit. I've struggled to deal with bigger lumps of ear wax.'

'Trust me, Miles,' whispered Agatha. 'This will be money

well spent.' She removed a twenty-pound note and dangled it invitingly at arm's length. Super, predictably, snatched at it with greedy fingers, but somehow missed completely and almost fell off his bike. 'You can have the money,' began Agatha, holding the note against her chest, 'and I don't even want you to keep an eye on the Audi. I've got Olaf for that. But I do want some information.'

'I'm not a grass,' insisted Super.

'Of course not,' said Agatha. 'But you're not stupid, either. I'm guessing you know everything around here. Everything *and* everyone. Let's not pretend otherwise. So, who better to help us than you?'

Super screwed up his face. Partly intrigued, mostly confused.

'We're looking for a woman,' continued Agatha. 'Mid-twenties. Black. Attractive. She's called Mercy. Do you know her?'

Super eyed them both suspiciously. 'You two pigs in blankets?'

Agatha and Miles exchanged glances.

'Plain-clothes police,' explained Super. 'It's only cops who come round here asking questions.'

Agatha shook her head. 'No, we're not. I promise. Mercy's not in any trouble. We're friends of hers. We just want to talk. She doesn't live here, but we think she might have been staying in somebody else's flat for the past few weeks.'

Super took it all in. Quickly decided he didn't like what he was hearing. 'I'm no grass,' he repeated. 'Besides, I've never heard of her. There are hundreds of people living in the Rocketway. Loads of pretty black girls. She could be anyone.' Raising his hand, he dismissed them with a flick of his wrist. 'No, can't help you. Keep your money. Laters.'

And, with that, he was off, his legs going like the clappers as he raced back towards the Rocketway.

Without another word, Agatha made her way back to the Audi and ducked inside.

'What now?' asked Miles, as he joined her on the back seat.

Agatha held up a finger. 'Patience. This shouldn't take long.'

'What shouldn't? It was a nice try, but I don't think it worked. Surely we should—'

'Be quiet and wait,' said Agatha sternly. Staring out of the window, she watched as Super rode around in circles at the entrance to the flats. Then, without warning, he leant the bike against the wall and disappeared inside.

Agatha was out of the Audi a moment later.

'Where are you going?' asked Miles, hurrying after her.

'To get Mercy,' she replied, striding towards the entrance. 'You heard Super. He's not a grass. But I bet he's fiercely loyal to all those who live in the Rocketway. Let's find out for sure, shall we?'

CHAPTER NINE

Super led them all the way to the seventh floor.

He used the stairs, probably through necessity rather than choice, out of order being the order of the day for the only two lifts available. A boy of his age could move at speed though, much to Agatha and Miles's despair. Eventually they caught him up, moments before he came to a halt at one flat in particular.

Number one hundred and twenty-eight.

Concealed behind a concrete pillar, they had a good view of Super as he clenched his fist and knocked repeatedly. He stopped when the door opened just an inch. Leaning forward, he spoke at a thousand miles per hour, but they couldn't hear what he was saying. He nodded at the reply, spoke again, and then the door closed. Whoever was inside had never revealed themselves.

They waited until Super had headed back down the stairs before they weighed up their options.

'That was helpful,' remarked Miles, gesturing towards the flat in question. 'There could be anyone in there.'

'Yes, there could,' mused Agatha, 'but let's not dismiss it so hastily.'

Emerging from behind the pillar, she made her way across the landing. Reached the door and knocked.

A reply came almost instantly. 'Who is it?'

'The council,' said Agatha.

'Have you come about the boiler?'

'Amongst other things.'

That seemed to swing it. The key turned, the lock clicked, and the door opened. Not an inch this time, but all the way. There was a man stood in the doorway. Shorter than average, stocky rather than overweight, he was dressed in a red tracksuit and checked flat cap.

'You don't look much like the council,' he said sceptically.

'Looks can be deceptive,' insisted Agatha.

'You're not the police, are you? Wouldn't do for me to be seen talking to your lot on my doorstep.'

'You're the second person to ask us that.' Agatha paused. 'No, we're not the police. And we're not the council either,' she admitted. 'It's a stab in the dark, but we'd like to ask you a few questions about a friend of ours. Mercy Mee—'

'Never heard of her,' said the man quickly. *Too* quickly. Impossible for either Agatha or Miles to miss.

'We think she may live somewhere in this block,' said Miles. 'She's hiding out, but she doesn't need to. If there's anything you want to tell us, Mr ...'

'Nimble,' said the man. 'Just Nimble. Always has been,

always will be. From the day I was born until the moment I drop dead. Which might come sooner than I'd imagined if I keep rambling on to a couple of straights like you two.' He stuck his head outside. Looked up and down the landing. There were noises coming from one end of the floor. Shouting and laughing mixed with the general hubbub of stomping feet. 'Can you two handle yourselves?' asked Nimble, out of the blue. 'You know, in a punch-up?'

'Not at all,' lied Miles.

Nimble groaned. 'It's not safe around here, not even in broad daylight. Aw, stuff it. Come on in. But I've not got long so don't keep me chatting. I'm off out soon.'

'Anywhere nice?' asked Agatha, as she crossed the threshold and entered the flat. She waited for Miles to join her and then closed the door behind him. They were in now. The only way they would leave was of their own accord.

'Come Fight With Me,' said Nimble, leading them along a narrow hallway into a cramped sitting room. 'It's a boxing club. *My* boxing club. I'm trainer to the talent of tomorrow. Mentor to the mean and magnificent. And here's one of them now.' Nimble nodded over at a long-limbed boy sprawled out on the sofa. 'This is Solomon. He's staying with me for a while until he gets his shit sorted out.'

Agatha nodded whilst her mind worked overtime. She knew exactly what shit the boy had to sort out. Largely because she knew exactly who he was. Solomon Duggan. Stepson of the recently deceased Errol Duggan. The man that Mercy had been accused of murdering. Hopefully wrongly accused. Agatha was only guessing, after all. She had no definite confirmation. She needed Mercy for that. Which reminded her ...

'We haven't got long, so let's get straight to the point.' Agatha pointed at Nimble and then the sofa. 'Sit down.'

'I ... um ... don't want to,' he mumbled in reply. 'I'd rather stand.'

'You don't get to decide,' said Agatha firmly. 'If I tell you to sit, you sit.'

A brow-beaten Nimble moved Solomon's legs out of the way and then slumped down beside him. 'This is my flat,' he grumbled.

'For now,' shot back Agatha, 'but circumstances have changed. You don't know what you've just invited into your home. We were telling the truth out there. We're not the police. No, we're worse than that. We don't abide by their rules and regulations. We're not governed by the law. So, I'll ask you again, and this time I suggest you consider your answer carefully. I know that Mercy Mee has been here. Now, we could turn the place over, but I'd rather save everyone the hassle. Where is she?'

'I don't know,' said Nimble, avoiding eye contact.

'Honestly, we don't,' chipped-in Solomon.

Agatha gently shook her head. 'You're making a big mistake. I didn't want it to come to this, but ...'

Without another word, Miles removed a handgun, a Glock 17, from inside his coat. Striding across the room, he pressed it against the side of Solomon's temple.

'Whoa!' Nimble practically jumped up off the sofa. 'There's no need—'

'There's *every* need,' insisted Agatha. 'Now, my colleague here has got an itchy trigger finger and an unnatural obsession with blood. I'm guessing you've got about five seconds before he squeezes. Five ...'

'No way,' said Nimble, frantically shaking his head. 'You're having us on. This ain't happening—'

Agatha ignored him. 'Four.'

'Don't,' whimpered Solomon. He was sat bolt upright. Frozen solid with fear. 'Do something, Nimble. Please ...'

'Three.'

'Okay, okay, we know Mercy,' Nimble admitted. 'She's a friend. She comes to the boxing club. But we don't know where she is—'

'Two.'

'We can take you there,' Nimble spluttered. 'To Come Fight With Me. We can all look for her—'

'One.' Agatha nodded at Miles. He wasn't looking in her direction, though. His eyes, instead, had strayed towards the doorway.

There was somebody there. Somebody familiar. Somebody missing in action.

Until now.

'What the hell do you think you're doing?' cried Mercy.

CHAPTER TEN

'Put the gun away, please.'

Miles did as Agatha suggested, tucking the Glock back inside his coat.

'That was a horrible thing to do,' said Mercy. Still stood in the doorway, she was shifting her gaze from Agatha to Miles and back again, undecided which one was most deserving of her wrath. 'Look what you've done to Solomon. He's scared stiff. You were never going to shoot him though, so why play games?'

'Needs must,' said Agatha. 'Sometimes it's best to go in a little heavy-handed. It brings about a quicker conclusion. We were desperate to find you—'

'And now you have,' said Mercy.

Agatha nodded. 'It's good to see you again, Miss Mee. You're looking well.'

Mercy sniffed away the compliment.

'Friends of yours, Mercy?' asked Nimble, breathing a little easier as he gestured towards Agatha and Miles.

'Friends? No, friends don't force their way in to other people's homes and make threats,' she shot back.

'Miss Mee works for me,' explained Agatha. 'She's part of my team. A vital cog. She's been gone too long.'

'I thought she did charity work,' said Nimble, confused. 'Mostly voluntary.'

'Yes, that's one way of putting it.' Agatha turned to Mercy. Held up her hands by way of an apology. 'You're right; it was a horrible thing to do. And underhand. And beneath me. And yet unfortunately necessary. We knew you were close, but we needed to draw you out.'

'Can you imagine what it must've felt like for Solomon?' asked Mercy, not ready to forgive so quickly. 'He's just lost his step-dad.'

'How could we forget?' remarked Miles. He held Mercy's gaze. 'How could *you* forget?'

'What's that supposed to mean?' she spat.

Miles held up his hands. 'No judgement here. You'll do anything to stay alive when you're out there on the street. Kill if you have to—'

'Mercy didn't kill anybody.' Solomon had found his stomach again, and with it came his voice. 'She wasn't even there when he died.'

'So, why did she go on the run then?' pressed Miles. 'That practically screams guilty.'

'I had no choice,' insisted Mercy, shaking her head. 'They wouldn't have believed me. The police. The judge and jury. The evidence was pretty damning. It *is* pretty damning. I had to do something. I had nowhere to go—'

'So, you came to the one person who you knew you could trust,' said Nimble. Puffing out his chest, he smiled at Mercy. 'I'm honoured.'

'And I'm grateful that you took good care of her,' said Agatha. 'You'll be financially reimbursed, I promise. Now, however, we'll be taking her off your—'

'I'm not going anywhere!' A slight twitch in the corner of Mercy's eye suggested the cogs had started to turn. She was planning her escape. Get out of there and start again.

'Relax,' said Miles, sensing her agitation. 'We're on the same side. *Your* side.'

'Yeah, right,' sneered Mercy. She was already backing away. Blink once and she would be on her toes. Twice and she would be gone.

Moving towards the door, Miles reached out to grab her.

At the same time, Solomon leapt up off the sofa and jabbed Agatha's number two with a straight left. He caught him on the jaw, the force enough to rock Miles from side to side.

'Leave her alone!' shouted Solomon. 'You know nothing! You haven't got a clue!'

Miles steadied himself. The blow had caught him off guard. He hated to admit it, but he had clearly underestimated the boy on the sofa. He wouldn't make the same mistake again, though.

Without missing a beat, Miles removed his Glock and pointed it at Solomon's chest. No words. No explanation. Simply immobilise the threat.

'Stop this!' said Agatha, stepping between the two of them.

'We're not at war with one another.'

'Sure feels like it,' muttered Mercy.

'Well, we're not,' insisted Agatha. She glared at Miles until he returned the gun to his pocket. 'Miss Mee, surely you don't need me to spell things out for you. We're not here to arrest you. We need you back. The others need you back.'

'And you're not listening,' said Mercy. 'If I step foot outside this flat, I'll be picked up by the police.'

Agatha waved away her concerns. 'Not anymore, you won't. You're in the clear. I have the Chief Constable's word on that. You're no longer a suspect in the murder of Errol Duggan.'

Mercy switched her attention to Solomon. Just the slightest of glances. Beyond subtle, but unerringly deliberate. 'Who is in the frame, then?'

'I neither know nor care,' replied Agatha bluntly. She regretted it at once. 'Sorry,' she said, addressing Solomon. 'That was quite insensitive of me. This must be very traumatic for you.'

'Not particularly,' Solomon shrugged. 'I just don't want Mercy to get into any trouble. She's innocent.'

'You seem pretty sure about that,' said Miles. 'Something you're not telling us.'

'Leave it,' said Mercy. 'Solomon's a good kid. He doesn't need you throwing accusations about.'

Miles rubbed his jaw. 'I throw accusations. He throws punches.'

'Just think about what you say in future,' said Mercy.

'Especially if you want me to leave here with you.'

Agatha resisted the urge to smile. 'Ah, so you're thinking about it? That's a start.'

'Well, this flat's not exactly massive, is it?' said Mercy, turning her back on Nimble so he couldn't hear her. 'Certain smells don't disappear as quickly as you'd like.'

'There's plenty of space at Cockleshell Farm,' said Agatha. 'I think there's even a room with your name on it.'

'Yeah, next to Tommy's,' frowned Mercy.

'Yes, well, that's unfortunate,' said Agatha hastily. 'They all miss you, though. You were the glue that bound them together. Miss Carrington-Finch, in particular, seems to have lost her way a little in your absence. She misses your guidance.'

Mercy rolled her eyes. 'Now you're just trying to guilt trip me.'

'I'm just being honest,' said Agatha. 'Miss Carrington-Finch is just one of many reasons you should come back—'

'And another is my bed,' chipped-in Nimble, out of the blue.

He regretted it instantly when Mercy spun around. Stared him out. 'What you talking about?'

'Sleeping on the sofa's no good for a fella like me,' Nimble explained. 'My body's a mess. Be nice to get back between the sheets once they've taken you away.'

'Oh, thanks a bunch,' moaned Mercy.

Nimble pulled a face. 'That came out wrong. Not taken you away; just moved you on to pastures new.'

'I'm not a cow!' Mercy threw up her hands in despair. 'You're basically chucking me out, aren't you?'

'Well, two's company and you're a crowd,' said Nimble, wincing slightly as the words rolled off his tongue. 'I still love you. Just maybe not as much as I did when you first arrived. I'll tell you what. I'll help you pack your stuff up. It's the least I can do ...'

Mercy watched as Nimble leapt up off the sofa and squeezed past her on his way towards his bedroom. Once he was gone, she turned her attention to Agatha. 'Looks like I'm coming with you, after all,' she said awkwardly. 'It's either that or sleep rough.'

'You won't regret it.' Agatha walked over and rested a hand on Mercy's shoulder. 'Welcome back, Miss Mee. Let's go to work.'

CHAPTER ELEVEN

Rose was still dreaming about a brighter future when a car pulled up on the driveway at Cockleshell Farm.

She held her breath. Listened carefully. Heard the engine shut down and the doors open and close in quick succession. Footsteps across the gravel followed soon after. Hushed voices. More than one person. Any second now, they would reach the entrance.

Whoever it was didn't bother to knock. Instead, they walked straight in, closing the door firmly behind them. That was enough to get Rose up and off the bed. By the time she had left her room, she could hear the hum of conversation. Not just general chit-chat either, but something louder. Raised voices mixed with raucous laughter. To call it uncharacteristic was an understatement.

Rose hurried down the stairs. She followed the voices across the hallway and into the sitting room. Unsurprisingly, the space had filled up considerably. She could see Agatha and Miles, even though they had their backs to her, whilst Proud Mary was stood in the entrance to the kitchen, the slightest of smiles carved into her battle-hardened features. The absurdity of that alone wasn't lost on Rose as she shifted her gaze and saw Lucas and Tommy in the centre of the room. There was someone between them. A woman.

Rose edged forward, her view improving with every step.

'You're back?' she said stiffly.

Mercy turned and smiled. 'I'm back. Did you miss me?'

Question or not, Rose chose not to answer it. 'Where have you been?'

'Where have I been?' repeated Mercy. If she was trying to buy herself some time, then it was all in vain. 'Nowhere,' she replied. 'Not really. It doesn't matter.'

'You been on holiday?' asked Tommy. 'That's not fair. I'd love a trip away. The sun on my back, surrounded by a bevy of bikini-clad babes—'

'Nobody has been – or will be going – on holiday,' said Agatha, cutting through the small talk. 'I appreciate you haven't seen each other for several weeks, but the catch-up will have to wait. For now, we have work to do. Purely surveillance. Nothing too taxing. I'd like you to team up in pairs. Two in the day, two at night. Any preferences?'

Rose forced herself to speak up. 'I've arranged to meet Rupert tomorrow afternoon.'

'Ah, yes, Rupert,' nodded Agatha. Her face gave nothing away.

'Rupert?' Mercy looked around the room. 'Who's Rupert?'

'Rose's boyfriend,' said Tommy, eager to stir things up.

'Somebody's in love.'

'He is not my boyfriend and I am not in love!' snapped Rose, the blood rushing to her cheeks.

'I'd still like to know who he is,' shrugged Mercy.

'Not now,' said Agatha hastily. 'That's a private conversation between the two of you. It does solve one particular problem, though. Miss Carrington-Finch can take the first night shift with—'

'I don't mind,' said Mercy.

'No, I'd rather you had a good night's sleep and wake up fresh tomorrow,' Agatha insisted. 'I think Mr O'Strife would be a better candidate.'

Tommy blew out in frustration. 'Seriously? Why me?'

'Why not you?' shot back Miles.

'Because Rose just ignores me. She never talks. She finds me annoying and I find her ... as dull as dog shit.'

'Good,' said Agatha. 'I don't want you to enjoy yourselves. I want you to concentrate. Both of you. Act like professionals.'

'How professional is it to fall asleep on the job? Because we all know that will happen at some point,' remarked Rose. She glanced at Tommy as she spoke, who reacted instantly.

'If I nod off, it's only because you've bored me into a coma. Try livening up a little. Stop being such a sad sack—'

'My word is final.' Agatha raised her voice to emphasise the point. 'This shouldn't be so difficult. You're all grown adults. You're not playing kiss chase in the playground. I don't care who you prefer. Who you'd rather socialise with. This is work.' The room fell momentarily silent after her outburst. 'Sorry,' said Agatha eventually. 'It's been a strange day. There's a horrible image of hairy nipples that I can't seem to shift from my mind.'

Tommy looked her up and down. 'Really? I would've thought you took better care of yourself than that.'

'Not mine,' said Agatha, taken aback. 'I haven't ... oh, forget it. The man we're watching is called Cole Burroughs. Ex-special forces. Decorated. Well-respected. And now recently retired.' She reached into her pocket. 'This is a photograph of him. He might have changed his appearance since then, though.'

Agatha handed the photo to Mercy. The man on show was dressed in military attire. Cropped hair and chiselled features. Strong chin and clean shaven.

'He's a good-looking boy,' said Tommy, snatching the photo from Mercy's grasp. 'Looks like I could have a bit of competition for a change.'

'Nah, the title of Stainmouth's biggest dickhead is yours for keeps,' grinned Lucas.

'I don't get it,' said Mercy, as the photograph got passed around. 'If everything you say about Burroughs is true, then why is he under surveillance?'

Agatha took a moment. Good question. And one she should really have been able to answer. Goose, however, as was his way, had been less than forthcoming with the facts. 'Let's just say that Cole Burroughs is a person of interest. You watch and report back to Miles, however mundane his actions. Hopefully, there'll be nothing to set the alarm bells ringing.'

'And if there is?' wondered Lucas. 'Burroughs has clearly got some skills. We haven't. We've just got Tommy.'

'Rude,' muttered Tommy. 'I've got skills. In and out of the bedroom.'

'There are four of you,' said Agatha, speaking over him. 'I'm sure you can find a way to deal with any situation. That's why we're here, after all. In Stainmouth. To make a difference.'

'No one ever told me that,' said Tommy. 'I thought we were being punished.'

'That's just you, I'm afraid, Mr O'Strife,' said Agatha, rolling her eyes at him. 'Right, Miles will be back at half-past-six to drive both you and Miss Carrington-Finch to your destination. I suggest you all take the opportunity to rest up whenever the chance arises. From tonight onwards, we'll be working twenty-four hours a day.' Agatha paused. Took in the four glum faces staring back at her. 'This is nice, isn't it?' she said, clapping her hands together. 'My Nearly Dearly Departed Club are back in business.'

CHAPTER TWELVE

Miles was a minute early when he parked the Audi up on the driveway at Cockleshell Farm.

Which made it six twenty-nine. Sixty seconds to go. Leaning back in his car seat, he began the countdown. Olaf had been given the night off, so he was flying solo. Get this done and dusted, and he had the rest of the evening to himself. A week ago and that thought alone would've been enough to give him the shivers. His old living quarters – the Black Hart Hotel – had been a festering pigsty of a joint. Agatha, however, had been true to her word and upgraded him. Now Miles had a room at the Nightingale, a much more salubrious establishment where Agatha herself resided. It was slightly old-fashioned, but in a good way. Blazing log fires and antique furniture. A better class of customer. Miles could already see himself running a bath in his room. Sinking into it. Scrubbing the Stainmouth scum off his skin.

Six-thirty.

Miles was about to press the horn when Rose appeared in the doorway. She looked nervous as she crept out into the darkness and approached the Audi. Of course she did. This, like most things in life, was way out of her comfort zone. Hardly that surprising for somebody who jumped when opening the fridge.

'Hi,' whispered Rose, as she shuffled onto the back seat.

'Evening.' Miles glanced over his shoulder. Watched her fiddle with her seat belt. 'Where's the other one?'

The other one being Tommy. Rose's only reply was a shrug. Fair enough, thought Miles. She wasn't his keeper. If anything, that was Agatha.

Thankfully, neither Miles nor Rose had to wait long before the door swung open and Tommy dived head first into the Audi.

'Wotcha', Millie. I was hoping my big Scandinavian chum would've been chauffeuring us around tonight.'

'He's got a night off,' said Miles. 'And I'm not chauffeuring you anywhere. I'm giving you a lift. After that, you're on your own.'

'Just the way we like it, eh, babe?' said Tommy, nudging Rose in the ribs. 'Tonight might just be the night you get lucky.'

Rose turned towards the window. Stared at her own reflection in the glass. She had this to endure for the next twelve hours. An endless stream of sexual banter and puerile jokes. It wasn't that she found Tommy threatening or offensive. Just irritating. And the more he irritated her, the more he seemed to enjoy himself. As was the norm, her thoughts drifted to Rupert and their meeting tomorrow. It was the only thing she had to look forward to. The only thing that could drag her through her first night shift.

Miles, too, was struggling to deal with that evening's assignment. 'Are you going to put your seatbelt on?'

'Don't need to,' grinned Tommy. 'I trust you, Millie. I'm sure you're a very capable driver.'

'It's the law,' sighed Miles.

'We're above the fuckin' law!' cried Tommy, laughing hysterically. 'We're Pleasant Agatha's invisible army. We can do what the hell we like!'

Miles gripped hold of the steering wheel. He was losing his cool. He could feel it slipping away, disappearing into the Audi's footwell. 'Just put your seatbelt on, or I'll get out of the car and put it on myself,' he spat.

Rose shifted closer to the window. Shut her eyes. Tried to take herself out of the situation.

'I'd like to see you try,' sneered Tommy. 'I'll tell you what is against the law though, shall I? Pretending to fasten a seatbelt so you can fondle another man's private parts without his consent. Just because I'm good looking, it doesn't mean I'm there to be groped at. I'm a human being; not a piece of meat.'

'Right ...' Miles pushed open his door.

And Tommy clipped in his seatbelt. 'You need to lighten up, Millie. It was just a bit of fun. No one can take a joke these days.'

Miles took the deepest breath imaginable, but it made no difference. Infuriated, he slammed his door shut and started the engine. Began to reverse so he could turn the Audi around and head back the way he had come along the driveway.

'Where are we going, anyway?' asked Tommy, leaning forward in his seat, resting his chin on Miles's shoulder.

Miles shrugged him off. 'You don't need to know.'

'Well, how long will it take?'

'Ten minutes.'

'Perfect.' Tommy sat back in his seat. Stretched out his arms so he could tickle the back of Rose's neck. 'Ten minutes is just enough time to tell you a story. Settle in, guys, because this is hilarious. Now, have either of you ever been forced to stick your entire hand up a donkey's bottom?'

CHAPTER THIRTEEN

It wasn't hilarious, decided Miles.

A few seconds in and he could've told you that. Tommy's story wasn't even vaguely interesting. It was childish. Overly vulgar. Ridiculously drawn-out. Oh, and also completely untrue. No donkeys had been harmed in the creation of this wild fabrication. Tommy was talking out of his arse, no pun intended. The best bit about the whole thing, in fact, was when it was over.

The ten minutes were up.

They had arrived.

Miles parked up away from the streetlights. The sign said Haversham Way. A smart, modern cul-de-sac with ten townhouses on each side of the road. All painted white. All three storeys high. All as …

'Expensive as fuck round here,' remarked Tommy, practically drooling as he pressed his face up to the window.

'Cole Burroughs lives at number eight,' began Miles. 'We've got access to number seven. It's directly opposite. There's no one living there at the moment, but there's still some furniture scattered about. Whatever you do, don't turn any lights on. You'll only draw attention to yourselves. All the surveillance equipment is in the front bedroom on the first floor. You'll have a perfect view of Burroughs's sitting room and bedroom from there. Reports suggest that's where he spends most of his time. Take photos if you like, but all we really need to know are his whereabouts.'

Miles passed the keys to Rose. There were two on a key ring. Front and back door. 'Only enter through the back and then he won't see you. There's a passageway that runs all the way along the rear garden, and number seven is clearly marked on the gate.'

'And what if he does the same?' wondered Tommy. 'We'll never see him leave if he only goes out the back.'

'That's not possible,' said Miles. 'All the even numbers have got a brick wall at the rear of the property. Something to do with the old steel works. It's a bit of an eyesore. The wall's too tall to climb, even for someone like Burroughs.'

Tommy screwed up his face. 'Someone like Burroughs?'

'A professional,' explained Miles. 'Everything you're not.'

'Is he definitely in the house now?' asked Rose.

Miles nodded. 'There's an unmarked police car over the road that says so. Once you're in place, I'll give them the word to depart. Then you're on your own.'

'I'll be on my own alright,' snorted Tommy. 'If anything goes wrong, I'm sure Rose will be shaking in the corner whilst I—'

'Speak incessantly until someone punches you in the mouth,' finished Miles.

'Yeah, probably,' Tommy had to admit. 'Still, it's all good fun, isn't it? Right, one last question, and then you can run back to Pleasant Agatha like a good little boy. Is there any food in there? Biscuits? Crisps? Cakes? I'm not on about knocking up a sodding lasagne; I just want to eat. Because let's be clear here, Millie, I'm starving. And, as everyone knows, I don't do my best work on an empty stomach.' Tommy took a breath. Waited for a reply that wasn't forthcoming. 'So, is there?'

'Is there what?' Miles was barely listening, his mind fixed firmly on the bath in his hotel suite.

'Food!' shouted Tommy.

'Yes ... probably ... I don't know.' Miles glanced over his shoulder. 'What about you, Rose? Is there anything else you need to know?'

She shook her head as she climbed out of the car. Tommy did the same, albeit with a chorus of mumbled expletives aimed fairly and squarely at his driver.

Miles lowered his window. 'Lucas and Mercy will be here to take your place at seven tomorrow morning. They can borrow Proud Mary's Mini, and then one of you two can drive it home.' He turned to Rose. 'Good luck.'

'She won't need luck when we're together,' said Tommy. 'She'll need a cold shower. Probably one every hour if she's going to keep her hands off me.'

With that, he gave Miles the thumbs up, patted the Audi's bonnet and set off along Haversham Way.

Rose scampered after him. 'Back door,' she whispered.

'Oh, yeah.' Tommy performed an exaggerated u-turn before doubling back on himself.

'I don't envy you,' said Miles, smiling at Rose as he raised his window. The Audi was back on the move a moment later.

Rose caught up with Tommy and the two of them made their way along the passageway at the rear of the property. One of them walked slowly, almost on tip-toes, whilst the other skipped and bounced and danced like a hyperactive five-year-old. Rose had never seen him this animated before, something that Tommy was only too keen to confirm.

'This is exciting, isn't it? Our first home together. Just you and me. How romantic!'

Rose stopped at a wooden gate marked with a number seven. Pushing it to one side, she was surprised at the size of the garden compared to the house. Or rather, the lack of garden. Several short steps later, she reached the back door. Slotting the key into the lock, she turned it until it clicked. Slowly lowered the handle.

'Would you like me to carry you over the threshold?' asked Tommy.

'I'd rather you didn't touch me at all.' Rose stepped inside. Waited for Tommy to join her and then closed the door, careful to lock it behind them.

She wanted to switch on the light, but remembered Miles's warning. Instead, she waited for her eyes to adjust. They were in the kitchen. A polished wooden floor, white walls, and a high ceiling. Granite work surfaces and sleek units.

'Ah, this is a piece of me,' said Tommy, taking it all in. 'We should have a party. Get some girls round.' He paused. 'And men. You know, to balance it out. I'm not greedy. Ask them to bring their own drinks, though. Set up a sound system. Call the local dealer. Get some coke—'

A glare from Rose brought Tommy to an abrupt halt.

'Coca-Cola,' he finished awkwardly. 'Other soft drinks are readily available, of course. What do you reckon, Rose? Agatha will never know. You can even invite old mole face. Rupert, I mean. What do you reckon? It'll be our little secret. What do you reckon, Rose? What do you reckon?'

Tommy had asked the same question four times. Thankfully, Rose only had to answer it once. 'No. It's not happening.'

With that, she passed through the kitchen and entered the next room on the ground floor.

The sitting room.

A large rectangular space, it had the same wooden floor and white walls as the kitchen. There were several armchairs and a small coffee table in there, but that was it.

Tommy was still muttering something unintelligible under his breath by the time he caught up with her. 'You're torturing me, Rose. Denying my inner-party animal a night of fun.'

Rose squeezed past him and made her way up the stairs. The first floor comprised two more large rooms. The room to her left was empty except for a double bed, unmade, but piled high with sheets and blankets. It was the room to her right that really drew her attention, though. This was the surveillance room that Miles had mentioned. There were two tripods set up by the window, one for an enormous pair of binoculars, and the other for a long lens camera. There was an office chair beside them, no doubt so you could roll across the wooden floor at will, moving from the binoculars to the camera whenever the need arose. Behind that, there were two more chairs, recliners, designed purely for comfort, not practicality.

Tommy grabbed a blanket from the other room. Wrapped it around his shoulders. 'Gonna' need this. It's fuckin' freezing in here.'

Rose wandered over to the window. Opened the blinds just a fraction. She could see number eight. It was identical in size and layout to the house they were currently hiding out in. There was a light on in the sitting room, but no sign of a man who could've passed for Cole Burroughs. No sign of anybody, in fact.

'What now?' she asked. She was speaking to herself as much as anyone.

Tommy answered, regardless. 'Now we wait,' he sighed, slumping down onto one of the recliners. He pulled the lever and his legs rose into the air. 'Let's be serious. We're only here, in this house, because the geezer across the road is a complete nutcracker. Still, at least it should be entertaining. With any luck, he'll set fire to the entire street and then burn his own genitals, and all for our viewing enjoyment. Pass me the popcorn, Rose. Hopefully, we won't have to wait long for the fun to begin.'

CHAPTER FOURTEEN

On the other side of Stainmouth, in the village of Croplington, somebody else was in desperate need of entertainment.

'Two weeks,' moaned Mercy, as she paced the sitting room at Cockleshell Farm. 'Two weeks I've been stuck in that poky little flat. Two weeks with two fully grown yet practically feral men who can't seem to stop farting and burping and scratching and sweating and weeing on the toilet seat and ...' She paused for breath. 'And then I'm out. I'm free. No more hiding away. And what happens? I'm stuck again. Stuck in here. With you.'

'At least I don't wee on the toilet seat.' Lucas shifted from one side of the sofa to the other to get a better view of the television. It was all to no avail, though, due largely to the amount of times Mercy wandered in front of the screen. 'I don't do any of that other stuff either,' Lucas added, just in case she was wondering.

'This is depressing,' said Mercy, ignoring him. 'We're young. Young-ish. We should be out there doing something. Anything.'

'No money, no friends, no point.' Lucas said it like a mantra he repeated regularly throughout the day. 'Besides, I'm trying to watch the TV. Emphasis on trying.'

Mercy continued to pace up and down as a different thought entered her head. 'What can you tell me about this guy that Rose has been seeing?'

'Rupert?' Lucas shrugged his shoulders. 'Not much, really. He seems pretty normal. Quite boring. Not that dissimilar to Rose.' He checked himself. 'Sorry. That was harsh. No, there doesn't seem to be much to worry about, but Agatha got a whiff of something and insisted we follow him. In the end, Tommy got too close and Rose spotted him. She wasn't happy, as you can imagine.'

Mercy nodded. 'At least that explains why she was in a bad mood earlier.'

'Does it?'

Mercy stopped pacing. 'What's that supposed to mean?'

'Think about it. It wasn't me and Tommy who walked out on her without a word. She's been funny ever since. Quiet. Withdrawn. Even more so than usual. Then she met Rupert.'

'I'll talk to her,' said Mercy. 'I had my reasons for leaving.'

'Which are?'

Mercy hesitated. She had no wish to go into things now. How Errol Duggan had died was still a secret that only one other person was privy to.

'Which are?' repeated Lucas.

Mercy was about to speak when Proud Mary marched straight past her and sat down in her favourite armchair. Turning towards Lucas, she held out her hand. 'My programme is starting soon.'

As if that was the special code, Lucas stood up and passed her the remote control.

'Cross your fingers it's not the one about knitting,' he whispered to Mercy on his way back to the sofa. 'I hate that programme. It's next level tedious. Proper dull.'

'It's Timeless Yarns,' said Proud Mary, confirming Lucas's worst fears as she jabbed at the controller. 'They're knitting tank tops tonight. I can't wait.'

Lucas rolled his eyes. 'Me neither.'

'I can knit you one for Christmas if you like,' offered Proud Mary. 'Keep you warm whilst you help me muck out the pigs.'

Lucas slowly exhaled. 'Why not knit me six more and I can wear a different one for each day of the week?'

Proud Mary wasn't listening, though. Her attention, instead, had switched to Mercy. 'Why are you standing up? Have you got an announcement to make?'

Mercy shook her head. 'No. I was just—'

'Then sit down,' demanded Proud Mary. 'And stop talking. It's about to begin.'

Mercy took a seat on the sofa as the theme tune kicked into life. It was less than ten seconds before she started tapping her feet. Clicking her fingers. Shuffling from side to side. Eventually, she edged closer to Lucas. Whispered in his ear. 'We need to get out of here—'

'Shush.' Proud Mary pressed a finger to her lips before pointing towards the kitchen. 'One more word out of you two and I'll fetch my shotgun.'

Mercy kept her gaze fixed on Lucas. When he finally looked at her, she nodded towards the door. It was more than just a hint; it was a silent instruction.

'Do you two know what's upstairs?' asked Proud Mary out of the blue.

Mercy glanced up at the ceiling. 'Well ... um ... our bedrooms.'

'Correct,' said Proud Mary. 'Feel free to head that way any time you please. I won't get lonely. I enjoy my own company from time to time. And this is one of those times.'

With that, Lucas jumped up from the sofa and hurried out of the sitting room. When he reached the hallway, he dashed up the stairs. Mercy watched him all the way, a little put out that he hadn't warned her. Now she was stranded.

'One down,' said Proud Mary. She stretched out her legs and groaned. 'My feet are in tatters. It's not right keeping them stuffed inside wellies all day. Wouldn't be surprised if I've got a severe case of trench foot coming on. Be a dear, Mercy, and give me a foot massage, will you? Try to bring these trotters back to life.'

Mercy watched in horror as her elderly landlady removed her socks one at a time. 'I mean ... it's not that I don't ... I should probably go and see Lucas ... he was looking pale ... he might be feeling sick,' she said, stumbling over her words as she scrambled up off the sofa and exited the sitting room, stopping only to close the door behind her.

'Two down,' smiled Proud Mary. Picking up the remote, she increased the volume. 'Good riddance to bad company.'

Out in the hallway, Mercy scowled at Lucas as he made his way back down the stairs. 'Thanks for that. You could've told me you were leaving.'

'I forgot about this.' Lucas waved a folded sheet of paper in her face. 'Agatha gave it to me.'

'What is it?' asked Mercy, pushing it out of her eyes so she could see better.

'It's our evening's entertainment.' Lucas snatched the keys to Proud Mary's Mini out of the tray by the door. 'Let's go for a drive, shall we? I'll tell you all about it on the way.'

CHAPTER FIFTEEN

Tommy was right.

They didn't have to wait for long. No, not for Cole Burroughs to completely lose his shit. That would come soon enough if Tommy had his way. But for Burroughs to show himself.

Or for *someone* to show themselves.

It was Rose who noticed him first. Sat by the window, she was using the binoculars to see through the slightest of gaps in the blinds. The lights were on and the curtains were wide open in the house opposite when, without warning, a man crossed the length of the sitting room. He stopped at the window and crossed his arms. Stared out into the darkness.

'Tommy,' whispered Rose. Why was she whispering? Nobody could hear her. 'Tommy,' she said, only slightly louder. 'Come here.'

He arrived shortly after, huffing and puffing as he came wandering up behind her. He had already explored the rest of the house and the results were in. Three out of ten. A huge disappointment. The top floor was completely bare, whilst the fridge and most of the cupboards in the kitchen were practically empty. They would have to go out before long for provisions. Spend money they didn't have. 'What is it?' he asked grumpily.

'Cole Burroughs,' said Rose. 'I can see him.'

And then she couldn't. Without another word, Tommy had nudged her to one side so he could take her place by the binoculars and focus on the man in question.

And then question the man in question's questionable appearance.

'That's not him,' frowned Tommy, squinting for a better view. 'He doesn't look a bit like the guy in the photograph.'

True, thought Rose. The man in the window opposite had straggly hair that covered his ears, a thick beard and dark eyes that disappeared into his skull. He dressed entirely in black. Hoodie. Combats. Woolly hat and gloves. If anything, he looked like a burglar. Wait ...

'You don't think—'

'Not if I can help it,' said Tommy, interrupting her. 'Spend too much time in your own mind and you realise how shitty everything is these days. Better just to bury your head in the sand like an ostrich. A *sexy* ostrich. Are you listening to me?'

The fact that Rose didn't answer him suggested she wasn't. 'It's definitely the right house,' she muttered under her breath. 'Number eight. Miles never said if there would be anybody else there, though.'

'He's a bit creepy,' remarked Tommy, refusing to give up the binoculars. 'Not Miles. Well, yes, Miles, but I was talking about this fella. Wouldn't want to bump into him in a dark alley with my jeans pulled down around my ankles?'

Rose took a moment. 'I don't understand.'

'Why not? You can't run away if your jeans are around your ankles. You'd just trip over.'

'No, I get that. What I can't quite figure out is why they're around your ankles to begin with.'

'You've not met the same women I have,' explained Tommy. 'Al fresco dining for the working classes. Jeez, your furry-faced pal here is freaking me out.' Tommy moved away from the binoculars. 'Tell me when he does something of interest. Picking his nose or scratching his arse would be a start.'

Rose couldn't help but agree. All the man – the potential Cole Burroughs – was doing was gazing at the street outside. Her best guess was that he was trapped inside his own thoughts, something that Rose knew all too well. She could sympathise with that. She had a heart, after all. Tommy, in contrast, had probably ripped his out and sold it for a gram of cocaine and a doner kebab on a night out.

Which went a long way to explain why he was currently heading for the exit. Maybe he would check the kitchen one more time. Just in case. No one deserves to go hungry in this day and age, especially not a growing boy with a huge appetite and an ever-expanding ego.

Rose took his place behind the binoculars. 'Fuck.'

That one word was enough to stop Tommy in his tracks. It wasn't the word itself, but who had said it. Rose rarely ever swore, so when she did, you knew it was serious. 'What's up?'

'Burroughs ... if it is Burroughs ... is leaving the house.' Rose reached for a pen and paper to log his movements. 'What do you think we should do?'

'I thought that would've been obvious.' With that, Tommy set off down the stairs at a gallop. 'What you waiting for, Rose?' he called out. 'The target is on the move ... and so are we!'

CHAPTER SIXTEEN

Mercy tried to read the sheet of paper as she bounced up and down in the passenger seat of the Mini.

Tried *and* failed. Not that surprising, really. It was dark outside, which, somewhat inconveniently, meant it was also dark in the car. Add that to the potholes and pitfalls that lined many of Stainmouth's roads and she was fighting a losing battle that, if she was being honest, she had already lost some time ago.

'You've gone very quiet,' remarked Lucas. 'Are you still awake?'

Mercy had been staring at the paper for over three minutes now. It was written in English. Maybe. Could've been Arabic for all she knew. 'Go on. You'll have to spell it out for me.'

Lucas eased the Mini around a typically tight bend. 'It's a list—'

'No shit.'

'A list of places.'

Mercy waited. 'Is that it? A list of places? Like a tour of Stainmouth's most popular attractions? The abattoir. The sewerage works. The cabbage factory.'

'I didn't know Stainmouth had a cabbage factory.' Lucas weighed it up. Did it matter? Probably not. 'Agatha asked me and Tommy to keep tabs on Rose's boyfriend, right? Well, that's a list of all the places he frequents. I thought we could do a bit of gentle spying before bedtime. See what he's up to. Better than hanging out with Proud Mary.'

Mercy nodded. That was a pretty good idea in all honesty, not that she'd ever admit it. 'I still can't read what it says, though.'

Lucas removed a hand from the steering wheel. 'Give it here.'

'Don't crash,' said Mercy, passing him the paper.

'Oh, thanks for the reminder.' Lucas kept one eye on the twisty, turny bends as he glanced down at the list. 'I looked at this back at Cockleshell Farm, so it's fresh in my memory. Paperworks Printers. I'm guessing that's where he works, but they're closed at the moment. Same with the library. After that, it's the Mucky Duck.' He side-eyed Mercy. Smirked. 'You don't know what that is, do you?'

'Educate me, smart arse,' she replied sharply.

'It's a pub. I asked Proud Mary. She said it's a bit of a dive, but it's worth checking out.'

'Fair enough. Do you know where it is?'

'What do you think?' Lucas tossed the sheet of paper back to Mercy. 'Mucky Duck, here we come. I'll get us there in the blink of an eye.'

***

Not true.

The average person blinks somewhere between fifteen to twenty times a minute. And it was over five minutes before Lucas swung the Mini into the pub car park and searched for somewhere to pull up. The laborious process that followed comprised a great deal of reversing, straightening, and constant muttering under his breath. Not to mention numerous swear words and a peculiar squeal that sounded uncannily like a strangled goat.

'Happy now?' asked Mercy, once the Mini had finally come to a halt.

'Not particularly,' frowned Lucas. 'I'm slightly wonky. Maybe I should—'

'Maybe you shouldn't. Just forget about your parking and concentrate on what we're going to do next. This is your plan, after all.'

'Is it? Oh, I was hoping you might take the lead now. You're good at that.'

Mercy shook her head. Why couldn't any of them ever think for themselves? How had they coped for the past few weeks without her? She took a breath, all set to vent her frustration, when Lucas placed a hand across her mouth, shutting her up immediately.

'Be quiet a sec,' he whispered, peering through the windscreen. 'I think—'

'That if you ever do that again, I'll knock you clean out,' said Mercy, finishing his sentence once she'd shifted his hand.

'No, forget that. Look outside … I can't tell if it's … yeah, it is. It's definitely him. There.' Lucas pointed across the car park. 'That's Rupert. That's the boyfriend.'

Mercy leant forward and watched as a man wandered straight past the Mini. He was of average height, average build, average all over. Thick hair swept back into a side-parting. A large mole covered much of one cheek, whilst both his hands clutched hold of a battered leather suitcase that he struggled to lift off the ground. 'Are you sure?' Mercy asked.

Lucas nodded. 'Ninety-per-cent. Ninety-five. It's not like we're the best of friends, is it? The thing is, if it's not him, then it's someone who looks a lot like him going to a place that he hangs out in. What are the chances of that?'

'Slim to impossible.' Mercy was still focussed on the man as he made his way towards the entrance to the pub. Then he disappeared from view. 'Has Rupert ever seen you before?'

'No,' said Lucas, without thinking. When he did think, the answer was the same. 'He only saw Tommy. I stayed out of sight at all times. Why?'

Mercy opened the door and climbed out of the Mini. 'I fancy a drink in the Mucky Duck. Care to join me?'

CHAPTER SEVENTEEN

'Hold my hand.'

It was Tommy who made the unexpected demand. And it was Rose who dismissed it with a frantic shake of her head.

'It's nothing weird,' Tommy insisted. 'We just have to play the part. If matey boy Burroughs turns around and spots us, it'll look better if we're holding hands. Like boyfriend and girlfriend. You'd be punching, of course, but needs must. What could be more normal than a pair of young lovers out for an early evening stroll? Better that than two odd-bods walking a metre apart, practically sprinting to keep up with each other.' Tommy paused. 'If you think you can get pregnant from holding hands, you're wrong. You know that, don't you?'

Rose glared at him out the corner of one eye. How naïve did he think she was? No, don't answer that. With no witty comeback of her own, her initial response was to ignore his request. Dig her heels in. Stubborn for the sake of it. It was never more than a passing thought, though. Largely because Tommy's idea was built on stable foundations. It made sense. Unfortunately.

'Now, that wasn't so hard, was it?' grinned Tommy, as Rose took his hand. 'We make a lovely couple, don't you think?'

No, thought Rose, but it was dark and they were moving at speed, so maybe nobody would notice.

And if nobody noticed, then neither would Cole Burroughs. At that very moment, he was about thirty metres ahead of them. Shoulders hunched, hands in pockets. Neither walking fast nor slow. Like he wanted to get somewhere, but was in no rush to do so.

'Where do you think he's going?' wondered Rose, hurrying herself along.

'How the hell am I supposed to know?' replied Tommy. 'I'm not a psychic. He should think about getting his haircut, though. And a shave. Women aren't interested in the caveman look. I mean, if that's what his head looks like, imagine what's going on inside his underpants. Small animals have probably set up home there amongst the undergrowth.'

Fortunately for Rose, she had switched off a long time ago and didn't have to imagine any of that. She couldn't be certain, but something had changed in the distance. Burroughs seemed to have come to a halt.

Rose gripped Tommy's hand until the two of them slowed in unison. 'What's he doing?' she whispered.

Burroughs vanished from view before either of them could answer that question. That was the cue for them to increase their pace. A steady walk. Nothing unusual about that. It didn't take long for them to realise that he hadn't vanished in the magical sense of the word, but simply entered a building.

Grab & Go.

A corner shop. Convenience store. Independent retailer. Take your pick. Like a blast from the past, it was small and compact, with seventies decor and poor lighting. Tommy guessed that the shop would be fit to burst whilst the prices would be sky high. The supermarket big boys hadn't moved in to this part of town yet and forced the little guy out of business. Simply staying open was a success. Making a profit from day to day was the stuff of dreams.

'Where are you going?' asked Rose, as Tommy made his way towards the entrance.

He spun around. Pulled a face. 'Inside.'

'Really?' Rose scurried after him. 'You can't. I mean, he might see you.'

'I can ... and I don't care,' insisted Tommy. 'It's a shop – not his fuckin' knicker drawer. Besides, there's stuff I want to buy. You coming in, Rose? Good. And don't forget your purse.'

Rose drew a weary breath. She didn't own a purse. That didn't stop her from entering the shop though, preferably before Tommy did something they would both regret.

By the time she had caught him up, he was already taking in his surroundings. The floor space was seriously limited, but the aisles were narrow and the shelves were full. Grabbing a basket, Tommy was back on the move a moment later. Snatching at items of interest, he opted mainly for sugary treats aimed at hyperactive toddlers. Zoo animals and aliens featured primarily on the wrappers. A short-term high in exchange for a lifetime of diabetes.

'Why do you need all that?' asked Rose, keeping pace with him as he slipped between the aisles.

'Snacks for the house,' said Tommy. 'Don't worry; I'll share it with you. It'd be rude not to. Especially seeing as you're paying.'

'Aren't you forgetting something?' Rose rested a hand on Tommy's forearm before he could pick up any more food. Spoke in a hushed voice. 'Where's Cole Burroughs?'

'Somewhere,' said Tommy. 'We'll find him when I'm finished.' That was his cue to look around for the till. He found it at the opposite end of the store. And stood behind it, a shop assistant of the female variety. Early-twenties at most. Heavy on the make-up. Unnecessarily so, Tommy decided. Whatever she was trying to hide, there was no need. She was alright. Decent even. In a world of few opportunities, and even fewer opportunities to act upon those few opportunities, she was an unexpected bonus. And what better way to liven up her dull shift than a spot of interaction with Stainmouth's newest sex symbol. The thinking woman's crumpet. Not forgetting all the less intelligent women as well. No need to discriminate against them. They had feelings, too.

Thoughts flying, Tommy raced out of the aisle with his eyes fixed on the young assistant behind the counter. If she looked up, caught his eye, he would greet her with a wink. No, too much. Just a smile would do the trick. Break her in gently. When the smile was returned, and the girl was onside, he would start the chat. The chat that had served him well throughout the years. And his opening line ...

Tommy's brain was still mulling it over when he crashed into another customer. They had approached from a different aisle. Appeared on Tommy's blindside. The *clang* of baskets was enough to wake the shop assistant from her slumber. She glanced up, but things had changed. Suddenly she was old news. Tommy was no longer looking at her.

Instead, he was staring at the man he had bounced off.

A man with long, straggly hair and a thick beard.

A man dressed all in black.

Hello, Cole Burroughs. Fancy seeing you here.

CHAPTER EIGHTEEN

The best thing about the Mucky Duck was that you would never feel overdressed, whatever you were wearing.

The worst thing about it was everything else. From the wallpaper to the carpet, not to mention every scuff and stain in between, the pub was well overdue a makeover. Although *well overdue* was just a polite way of saying desperately in need of. And *desperately in need of* was just an even more polite way of saying beyond hope. Still, at least the pub was easy to sum up. No need to beat around the bush.

'This is a dump,' remarked Mercy, within three seconds of stepping inside the premises.

'Keep it down,' said Lucas. 'We're already getting eyeballs from the other side of the room. We don't want to get on the wrong side of the regular clientele if we can help it.'

The *regular clientele* were all sat together around one large table. Ten of them in total, all men. An unglamorous combination of shaven heads, bloated faces, and patchy stubble. Faded tattoos on flabby arms. Hunched over, they were deep in conversation.

At least, they *were*.

Now the conversation had ceased as they turned towards the doorway. Ten pairs of eyes staring in disbelief at the two new arrivals. There was no sign of Rupert, though. If he was in there, then he must be hiding in the lavatory.

Mercy and Lucas had barely reached the bar when a woman appeared from the other side. She was mid-fifties at a guess. A curly head of red hair fighting to stay out of her eyes. Small in size, but still in good shape for her age, something she was keen to show off judging by her ample cleavage and thigh-length skirt. Lucas nodded at her by way of a greeting. She returned the gesture with a scowl, which she soon turned to words.

'What do you think you're doing in here?'

Lucas pointed at himself. 'Who? Me personally?'

'Both of you,' said the barmaid.

'Getting a drink,' replied Lucas. That was true. Or had been. Maybe not now if her reaction was anything to go by.

'Not possible, I'm afraid.' The barmaid glanced over at the regular clientele before leaning over the pumps. When she spoke again, she had dropped the volume to little more than a whisper. 'Just go. Now. Don't hang around and you might be alright.'

'You need to work on your customer service,' frowned Mercy. 'This place isn't exactly heaving, is it?'

The barmaid shook her head. 'You're not listening. I don't want to be here. I don't think like them. But a job's a job, right? I need the money.'

Lucas held her gaze. Either the woman was completely

insane, or there was something else troubling her. Something yet to be explained.

'I'm trying to ... oh, shite.' The barmaid turned at the sound of scraping chair legs. One of the men had stood up from the table. He was big, bald and barrel-bodied. The last of which probably reminded him.

'Haven't you got a barrel to change, Donna?'

It was less of a question and more of a demand. The barmaid responded with a nod and a smile. Her last action before she headed towards the basement was to pull a face at Lucas. What was that? A look of disgust? Or an apology?

The man moved behind the bar. Looked them up and down. 'Is this a joke?' he asked.

Lucas shrugged. 'Not intentionally. Have we done something to upset you?'

The man threw back his head and laughed. That was the cue for the rest of his table to join in.

'Oh, you've done a lot to upset me,' said the man. The laugh ended abruptly. 'You know what you two should've done? Listened to Donna. She's got your best interests at heart. She's not quite as ... *dedicated* as the rest of us.'

'I haven't got a clue what you're talking about,' admitted Lucas.

The man jabbed a finger at the door. 'You should've left when you had the chance.'

Mercy peered over her shoulder at the exit. 'The chance hasn't gone away.'

'Hasn't it?' The man gestured towards the table. At the hostile faces staring back at him. 'We're a tight-knit bunch here at the Mucky Duck. We're solid. We think the same. What we don't like is your kind invading our space ... polluting the atmosphere.'

'Our kind?' Mercy felt her hackles rise. 'What's that supposed to mean?'

'I thought that would've been pretty self-explanatory, sweetheart,' hissed the man. 'You're not welcome here. Never have been, never will be.'

Lucas looked over at the table. Others were rising from their seats. Reinforcements if things turned nasty. Well, there was no way that was about to happen. To go two on ten would've been suicide. Only a fool would think they had a chance.

Only a fool ... or Mercy.

Lucas tried to grab her arm, but was left clutching at thin air when she easily shrugged him off. 'Is this because we're black?' she asked, going eye to eye with the man behind the bar.

He smiled. Cracked teeth and a lop-sided grin. 'Read the room,' he spat. 'Of course it's because you're black. Now, what you gonna' do about it?'

CHAPTER NINETEEN

Tommy momentarily froze at the sight of Cole Burroughs.

Emphasis on momentarily. A second or two at most. Then he was back. Bobbing up and down. Rolling his shoulders. Burroughs's face was expressionless, his glare icy cold, but Tommy either didn't notice or didn't care.

'Apologies,' he boomed. To Rose's despair, Tommy had chosen to use a different voice. Bold and brash. At least a class higher with echoes of a privileged education. 'I failed to see you on the horizon, old chap, and for that, I am well and truly sorry. I was …' He glanced at the female assistant behind the counter. Raised an eyebrow. 'Distracted. Easily done under the circumstances.'

Burroughs didn't bat an eyelid.

'Next customer,' the assistant called out.

'After you, my good man,' said Tommy, waving him past. 'I wouldn't wish to stand in the way of you and your …' He peered into Burroughs's basket. 'Whiskey. Two bottles. That's quite the evening you've got planned for yourself there.'

Burroughs nodded. Stepped forward without a word.

At the same time, Tommy slipped in behind him. Smiled at Rose. She didn't smile back. If anything, she wanted to strangle him. What was he thinking, the bloody fool? One minute of madness and he had put the entire operation at risk. Put *them* at risk. And for what? Just to be a smart arse? To play up to an imaginary crowd who weren't even watching?

Burroughs paid for his shopping before loading the two bottles into a plastic bag. He left the shop soon after. Rose's first thought was one of fear. Fear of losing him. For Tommy, however, that thought couldn't have been further from his mind.

'Hello ... um ... I don't think we've been introduced,' he said, strolling up to the counter.

The shop assistant pointed at her name badge.

Straining his neck, Tommy focussed on the tiny lettering. 'Candice. That's nice. So, Candice, what time do you get off tonight?'

Rose elbowed him gently in the ribs. 'What do you think you're doing? We need to—'

'Patience,' said Tommy, raising a hand. 'Let Candice speak.'

'What time do I get off? When the shop closes,' mumbled Candice. She kept her head down as she scanned the shopping.

'Yeah, well, that makes sense I suppose,' muttered Tommy, knocked slightly off his stride. 'Maybe I could meet you after work. Show you what Stainmouth has to offer.'

Candice didn't look up.

'Or maybe another time,' pressed Tommy. 'A spot of lunch.

Dinner. Or just a drink. You name it.'

'Seriously?' hissed Rose. 'You're doing this now. He's going to get away.'

Candice glanced at Rose. 'I don't think your girlfriend would be thrilled.'

'Oh, she's not my girlfriend,' blurted out Tommy. He took a step to one side, leaving a gap between them as if to prove the point. 'She's my—'

'Carer,' chipped in Rose. 'I look after him. Pretty much all day, every day. He can't be trusted out in public by himself. He talks too much. To people like you. Women who ... you know ... don't like it—'

'That's bullshit,' cried Tommy.

Candice, however, had swallowed it hook, line and sinker. Nodding at Rose, she then turned her attention back to Tommy. 'That'll be sixteen pounds and forty-three pence, please.'

'Don't listen to her,' said Tommy, clearly aggrieved. 'She's lying out of her arse. She hasn't got a clue ... erm ... can you lend me some money please, Rose?'

Rose squeezed in front of him and handed Candice a twenty-pound note. She waited for the change and then took the bag of shopping. Left the shop. And, for the time being at least, Tommy as well.

'Right,' he said, rubbing his hands together. 'Now that she's gone, we can get to know each other a little better.'

Candice had moved on, though. To the next customer in the

line. And then the one after that. And the one after that.

A disgruntled Tommy was reunited with Rose outside the shop.

'What did you do that for?' he moaned. As an after-thought, he snatched the bag out of her hand, not as an act of chivalry but because they were his snacks and he was no longer in the mood to share them.

'We were going to lose Burroughs,' said Rose. She pointed at a shadowy figure in the distance, as if to prove that it hadn't quite come to that.

'No, we weren't,' argued Tommy. 'We know where he's going. Back home. To get stuck into the whiskey and then pass out on the sofa. Can hardly blame him either.'

'And what if he doesn't?' asked Rose, as the two of them started to walk.

'He will,' insisted Tommy.

And yet he didn't.

Without warning, Burroughs took a left turn and drastically changed his route.

'Yeah, alright, clever bollocks,' Tommy muttered. 'No need to look so smug about it.'

Rose didn't look smug, though; just pensive. She watched as Burroughs carried on for a while before he crossed the road and made his way down a narrow side street.

'I would've thought this was a dead end,' said Tommy, as they edged closer.

Rose turned to him. Frowned. 'Now you're just trying to

scare me.'

The street was quiet and what little noise there was came from blaring televisions and the occasional crackle of shining street lights. Street lights that seemed to be rapidly decreasing in number with every step.

Rose grabbed Tommy's hand and squeezed with enough force that he almost yelped. 'What if he knows we're following him?' she whispered. 'What if he's going to confront us ... and we're trapped ... and—'

'Chill out.' Tommy laughed. Not because he found it funny, but because he didn't want to show how nervous he really was. 'You've forgotten who you're holding hands with. I'm like a tiger in the wild. I don't fight clean; I go in dirty. I've knocked out bigger men than him before breakfast.'

Tommy was talking, Rose was listening, but neither of them believed what was being said.

'We should turn back,' suggested Rose, filling in the gap when Tommy finally paused for breath. 'I don't like it.'

Tommy tensed up. 'It'll be fine,' he said unconvincingly.

The houses were coming to an end. As was the street itself. Burroughs was getting harder to spot, his dark clothes blending in effortlessly with the night sky. So hard, in fact, that ...

'Where's he gone?' said Tommy, his eyes darting this way and that.

They had both slowed their step without a word being passed between them. Without warning, Tommy spun around. He had sensed something by his shoulder, but there was nothing there.

By the time he had turned back, Rose had let go of his hand and walked over to a metal gate. It was chained up for the evening. There was a sign hanging from the railings, though.

'St. Benedict's Cemetery,' she read out loud.

'Wonderful.' Tommy closed his eyes as his stomach turned somersaults. 'What could be better than a stroll through a graveyard in the dark with a crazed psychopath? You lead the way, Rose. I'll be right behind you.'

CHAPTER TWENTY

His arms around Mercy's waist, Lucas dug his heels into the pub carpet before she could make her move.

It wasn't a lucky guess. He knew her well enough by now to know that her heart would overrule her head and she would react angrily. Fists first. Everything else after. Attack ... attack ... attack. All he could think about were the odds, though.

Ten on two.

That wasn't just a little tricky; that was undeniably impossible.

'I want to see the landlord,' demanded Lucas, desperate to find another solution.

'You're looking at him,' said the man behind the bar. 'This is my pub. The name's above the door. Barry Blackstock.'

Lucas had to use all his willpower to stop himself from smiling. 'That's a bit ironic, don't you think?'

Blackstock curled his top lip into a snarl. 'Why?'

'I thought that would've been self-explanatory,' said Lucas, mimicking the landlord. His next approach was far less confrontational. 'Listen, we only came in here looking for someone. We don't want any trouble—'

'Don't we?' spat Mercy, straining to free herself.

'No, we don't,' Lucas insisted. 'The man we're looking for ... Rupert—'

'Rupert?' Blackstock snorted. 'There are no Ruperts in here.'

'Fine. Then we'll leave you to it.' Lucas, still holding onto Mercy, tried to shuffle backwards towards the door.

'Yeah, you do that,' said Blackstock, waving them away with an arrogant flick of the wrist. 'Get out of my pub. Get out of my town. Get out of my country.'

'That's it!' Mercy pushed Lucas away and raced forward.

At the same time, Blackstock smashed a pint glass against the bar. Held the jagged remains at arm's length. 'Go on,' he growled through gritted teeth. 'Just you try it, bitch. Give me an excuse to scar that pretty little face of yours.'

Mercy skidded to a halt. She hadn't stopped her attack; just reevaluated the situation. A weapon had been drawn, and that weapon did damage. Don't dive in head first and suffer the consequences. Hold back. Pick your moment. Two blows would do the trick. One to disarm, one to inflict some damage of her own. And yet she couldn't get close enough to do either.

Think. There had to be another way.

Reaching behind her, Mercy picked up a stool from under an empty table and got ready to launch it at the landlord.

'Mercy, no!' shouted Lucas.

'Yeah, Mercy, listen to your fella,' said a grinning Blackstock. 'If you throw that at me, then my friends here will be forced to retaliate. We'll tell the police it was self-defence and we'll get away with it. That's if we bother to tell them at all. I'm guessing nobody knows you're here. A dead body won't be so hard to dispose of.' He glanced at Lucas. 'Two dead bodies might be slightly more difficult, though.'

Lucas moved in front of Mercy, blocking her line of sight. 'Give it here,' he said, taking the stool from her grasp before she had a chance to throw it. Placing it down by the table, he then turned his attention to Mercy herself. Moving swiftly, he secured her by the arms and dragged her towards the exit.

'This isn't the end,' barked Mercy, eyeballing the landlord.

Blackstock pretended to shake. 'Any time, any place, darling. But you'd better bring an army because I'll bury you.'

That was the last thing Mercy heard before Lucas bundled her out of the door and into the car park. He had almost dragged her all the way to the Mini when Mercy finally shook him off. 'What do you think you're playing at?'

Lucas staggered backwards. 'Saving your skin,' he said once he'd regained his balance. 'You didn't stand a chance in there. They'd have murdered you.'

'I don't care,' cried Mercy. She kicked the Mini's tyre. Swung a fist wildly at thin air. 'Do you hear me? I do not care.'

'Not now perhaps, but you will do,' insisted Lucas. 'Right or wrong, it's always best to walk out of somewhere alive. They taught me that in the force.'

Mercy turned away from him. Tried to control her breathing. He had a point. A *good* point. Of course he did. But that didn't make the situation any more bearable.

'Barry Blackstock just racially abused us,' she muttered under her breath. 'And then threatened to kill me. He can't just get away with that.'

'I'm not going to argue with you, but if you want to go head-to-head with him, then you have to do it when the time is right. On your own terms.' Lucas placed a hand on Mercy's shoulder. Expected her to shrug it away, but she didn't. 'We need to get our heads back in the game. This is about Rose, remember? Nobody else. Rupert might not have been in the Mucky Duck, but he is somewhere. People don't just vanish.'

No, they don't, thought Mercy. Which got her thinking some more. 'Come on,' she said, storming back towards the pub.

'Not now,' pleaded Lucas, hurrying after her.

'No, not now,' said Mercy, avoiding the entrance. 'Barry Blackstock will keep. But you heard him. He said there's no one called Rupert in there. So, where did he go?'

She set off around the side of the Mucky Duck. She was out of sight of the car park, but if Rupert hadn't entered the pub, then he must have gone this way instead. Still on the move, Mercy almost tripped over an iron stairway at the side of the building. Also known as a fire escape to those of a nervous disposition, it led all the way to a top floor door.

Lucas watched as Mercy took to the steps. Started to regret that he had ever set foot outside Cockleshell Farm. 'Surely we should get out of here before Barry and his bigot boys come looking for trouble.'

'Just give me a minute,' said Mercy. The higher she climbed, the more she could hear. Shouts and screams mostly. Coming from somewhere behind the door.

Mercy stopped when she reached the top step.

Lucas was right behind her. 'What's going on in there?'

Mercy didn't reply. Instead, she let her actions do the talking.

Pulling down on the handle, she raced into the room before coming to a sudden halt. There was something there, pointing straight at her, glistening in the bright lights.

Something long and sharp, only inches from her face.

Something that looked remarkably like a sword.

CHAPTER TWENTY-ONE

St. Benedict's Cemetery had been locked up for the night.

But there was still a side gate.

A side gate that Cole Burroughs had used to gain access.

'We're not really going in there, are we?' asked Rose. She decided against holding Tommy's hand and moved up to his arm instead, clutching it tightly.

'It's just a cemetery,' he said, feigning nonchalance. That much was true, at least. It *was* just a cemetery.

'I think it's a trap,' panted Rose, struggling to breathe properly.

'Yeah, well, you would do.' Tommy did, too, but kept that particular detail to himself. 'Come on,' he said, practically dragging her along. 'Let's not stand around like a pair of victims. There are two of us. Strength in numbers and all that. Me and you versus a complete nutcase.'

They passed through the gate in single file before walking side by side along a path that broke off in numerous other directions around the cemetery. There were gravestones on either side of them of all shapes and sizes.

'God help me if I end up in here,' remarked Tommy. 'Six feet under being munched on by worms and fuck knows what other insects. I can't think of anything worse.'

'You wouldn't have to think about it at all,' replied Rose. 'You wouldn't even know it was happening. Not if you were dead.'

'You're a cheerful little soul, aren't you?' Tommy strained his eyes for a better view of their murky surroundings. 'I think Burroughs is playing games with us. He probably fucked off out of here ages ago. He's given us the slip—'

Rose came to a sudden halt. Pulled hard on Tommy's arm to stop him, too. He was about to protest when she put a finger to her lips. When she was sure he understood, she pointed along the length of the path towards an overhanging tree less than twenty metres from where they were standing. There was a wooden bench beneath the lowest of the branches. A wooden bench with somebody sat on it. A man, dressed all in black. Leant forward, he had his head in his hands.

Cole Burroughs hadn't given them the slip at all.

Tiptoeing backwards, Tommy's eyes darted in every direction as he searched for somewhere to hide. There was one gravestone that stood out in particular. A huge stone affair depicting an angel with open wings. Grabbing hold of Rose, he pulled her behind it. Crouching down, they huddled together, keen to make themselves as small as possible.

'What's he doing?' frowned Tommy.

'I'm sure we'll find out soon enough,' said Rose, fearing the worst.

And she was right. In the time it had taken them to hide, Burroughs had lifted his head and chosen to stare into the black void that surrounded him. He shuffled slightly and kicked the shopping bag by his feet. As if that was all the encouragement he needed, he reached inside and removed a bottle of whiskey. Unscrewing the top, he put it to his mouth and took a huge gulp. There was a momentary delay as the liquid disappeared down his throat before he coughed and spluttered. Then he repeated the process.

Rose leant in closer. Whispered in Tommy's ear. 'Do you think he's seen us?'

Tommy gently shook his head. 'Not a chance.'

Back on the bench and Cole took another mouthful. Wiped his mouth on his sleeve. 'You can come out,' he said, his voice breaking through the eerie silence of the cemetery grounds. 'I know you're there.'

Bollocks.

Tommy ducked down even more, tucking his head into his shoulders as he cursed under his breath.

A few seconds later, Cole spoke again. 'I'm not going to hurt you. I promise. I just want to know what you're doing.'

Rose stared at Tommy, but all he did was shake his head.

'I don't like being followed.' Cole took another drink from the bottle. It gave him a moment to choose his words carefully. 'There are things I have to do. Bad things. And I don't want anyone to get in the way.'

Tommy held his breath. He had a tickle in his throat that

could only be cured with a cough.

'Have it your way.' Cole screwed the top back on the bottle, put it in the bag, and stood up. 'Don't say I didn't warn you,' he said, heading back towards the exit at a steady pace. He passed Tommy and Rose and their angel gravestone, but kept on moving. 'There's a dark cloud looming,' he called out. 'Whatever you do, don't get caught beneath it.'

CHAPTER TWENTY-TWO

Mercy raised her hand to block the sword.

It was an instinctive reaction. The best of two evils. No one wants to get stabbed, but if it's going to happen, then it's better to get slashed across the palm then poked in the eye. She waited for the inevitable pain at the point of impact. Searing and red-hot. Followed by the flow of blood as it spurted from the open wound.

She was still waiting when the sword broke off in her hand.

'I am so sorry!' cried a woman in a white toga, open-toed sandals and something that looked unerringly like a beekeeper's hat. Backing away from the door, she lowered her half of the sword. Her cardboard sword. Wrapped in tinfoil. 'I had no idea you were there—'

'Wrong! Wrong! Wrong! This isn't in the script! Who told you to improvise? Ah, I see we have fresh meat in attendance ...'

Mercy looked on in bemusement as a peculiar man approached from the other end of the room. He was as round as he was tall, with an extravagant moustache and rosy red cheeks.

Dressed in a pink roll neck jumper, flared trousers and a black beret, he waddled towards them like a human penguin on ice. Arms by his side, head wobbling, a broad grin spread across his face.

'Welcome to the Stainmouth Amateur Dramatic Society,' he bellowed. 'My name is Montgomery Wingston, but you can call me Bingo. I am the writer, the director, the ... genius behind this whole production. And these ...' Bingo opened his arms and gestured around the room. 'These are my children.'

Lucas cast an eye over the assembled throng. There was at least twenty people in there. A mixed bunch, men and women, ranging anywhere from eighteen to eighty. All were dressed up, but it was hard to pinpoint what they were supposed to be wearing. A tunic here, a table cloth there. Even a suit of armour.

'What play are you performing?' asked Lucas, genuinely interested.

'Play?' Bingo gave a little chuckle. 'Oh, this is more than a play, dear boy. This is my masterpiece. My magnum opus. This is the Lord of the Rings.'

'Wow!' Lucas pulled a face. 'That's a big book to tackle.'

'It's a little ambitious, yes,' admitted Bingo, 'but why limit ourselves to the tried and tested when we can reach for the stratosphere?' He paused. Studied the two new arrivals with a critical eye. 'You're not looking to audition, are you? We are missing a Gandalf, but neither of you quite fit the bill. You're nowhere near ... *wizardy* enough for my liking. As elves, however—'

'No, we're not looking to audition,' said Lucas hastily. He continued to take in the room. Picked out the individual faces. 'We were looking for a friend of ours. We thought he came in here, but maybe we were ...'

Lucas stopped talking when he met Rupert's gaze. That was him alright. Yes, he was wearing a fake beard and a long, green cloak, but there was no doubt about it. If nothing else, it was his mole that gave him away.

'Maybe you were ...?' wondered Bingo.

'Wrong,' said Lucas, shaking his head. 'Our friend isn't here. Sorry for gate-crashing rehearsals.'

Bingo hopped forward. Drew them in closer. 'Whatever you do, don't ask downstairs.'

'Been there, done that,' sighed Mercy.

Bingo pressed a hand to his forehead. Practically swooned. 'Oh, my, they're horrid, aren't they? Frightful, frightful people. We avoid them the best we can, but sometimes it's nigh on impossible. Every minute of every day I question my motives, whether feathering their hateful cap with our honest pennies is the right thing to do, and yet there's no other option. We've been barred from every church hall and community centre in the surrounding area. They call it noise pollution; I call it blatant prejudice. Heathens, the lot of them. We're being persecuted for our art.' Bingo pretended to wipe a tear from his eye. 'Sometimes a room above a pub full of racist thugs is the best that life has to offer. Maybe there's a metaphor in there somewhere.'

'Yeah, give up whilst you still can,' muttered Mercy under her breath.

'Never, my dear,' Bingo barked back at her. 'We have our first performance in two weeks. Five nights of open air magic on Rafter's Green. Pray for fine weather, I implore you. You're welcome to come and watch, of course. Bring your friends and family. It's all free, naturally, although a bucket may get passed around at the finale. Alas, one cannot feed oneself on acting talent alone.'

'No, I ... erm ... don't suppose one can,' mumbled Lucas.

'We really need to go,' insisted Mercy, edging away.

'Then be gone,' roared Bingo. He bounded towards the door and threw it open. 'The night is young and we have a lot to do. Goodbye, good luck and good tidings. Until we meet again ... in two weeks ... on Rafter's Green.'

With that, Bingo physically forced them out of the door before slamming it shut behind them.

'Well, that was one way to end this weird and wonderful night,' remarked Lucas.

'I'm not sure which one was worse,' said Mercy. 'Barry or Bingo? On second thoughts, scratch that. I know exactly which was worse. And it's the one I'd like to punch in the face.'

'Bingo doesn't deserve that. You'd knock his beret off.'

'Funny,' groaned Mercy, as she set off down the steps. 'What about Rupert? Was he in there?'

Lucas nodded. 'Yeah, I clocked him just before Bingo sent us packing. So, what does that tell you? That Rupert's into his amateur dramatics? That he's an actor?'

'He's not just an actor,' said Mercy, correcting him. 'He's a *bad* actor. So, ask yourself this. Is Rose the kind of person who would fall for the lies and deceptions of your bog-standard fraud?'

'Maybe he's not like that,' said Lucas, as he hopped off the bottom step and turned towards the car park. 'Maybe he's just a nice guy.'

'Yeah, maybe,' mused Mercy. 'Only time will tell, I suppose. Until then, we'll have to keep an eye on Rose. At least she can't get into any trouble tonight. Not stuck in that house with Tommy. Do you think they've seen him yet? Cole Burroughs, I mean?'

'Probably not,' said Lucas. 'I've done surveillance before, remember? Half the time you're not doing anything, and the other half you're doing even less than that. It's mind-numbingly boring.'

Mercy threw up her arms. 'Yeah, well, sometimes boring is good. It was boring at Cockleshell Farm, and we probably should've stayed there. Boring can't get you into trouble, can it? Or worse, get you killed. With any luck, Cole Burroughs will be the most boring man on the planet and this will all be for nothing. We can only hope,' she sighed, climbing into the Mini. 'Cross your fingers.'

CHAPTER TWENTY-THREE

It was gone midnight when Rose next saw him.

Him being Cole Burroughs.

They had been back at the townhouse on Haversham Way for over four hours. Until then, Burroughs had kept a relatively low profile. But then so, too, had Tommy. Ever since they had returned from Grab & Go – via St. Benedict's – he had just sat in the recliner behind Rose and the surveillance equipment, stuffing his face with as much food as he could squeeze in at any one time. Sporadically, he offered some to Rose, or reminded her about how he could take Burroughs with his eyes closed, or how he might nip back to see Candice tomorrow and tell her it was all a sick joke, and he wasn't some twisted pervert who wet himself at the sight of a woman, and he was actually a great guy who would show her a good time, even if he was living off the peanuts that Agatha Pleasant occasionally fed him, and then ...

Then he must've fallen asleep. Because the next time Rose looked, he had scurried off to the other bedroom so he could crawl under the blankets and settle down for the night in a sugar-induced coma. Eyes closed and mouth open, drool trickling down his chin, surrounded by wrappers and packets and crumbs and bigger chunks that had somehow missed their target and stuck to his clothes.

Not that Rose was complaining. This was the Tommy she liked best. The Tommy who wasn't talking. Who wasn't even in the same room as her.

But the sight of Cole Burroughs after midnight had made her, first, shiver, before wondering if she should wake Tommy from his unscheduled slumber.

Standing by his sitting room window, Burroughs had crossed his arms and stared at the house opposite his own. He stayed that way for some time, whilst Rose tried to convince herself that everything was fine. He didn't know she was there. He couldn't see her.

So what was he looking at?

It was half-twelve when Burroughs finally walked away. The light in his sitting room went out, before the light in the first-floor bedroom replaced it. The curtains were already closed, so Rose couldn't see anything. Shame. If she was being honest, she would've liked to have seen him getting undressed. No, not like that, she told herself. She'd leave that kind of thing to Tommy. But here was a man who hid behind his long, straggly hair and thick beard. He wore ill-fitting clothes that hung off him. He was practically faceless, shapeless. What was he like under the camouflage? Handsome or ugly? Wiry or bloated? Or just normal, because that's what most people were at the end of the day. Perfectly average. Bland and forgettable.

But if Cole Burroughs was so normal, why were they watching him?

The thoughts continued long into the night. One merged into another and so on and so forth. All the while, Tommy slept soundly. And Rose must've dropped off, too. Elbows on the windowsill, head in hands, eyes resting against the binoculars. Not comfortable, but it didn't need to be. Not for an unintended catnap. All was quiet on Haversham Way, and the silence allowed her to dream about Rupert.

Is that what he was now? The man of her dreams? Popping up uninvited when she least expected it. Invading her imagination. She could see him now, walking towards number seven. Stumbling slightly, looking nervous. He had more flowers. She wanted to call out to him, but she couldn't quite figure out how to open the window. Not to worry. He already seemed to know that you had to go around the back. She waited. Any second now. Sure enough, the door opened and closed.

And that was when she woke up.

For a split-second, Rose believed that Rupert was really there. Then reality came back with a bang. He had no idea where she was. Would never know. Besides, it was late. She glanced at her phone. Three thirty-six. That really *was* late. Early even. She stretched her arms above her head and smiled. The funny thing was, she could've sworn she had heard the back door opening and closing and ...

Rose held her breath. Listened carefully. A scraping sound followed a gentle click. Both were instantly recognisable, and both were coming from downstairs. From the kitchen, to be precise. The click of the light switch and the scrape of a chair being pulled out from behind the table.

Rose jumped to conclusions and landed on Tommy. Facts only. He was both greedy and selfish. At a guess, he had gone searching for second helpings and made as much noise as possible in the process.

Rose stood up and padded slowly towards the door, her only guide the streetlight outside. When she reached it, she peeked out onto the landing. The door to the opposite bedroom was closed. She moved towards it. Gently pushed it open. There was an enormous lump in the middle of the bed, swathed in blankets. A mop of hair on the pillow. Snoring was the final confirmation.

Tommy O'Strife was out for the count.

Rose shuffled forward, hands out, ready to wake him. Something stopped her. What if it was nothing? What if the noises downstairs were just the groans and grumbles of an empty house? The wind against the windows? A rattling fence? Not a light switch. Not a moving chair. If Rose woke Tommy for no reason, he would never let her forget it. Worse than that, he might be up for good, refreshed and reinvigorated, his twenty-four-hour motor mouth working overtime. He would talk and she would listen. He would talk and she wouldn't listen. It didn't matter which. He would talk regardless.

And that was why Rose backed out of the room as quietly as possible and closed the door behind her. She listened for what seemed like forever, but was actually a few seconds. Heard nothing but silence.

Against her better judgement, she took to the stairs.

It was the fear of the unexpected that frightened you, she decided. Maybe that was why she felt permanently on tenterhooks. Life was no longer mundane. Routine. It was unpredictable. Dangerous.

She was halfway down the stairs when she noticed the kitchen light was on. That was a bad start. She felt her pockets, but they were empty. She had a sudden urge to rush back upstairs and grab her phone. Call Mercy or Lucas. Maybe even Miles. But the same arguments reappeared just as quickly. The groaning house. The wind. The fence. Her imagination.

Or just Tommy. Bloody-minded and irresponsible, he could've raided the fridge at any time. Left the light on. If he had, if he was to blame for all of this, Rose would give him a piece of her mind. The piece that rarely ever showed itself. Not now, but tomorrow. When he had woken up. She would shout and scream and put him in his place.

Or just silently rebuke him. Yes, that was more her style. Not that he would notice.

Rose had reached the bottom step. Without thinking, she made her way towards the kitchen. The door was halfway between closed and open.

She lifted a hand and pushed.

Now it was just open.

It took a moment for her eyes to adjust to the light. To her horror, she was right about the scraping sound. A chair had been moved out from behind the table.

A chair that was now occupied.

'You wouldn't come to me, so I've come to you.' Cole Burroughs raised a hand, urged her to join him. 'Close the door and take a seat. I think it's about time we got to know each other.'

CHAPTER TWENTY-FOUR

Rose had forgotten how to breathe.

Usually, it required no thought at all. It was the most natural thing in the world. Now, however, it refused to come. It had got trapped in her throat.

Trapped by fear.

'Don't,' said Cole Burroughs, staring at her.

Rose swallowed. Forced out the two words she needed to make a sentence. 'Don't ... what?'

'Don't do anything stupid,' replied Cole. 'Don't shout or scream or go running to your friend upstairs. Don't try to attack me—'

'I ... I ... I would never do that,' stammered Rose.

'Good.' Cole gestured towards the opposite chair. 'Take a seat and we can talk.'

Rose could feel her legs beginning to give way beneath her. It took all her effort to stay upright. 'I don't want to. I'm ... I'm scared.'

'I know, but you don't have to be,' Cole insisted. 'I'm not

going to hurt you. You have my word. Once we've talked, I'll leave. I just want to know what's going on.'

Rose shuffled slowly towards the table. Rested a hand on the chair. Leant forward. 'I think I'm going to be sick.'

'Sit down and take a deep breath,' said Cole. He waited for Rose to do just that before he stood up slowly and wandered over to the sink. Turning on the tap, he poured her a glass of water, which he placed in front of her. 'There. Take a drink. Just try and calm down a little. I don't want you passing out on me.'

Rose sipped at the water. Tried to look anywhere but straight at Burroughs.

'What's your name?' he asked.

'Rose.'

'Okay, Rose. I'm Cole.'

'Yes, I know.'

'Of course you do.' Cole's eyes narrowed. 'You're not professionals, are you? You and your pal upstairs? You both stood out like a sore thumb when you were following me earlier. Then it just got weird in the shop. I tried to diffuse things a little in the cemetery, but I'm guessing it just freaked you out.'

'You knew we were there?'

Cole nodded. 'From the moment you left the house.'

Rose felt a prickle of irritation. 'Well, I heard you down here in the kitchen.'

'You were supposed to,' remarked Cole. 'I wanted you to come and investigate so we could talk. So, let's do that, shall we? You're watching me. I get that. I'm under surveillance. We've already gathered, however, that this doesn't come naturally to you. You're not the police …'

Cole waited for Rose to confirm it with a shake of her head.

'Who are you then? You can't just be nosey neighbours with too much time on your hands.'

'I'm nobody,' said Rose meekly. 'I don't know why I'm here and I don't know what I'm doing.'

'That's not true. Who are you working for?'

'This isn't working,' spluttered Rose. 'You get paid to work. This is just … life. My life. *Our* life,' she added, glancing up at the ceiling. 'We don't have a choice. Agatha tells us what to do and then we do it.'

'Agatha?'

Rose winced. She shouldn't have let that slip. And Burroughs wasn't the sort of man to let it pass without comment.

'Who's Agatha?' he asked, pressing home his advantage.

'I don't know. Honestly. She comes and goes … tells us what to do … and then we do it.'

'That makes no sense. I really hope you're not lying to me—'

'I'm not,' insisted Rose, the desperation dripping from her voice. 'Agatha asked us to watch you. We don't know why, but we haven't got a say in the matter.'

'Agatha … who? Has she got a surname?'

Rose took a moment. Was it better to tell the truth and stay on his right side, or lie through her teeth and run the risk of angering a man who could easily explode at any moment? No contest. Not really. 'Pleasant. Her name is Agatha Pleasant.'

'Thank you,' said Cole. His lips turned up at the sides, almost as if he was trying to force a sympathetic smile. 'I can see this is upsetting for you, Rose, and that's not my intention. The fact that you're watching me is hardly a surprise. It was almost inevitable. Especially once I'd shown my hand.'

'Your hand?'

Cole rested his elbows on the table. Clenched his fists until his knuckles turned white. 'There are some wicked men out there, Rose. I'm going to do the world a favour. I'm going to kill one of them.'

CHAPTER TWENTY-FIVE

Rose felt the colour drain from her face.

Had he really just said that? Openly admitted that he was about to kill someone? No, not someone. A man. A wicked man. That was a relief, thought Rose. He may have had murder in mind, but at least it wasn't hers.

Not yet, anyway.

'Do you want a proper drink?' Cole nodded towards the back door. Specifically, at one of the whiskey bottles he had brought from over the road.

'I don't really drink,' replied Rose.

'Maybe you should think about starting.' Standing up, Cole grabbed the bottle from the floor and moved towards the kitchen units. A quick search and he stumbled upon two shot glasses. 'Don't gulp it down,' he said, once he'd returned to the table and poured a measure of the spirit into each glass. 'Just sip it. It'll warm you up. Straighten you out a bit.'

Rose stared at the glass that Cole had pushed towards her. 'I don't know if I can trust you.'

'That's understandable,' said Cole. 'I've just told you I'm

about to kill someone. That's not all, though. There's a back story. The man I'm about to kill is a murderer himself. He took two innocent lives.' Cole shifted in his chair. Swallowed his drink whole and then poured himself another measure.

'I thought you told me to sip it,' said Rose.

'I've got used to it,' said Cole. 'Sometimes I don't even notice when it's going down ...' He stopped without warning. Slumped forward as if all his strength had suddenly deserted him. 'The man I'm going to kill is called Tobias Montague. And the two innocent lives he took ...' Cole visibly wobbled. 'They were my wife and daughter. Charlotte and Sophie. He destroyed my family.'

Rose lifted her head as the words filtered into her brain. 'I ... I don't know what to say.'

Cole waved it away. 'Nobody ever does. It only happened a month ago, so it's still raw. I don't normally like to talk about it ...' He let the sentence tail off so he could clear his throat. The story wouldn't tell itself, though. He had to keep going. 'Montague was driving whilst under the influence. He'd been drinking all day. Topped up with coke and amphetamines. He was speeding when he swerved around a parked car and mounted the pavement. That was when he hit them. They didn't stand a chance. He could've stopped ... done something ... anything to help ... but he didn't. He drove away. He didn't even go home. Just on to another party. The death of my family didn't even warrant a second thought.'

Rose put a hand to her mouth. 'That's horrible. I'm sorry. So sorry.'

Cole hadn't finished, though. 'The police arrested him and his two passengers, Claude Bonham and Abbie Simkin, the next day. They held them for twenty-four hours, questioned them, and then let them go. Montague was a free man.'

'Surely there was evidence ... witnesses ... there are cameras everywhere these days,' said Rose.

'None of that matters. Not if your father is Magnus Montague.' The blank look on Rose's face persuaded Cole to fill in the gaps. 'He's one of Stainmouth's only multi-millionaires. He's currently working out in Dubai, leaving Tobias free to run wild with the family credit card and an empty mansion. One call from Magnus and the police had little choice but to release his son.' Cole closed his eyes. Pressed his fingers against his temple. 'Thank you,' he said eventually.

'What for?' shrugged Rose.

'For listening. For not judging me. I'm not an evil man, but I'm about to do some evil things. My worry is you might get caught in the crossfire. I'd hate for that to happen.'

You're not the only one, thought Rose. 'I'm trying to understand ... I really am ... but I'm not sure I can keep this to myself,' she warned him.

'You don't have to,' said Cole. 'I'm prepared to face the consequences.'

'You'll go to prison. You'll get life for murder.'

'Then so be it. I don't care. Not anymore. Once Tobias Montague is dead, they can shoot me down in cold blood. I've got nothing left to live for.'

With that, Cole stood up from the table and grabbed at the half-empty bottle. He was out of the back door a moment later, no doubt heading for home. Rose watched him go and then kept on watching the door in case he returned.

He didn't.

He had said all he had to say. Revealed everything. Now it was Rose's turn to decide what to do with it.

To tell or not to tell. That was the question.

CHAPTER TWENTY-SIX

Cole Burroughs had left Rose at three fifty-three in the morning.

At half-past six, a more respectable time by anybody's standards, she called Miles. Who immediately called Agatha. Who insisted they both hurry to the townhouse on Haversham Way as fast as the speed limit would allow.

More luck than judgement, they arrived at the exact same time as Mercy and Lucas. Also known as the day shift.

Rose let them in through the back door, before Miles insisted they all sat in the front bedroom, blinds down, lights out, whilst Rose filled them in on everything that had happened. Step by step. Minute by minute. Every last detail. By the time she had finished, she was greeted with a stunned silence.

It was Lucas who finally spoke up. 'You don't seem very scared?'

'I was,' insisted Rose.

'Was? Not now?'

Rose took a moment to think. 'I don't know ... Cole Burroughs isn't ... he's not a bad man.'

'He told you he was going to kill someone,' said Lucas. 'The guy's a psycho in my eyes.'

'He's hurting,' said Rose.

'He's dangerous,' said Mercy.

Rose snapped back at her. 'You're not listening. None of you are. Burroughs was in this house. He could've done anything to me, but all he did was talk. He opened up about his family. I think ... yes, I want to help him. Not persecute him.'

'The thing is, Rose, you *would* want to help him,' began Mercy. 'That's you all over. You're nice. You think the best of people. You're—'

'Gullible,' finished Lucas.

'Oh, fuck off!' barked Rose.

Mouths fell open as shock waves raced around the room.

'I mean it,' Rose continued. 'Stop treating me like a fool. I'm not this stupid little girl that you all seem to think.' She spun around to confront Agatha. She was on a roll now. Couldn't stop herself. 'And you've got no right to spy on Rupert. It's got nothing to do with you who I choose to spend my time with.'

'It's for your own safety,' said Agatha calmly. 'We have to be certain—'

'No, *you* don't have to be anything,' cried Rose. 'It's my life. If I want to see Rupert, I will. And if I tell you that Cole Burroughs isn't a threat to me, then that's my opinion. You don't have to argue just because I said it.' She walked over to Lucas and held out her hand. 'Give me the car keys. I'm going back to Cockleshell Farm.'

His face split somewhere between a smile and a frown, Lucas placed the keys in her palm. 'I didn't mean to—'

'You did. You all did. You always do.' With that, Rose set off down the stairs, leaving the other four stood in silence before she slammed the door shut behind her.

'That went well,' sighed Lucas. 'You know you've hit a low when Rose starts swearing.'

'You can't blame her,' said Mercy. 'She's right about everything. We don't listen to her or trust her in the slightest. We treat her like a kid and that's not on. We need to do better. All of us. And Tommy. Yeah, definitely Tommy.'

'Talking of which ...' Agatha looked around. 'Someone's conspicuous by their absence. Where is Mr O'Strife?'

'Asleep.' Miles gestured across the landing. 'I can hear him snoring. Either that or there's a warthog living rent-free in here.'

'Well, wake him up,' demanded Agatha. 'Get him out here now. I want to hear what he has to say.'

Miles walked through to the other bedroom without another word. Taking hold of one corner of Tommy's blanket, he yanked it off the bed and tossed it to one side.

'Get out of it!' A fully dressed Tommy sat bolt upright, his arms swinging in every direction. It was only when he realised it was Miles that he stopped throwing punches. 'Oh, hello, Millie. If you wanted to join me, you only had to ask.'

'Get up,' said Miles sternly. 'We're all waiting for you.'

'Give me a chance, pal.' Tommy waited for Miles to leave before he rolled off the bed and shuffled through to the front bedroom. 'Morning all,' he yawned, stretching his arms above his head. 'What time is it? It's still dark.'

'You've got your eyes closed, moron,' muttered Mercy.

'Oh, so I have.' Tommy looked around at all the disapproving faces. 'Whoa! Nobody told me the whole gang was here. Minus ... the mouse.'

'Don't call her that,' spat Mercy, tensing up. Lucas read the situation and placed a hand on her shoulder. All he got in return was a scowl.

'Is that the same mouse that was confronted by Cole Burroughs early this morning?' asked Agatha.

Tommy responded with a shrug. 'Nah, you've lost me.'

'Cole Burroughs was in this house,' explained Miles. 'He broke in through the back door. Rose was alone with him. Anything could've happened to her. So, where were you?'

'Here,' insisted Tommy.

'Here?'

'In this house.' Tommy threw up his arms. 'I haven't been out, if that's what you're implying. We followed him to the shop and cemetery, but I haven't left her on her own.'

'You may as well have done,' said Mercy. 'You're no good to anybody asleep.'

'She could've woken me up,' said Tommy innocently.

'And why do you think she didn't?' Agatha rolled her eyes. 'Is it because she doesn't like you? Respect you? She thinks she'd be better off without you?'

'Ah, come on,' groaned Tommy. 'It was the middle of the

night and I fell asleep. Give me a break, eh?'

'I'll give you a break!' With that, Mercy lunged forward. Fortunately for Tommy, Lucas was right behind her. Miles wasn't too slow, either, and between them, somehow, they stopped her from lashing out.

'Calm down,' said Lucas, struggling to hold her back.

'Yeah, calm down,' repeated Tommy. He ended his sentence with a risky grin.

That was the catalyst for Mercy to break free. She had Tommy in her sights now. All she had to do was pick him off. A right-handed jab to the side of the head followed by a left-handed uppercut. Game over, dickhead.

She moved into position. Leant forward. And ...

Mercy spun a full one-eighty, unclenched her fist and slammed her palm against the wall. She cried out at the same time. Not in pain, but frustration. Sheer bloody frustration that had been pent up for weeks with no viable escape route.

'Have you all finished?' Agatha shook her head. 'This is unacceptable. I expect better. From all of you. We're a team. We work together. And as for you ...' She switched her attention to Tommy, who had finally dared to lower his hands. 'You haven't even asked how she is.'

Tommy screwed up his face. 'Who?'

'Are you being deliberately stupid?' said Agatha. 'Miss Carrington-Finch. You don't know where she is, but you haven't even asked about her. For all you know, she could be dead. Don't you care?'

'Of course I do,' insisted Tommy. 'I've just been asleep. Practically still am. I'm not thinking straight.' He hesitated. 'She's not, is she? Dead, I mean?'

'Thankfully not,' said Agatha.

Tommy nodded. 'Good. Yeah, that's ... great news. Listen, I'll go back to Cockleshell Farm and make it up to her. I'll cook her some breakfast. Run her a bath—'

'Stay away from her!' warned Mercy.

'I'm trying to be nice,' sighed Tommy. 'Okay, I get it. I've cocked up and now I've had my wrist slapped. Fine. Let's move on, shall we?' He held out his hand. Bypassed Mercy and focussed on Lucas. 'You got the keys to the Mini?'

Lucas tried not to smile as he shook his head. 'Not anymore. It's gone. Rose took it.'

There was a moment's delay whilst Tommy processed the information. 'Ah, bugger. Any chance of a lift?' he asked, turning to Miles.

'I'm not going that way, I'm afraid,' replied Miles, straight-faced.

Tommy felt his shoulders slump. 'Guess I'm walking then. It's not too far, is it?'

'About six miles,' said Lucas, enjoying himself too much.

'Okay.' Tommy turned towards the door. 'I'll see you all later. Hopefully. If I make it home. Don't suppose anyone would really mind if I didn't. Everyone hates me anyway. And all because I fell asleep. Not the worst crime ever ...'

His voice faded away as he slowly descended the stairs. Before long, he was just a mumble. Then the back door closed, and he was gone.

'You should have let me hit him,' moaned Mercy. That was aimed at Lucas. The next sentence, however, was reserved for Agatha. 'What do you want us to do now?'

Agatha pointed towards the surveillance equipment. 'Nothing's changed. Yes, Cole Burroughs may know that we're here, but he still needs to be watched. He's openly admitted to Rose that he's going to murder the man who killed his family. Whether that's right or wrong, we can't let him do that. Do you understand? If Burroughs does anything out of the ordinary, you need to report back to Miles.'

With that, she moved towards the exit.

'*Anything* out of the ordinary,' repeated Miles, before he followed Agatha out of the room. He caught up with her on the stairs. 'What now? Where are we heading next?'

'Oh, we've got a busy day ahead of us,' she replied. 'Best start it with a spot of breakfast.'

Miles raised an eyebrow. He wasn't expecting that. 'Lovely. Got anywhere in mind?'

'The Wild Boar Member's Only Club,' said Agatha. 'It's time we dragged that place kicking and screaming into the twenty-first century.'

CHAPTER TWENTY-SEVEN

Lucas knew it was going to be a long shift.

He'd done surveillance jobs back in the day. In his previous life. When he was still in both full-time employment as a police officer and full-time living as a normal human being. It had usually involved warm cars and an endless supply of coffee and doughnuts, much like in the movies. It was boring, yes, but that was all. Lots of things in life were boring. Deal with it.

This, however, was practically unbearable.

The house was cold, his chair was hard, and there was nothing to eat. That was three problems right off the top of his head. The fourth was who he had been paired with.

Mercy.

But an angrier version. More likely to go off the handle at the slightest of complaints.

Lucas had realised this a few minutes into their shift when he had raised his first objection of the day.

'It's bloody cold in here.'

Mercy's reply was savagely blunt. 'And what do you want me

to do about it?'

Wow. 'Nothing. Just saying.'

'Get a blanket.'

'This chair's rock hard as well.'

'Put a pillow under it.'

'I'm absolutely starving.'

'There's a shop not far away.'

'And I'm bored.'

'Do I look as if I care?'

Lucas ended it there. It didn't do to get on Mercy's wrong side. Not if you enjoyed having a full set of teeth in your mouth.

Still, there had to be a reason she was so irate. It couldn't just be him. Yes, he could be annoying from time to time, but he wasn't *Tommy* annoying.

'Do you want to talk about it?' he asked.

Mercy pulled away from the binoculars. Stared at him. 'Talk about what?'

'Last night,' said Lucas. 'At the Mucky Duck. You lost it—'

'They were racist scum!'

'I know. I was there as well. You had a right to get mad—'

'You didn't, though. You seemed perfectly calm.'

'No, I *was* mad, Mercy. I just didn't show it.'

'Good for you.'

'No, good for both of us,' argued Lucas. 'There were ten of them. If we had started fighting, they would've torn us to shreds.'

'Maybe not.'

'Oh, come on. We wouldn't have stood a chance. You know that, right? Admit it, you let your emotions get the better of you and it nearly ended in disaster. You were raging.'

'If you say so.'

The room fell silent. Mercy didn't move an inch from her position by the window, whilst Lucas paced the floor behind her. He hadn't quite finished, though. Not yet.

'I think you've got an anger issue,' he said. 'When the red mist descends, you can't control it.'

Mercy pulled away from the binoculars for a second time. 'What? Seriously? Just because I turned on a pub full of nobheads?'

'Not just that. What about earlier? With Tommy?'

'He was winding me up. Don't tell me you've never thought about punching him before?'

Lucas kept on pacing. 'Of course I have. Practically every single day. The difference is I've never done it. Besides, this isn't about me.'

'That's convenient,' snorted Mercy. 'Listen, I know I get mad occasionally—'

'All the time.'

'*Some* of the time,' said Mercy, correcting him, 'but I'm still in control. I would never put myself in danger. Or you. Or anybody.' She stood up. 'You are right about one thing, though. This is boring. Take over and I'll find us something to eat.'

Lucas nodded wearily as he took her place behind the binoculars. He slightly adjusted the setting and focussed on the house across the road. Until then, Cole Burroughs had been something of an enigma. Bits of him kept flitting into view as he wandered from room to room, but that was all. His feet across the carpet. The back of his head. Nothing to get worked up about.

That all changed when a bright yellow Honda Civic came to a halt on the pavement right outside of number eight.

Lucas watched in surprise as the door opened and the driver climbed out of the vehicle. 'Okay, maybe this is what Agatha meant by out of the ordinary.'

Mercy hurried back into the room. 'What is?'

'Cole's got company.' Grinning from ear to ear, Lucas looked over at Mercy in the doorway. 'And it's female.'

CHAPTER TWENTY-EIGHT

What a bunch of bellends!

Tommy had repeated that particular sentence over and over, out loud and under his breath, ever since he had left the townhouse. That was ten minutes ago. Now he was heading towards Stainmouth town centre. Not through choice, but because it was the only way he knew to go. Get there and he could always find some kind of transport back to Croplington. A taxi or bus. Cadge a lift maybe. Work his charm on some fifty-year-old divorcee who was going his way.

Yes, that's right. Cockleshell Farm please, Gloria. What's that? Would I like to come and look at your garden? That's one way of putting it. Me? Funny? Yeah, I know I am. And I'd love to come back to yours. I'm in no rush. There's nobody waiting for me at home. Only Rose. No, she's not my girlfriend. Probably wishes she was. Bit too dull for me, though. No, you're not dull, Gloria. Quite the opposite. My, what soft hands you have…

Whoa. Rewind. Tommy had forgotten about Rose when he was compiling his bunch of bellends. Well, not anymore.

Now she was right up there, slotted in neatly between Mercy and Lucas. Miles, naturally, was at the top. Always was, always would be. That stiff upper prick was practically begging for a slap across the chops. Agatha was probably at the bottom. She didn't irritate him as much as the others for some reason. Maybe it was her age. Respect for your elders and all that bullshit.

Tommy caught his reflection in a shop window. Stopped in horror. Christ, he looked rough. His tousled hair was trying its best to resemble a curly perm, whilst the bags under his eyes were so big they could easily have carried the contents of his pockets. He was jowly. He had no idea what that meant, but decided it suited the face that stared back at him. He could forget about Gloria; at this rate, he'd struggle to attract the dossers and deadbeats who sat on the street corners, sipping cans and sharing roll-ups. What had happened to him? He used to be razor sharp, with a swagger to match. Now he was lazy and lifeless and walked with a limp. That was only temporary, though. He had laid funny on one leg last night when he was asleep. Trapped a nerve.

There he was again. Making excuses. It probably explained why Candice had ignored him in the shop. And why Gloria would refuse to give him a lift in her Renault Clio. And, yes, Gloria did exist. Of course she did. There were thousands of Glorias out there. And every last one of them would think he resembled the contents of a bin wagon.

Well, not anymore, people. It was time to take back control.

Tommy didn't have to look too hard to find what he was

searching for. Across the road, turn right and there it was. *Sergio's Snips* in big white letters on a red background. Yeah, that would do. It would do nicely ... and yet it wouldn't. There was one slight problem. A slight problem that wasn't so slight, if Tommy was being honest. And, unlike last night, it wasn't as if he had Rose to rely upon. Now he was flying solo.

Right on cue, a man appeared in the entrance to the barbershop. He had a thick head of coiffured white hair and a wispy moustache. Dressed in a black shirt, unbuttoned to the chest and rolled up at the sleeves, and a stripy apron, he noticed Tommy immediately and waved him over.

'Hey, signor,' he called out. 'Why so glum?'

'Woman trouble,' replied Tommy, as he made his way across the road. 'No, not woman – *women*. Plural problems.'

'Now, that's something I can understand.' White Head stepped to one side. Gestured towards the open door. 'Why don't you come on in and tell Sergio all about it?'

'I'd love to, but ...' Tommy turned out his pockets as if to emphasise the point. 'I haven't got a pot to piss in. I'm stoney broke. Beggared and buggered.'

Sergio shrugged his shoulders. 'I'm not sure I—'

'I've got no money,' explained Tommy. A sickening feeling appeared in the pit of his stomach. What was it? Embarrassment? Shame? Or just hunger pains?

'You can owe me,' said Sergio, taking Tommy by the arm. 'I trust you, signor. You have an honest face.'

Yes, I do, thought Tommy, as he wandered into the

barbershop. At last. Somebody who saw him for what he was.

Sergio gestured towards the only chair. 'Take a seat and I'll see what I can do.'

'You'd have to be a bloody magician to sort this out,' muttered Tommy, as he slumped down in front of the mirror. 'I've seen better looking dog turds.'

'Signor, by the time you leave here, you'll be back to your best,' purred Sergio. 'So, what would you like?'

'A bit off here, a bit off there,' said Tommy, somewhat vaguely. He took in his surroundings as Sergio wrapped a gown around his shoulders, tying it at the neck. It was a small room, neat and tidy, but a little worn in places. Not that that was always a bad thing. 'Nice gaff,' Tommy remarked.

Sergio smiled as he picked a shaver up off a side table. 'I've had this barbershop for nearly twenty years now. Before that, it was my father's. I must be doing something right because the customers keep on coming back.'

'Cool,' nodded Tommy. And it was cool. Cutting hair for a living. Chatting all day. No one giving you shit, or trying to punch you, or expecting you to stay awake all night long.

'What about you?' asked Sergio, as he set to work. 'What do you do?'

Tommy blew out. 'It's hard to explain.'

'Try me. I hear a lot of strange stuff in here. You'd do well to shock me.'

'Well … it's kind of … a bit like …' Tommy sighed. 'Would you believe me if I told you I was part of a top secret undercover organisation?'

Sergio stopped shaving. 'If it's true, then I believe you.'

'Oh, it's true alright.'

'Then that is cool, too,' grinned Sergio. 'Are you like James Bond or something?'

Or something, thought Tommy. Still, why ruin a good story? 'Yeah, just like James Bond. The Stainmouth version. Not quite so glamorous.'

Sergio nodded enthusiastically as he swapped the shaver for a pair of scissors. He was enjoying himself. 'You got a gun?'

Only in my underpants. Loaded and ready to go. 'Yeah, I've got a gun. Not on me, of course. Don't need a gun when I'm getting my haircut. Not unless you mess it up.'

Sergio laughed. 'No chance, signor. A sophisticated guy like you deserves a classy haircut.' He leant forward. Practically whispered in Tommy's ear. 'I bet you get a lot of women throwing themselves at you, right?'

Chance would be a fine thing. 'A gentleman never tells.'

'Apologies.' Sergio patted him on the shoulder. 'I shouldn't have asked.'

'Don't worry about it.' Tommy found himself staring at his own reflection. The haircut was only halfway through, but he was looking better already. By the time Sergio had finished, he would be a new man.

Still gazing in the mirror, he let his eyes drift to the street outside. There was someone in the barbershop window. Someone familiar. Someone it might have been possible to ignore if it wasn't for the huge mole that covered much of their cheek.

'Something the matter, signor?' asked Sergio, sensing Tommy's agitation. 'You don't like what I've done so far?'

'What? No, it's got nothing to do with my hair.' Tommy tilted his head back. 'That man. Outside on the pavement. I've been following him.'

Sergio peered discreetly over his shoulder. Rupert was still there, but now he had turned his back to the window. 'That man?'

Tommy nodded. 'He might not look like much, but he's actually a top womaniser. He preys on the boring types who are desperate for the attention.'

'He's leaving,' said Sergio. Sure enough, Rupert had moved away from the window. 'You should go after him.'

'I should?'

'Of course. Go now. Don't let him get away.'

Sergio pulled the cover from around Tommy's neck. Practically tipped the chair forward until he fell out.

'What about my hair?' he protested.

'Your hair can wait – this cannot!' Sergio pointed at the door. 'Go get him, James Bond. Do it for the women of Stainmouth.'

Jumping to his feet, Tommy darted towards the exit. Sergio was right. Okay, so he wasn't exactly James Bond, but he was Tommy O'Strife. Man of action. That bunch of bellends had called him useless back at the townhouse. They had said he didn't care. Well, he did care. And he would prove it. Starting now.

Tommy stopped in the doorway. 'Keep that chair warm. I'll be back before you know it.'

Sergio stuck his thumb up. 'You have my word. Just take care of yourself. And stay out of danger.'

'Danger?' Tommy felt the need to puff out his chest. 'Ha! Danger's what I do best.'

CHAPTER TWENTY-NINE

Clifford Goose put a hand to his mouth and tried not to burp.

He blamed the lobster scrambled eggs. No, blame was a little harsh. If truth be told, they were absolutely delightful. Beyond delicious. Michel was a fantastic chef, no doubt about it. Hats off to him. Goose would tell him that the next time they crossed paths. Might even squeeze the recipe out of him with a bit of luck. He was the Chief Constable, after all. He got what he wanted and what he wanted he got. If Michel didn't like it, he could always leave Stainmouth and work in a different town. Be a shame, though. A massive shame.

'You still in the room, Clifford, or have you had a stroke?'

Goose looked up from his plate. Councillor Martin was staring straight at him, his mouth full to bursting point, stains splattered across the front of his napkin.

'Jolly decent of you to pay the bill, Clifford,' he grunted.

Goose nodded. Had he ever offered? Probably not. Still, no point making a scene. Not in public. He might have a word after breakfast, though. Nothing threatening. Just a gentle reminder in case Martin had forgotten who he was dealing with.

Only a fool would dare to fuck with the Chief Constable.

Leaning back in his chair, Goose took a moment to admire the dining room at The Wild Boar Club. At the members who occupied the other tables. Businessmen. Entrepreneurs. Academics. All successful. All well-respected.

All men.

Good, thought Goose. Not that he disliked women. Not as such. The ones that they invited from time to time he was particularly fond of. They were special women, though. They came with an eye-watering price tag, but they were well worth it. Immaculately turned-out and well spoken, elegant and sophisticated, they were as far removed from his ex-wives as you could possibly imagine. Nice. Yes, very nice indeed.

A distracted Goose was brought back to reality by an outburst from his breakfast companions. Huddled together, Councillor Martin was chuckling again, probably at his own joke, whilst another man, Professor Eccles, was tittering behind his hand like a naughty child. It was Martin's laugh that really grated, though. A raucous cackle, it seemed to send a shiver down Goose's spine before vibrating inside his bladder.

He stood up. 'Excuse me, gentlemen.'

'Don't try to sneak out whilst I'm not watching,' barked Martin. 'You're paying, remember?'

As if I could ever forget, you tight-fisted prick. That sentence stayed deeply rooted inside Goose's mind, though. Instead, he made his way across the dining room without another word leaving his lips. He passed the other tables and acknowledged each and every member accordingly. A nod here, a smile there. They knew him and he knew them. One big, happy family. The crème de la crème. Stainmouth's finest all gathered together in close proximity. Breathe in that rarefied air. You could bottle it and sell it for a fortune.

Goose crossed the lobby and entered the restroom. To his delight, it was empty. Thank God for that. No one asking questions whilst he tried to relieve himself. Choosing a urinal over a cubicle, he unzipped his trousers. Rummaged about a bit. Ah, there it was. A second later, the liquid began to flow. Staring up at the ceiling, he held his breath for a moment and then sighed. The novelty was wearing off. All this eating and drinking and general merriment was starting to get him down. Maybe he needed to get back to doing what he did best. Policing Stainmouth. Leading from the front. Your people need you. Men, women and children. Yes, he would do that. Now. And if not now, then straight after breakfast. Maybe another serving of lobster scrambled eggs would satisfy his cravings.

His mouth salivated at the prospect.

Before his balls curled up into his stomach at the sound of a voice at his shoulder. It was both unmistakably feminine and unnervingly familiar.

The stuff of nightmares.

'Good morning, Clifford. Have you got a moment?'

CHAPTER THIRTY

'A female?'

Mercy pushed Lucas to one side so she could get a good view of the mystery arrival. The binoculars were pointing straight at her, making her impossible to miss. Yes, she was a woman – well spotted, Lucas – but it was what she was wearing that really took Mercy by surprise. A headscarf and sunglasses covered much of her face, whilst a beige trench coat turned up at the collar concealed her entire body all the way down to her knees. Nice legs, though, thought Mercy. At least what she could see of them before the woman opened the door to number eight and entered without knocking.

'Someone doesn't want to be recognised,' remarked Lucas. 'Maybe she's famous.'

Mercy snorted that theory away. 'Cole Burroughs looks like he hasn't had a wash in weeks. I doubt anybody famous will be calling round soon.'

She watched for movement in the house across the road, but there was none. Maybe the two of them were in the kitchen. Or one of the back bedrooms. Why would they be in a bedroom?

Mercy berated herself. She was better than that.

Lucas, however, seemed to be on the same wavelength. 'I thought Burroughs had just lost his wife.'

'He has.'

'Well, that didn't take him long, did it? You know, to get back on the horse? Not that Headscarf Lady resembled a horse in any way.'

Mercy moved away from the binoculars. Scowled at him.

'Hey, I'm not one to judge,' Lucas insisted. 'It's his life. I just thought there'd be a longer period of ... erm ... abstinence.'

Mercy shook her head. She didn't want to snap back, but sometimes the urge was too strong. 'Bit cynical, don't you think? She could be a relative. A friend. A work colleague. We have to hang out together, but we're not up to anything, are we?'

'I wouldn't dare,' muttered Lucas.

Mercy ignored that. 'Headscarf Lady? Is that what you're calling her? Could be worse, I suppose ...' She stopped. Grimaced. 'Okay, so now they've closed the curtains in the sitting room—'

'Told you so.' A grinning Lucas had seen enough. Heading towards the door, he made his way out of the room and down the stairs. 'I'll leave you to your thoughts whilst I get us a coffee,' he called out. 'You might also want to admit that I'm the smarter one of this pairing at some point.'

'Dream on,' Mercy shouted back. 'You're not smart; you're just cynical. Unlike you, I'd rather keep my mind out of the gutter if I can help it.'

***

Headscarf Lady was inside for almost thirty minutes.

Mercy was still behind the binoculars when she emerged from the house, whilst Lucas was leant against the wall behind her. The coffee had come and gone, neither of them really aware that they had even drunk it.

'That was quick,' said Mercy, as the mystery arrival hurried back towards the Honda.

'Not really,' said Lucas, overly defensive. 'What now? Do we follow her?'

Mercy was all set to answer when the curtains in number eight began to open. Cole Burroughs was stood in the window. He had his hood up and his head down as he watched the Honda disappear into the distance. Then he disappeared himself, deeper into the house.

'Headscarf Lady isn't a suspect, but it is unusual,' said Mercy. 'We'll call it through to Miles, just to be on the safe side. Then we've covered our backs.'

'You're right,' said Lucas, nodding in agreement. 'No napping on the job our end. The last thing any of us wants is another Tommy situation.'

CHAPTER THIRTY-ONE

And yet Tommy's situation had changed.

Now he was less like a sleeping dog and more like a dog with a bone. Persistent. Stubborn. Relentless. Yeah, that would do. No need to over-egg it. Besides, his limited vocabulary had come to a floundering standstill with those three. There were no more words to fit the bill. None that he could think of, anyway.

Back on the streets of Stainmouth and Rupert was on the move.

He kind of sashayed, thought Tommy, not exactly in hot pursuit of his target, but keeping pace. A hip wiggle here, a booty roll there. Slightly effeminate. Threat level zero, which probably explained why Rose liked him so much. And why she didn't like Tommy. He strutted about as if his balls were too big for his underpants. Anyone could see that. Stand back and admire the view, people. Don't get too close because this bad boy's gonna' blow.

Well, you can tell by the way I use my walk, I'm a woman's man, no time to talk ...

That was him alright. Staying alive. Against all the odds.

Tommy strolled along the pavement as the thoughts bounced around his brain. What did Lucas say about following Rose? Don't dribble down the back of her neck. It made sense, actually. Not too close, not too far away. Yeah, he was getting good at this. Maybe he should write a book. Nothing too heavy, just your basic tips of the trade for wannabe spies. In brackets, sneaky beaks who enjoyed snooping on people. No, that sounded wrong. Proper creepy. Not a good angle. What it needed was a snappy title. *The Secrets of Spycraft*. Bore off. *The Art of Spying*. Nah, that sounded like a kiddie's colouring book. *Spy and Mash*. Just weird. *The Spy Society*. Bullseye. That had bestseller written all over it. Title locked in, it was time to open her up. Let the content flow. Break it down into chapters. Bullet points. Attention grabbers for your TikTok generation.

Tommy O'Strife's first rule of surveillance – keep the suspect in sight at all times.

That was good. Well, pretty obvious really, but you have to start somewhere. Rupert was in sight now. Ever onwards. Destination unknown. What would happen if he turned around? Picked Tommy out from the smattering of pedestrians who loitered close by? A problem like that needed a solution.

Tommy O'Strife's second rule of surveillance – don't follow from behind, follow from the side.

He crossed the road, safe in the knowledge that Rupert was less likely to look over to his right than behind him. What was that? About twenty-past-three on a clock. Yeah, Rupert was definitely more of a half-six kind of guy.

Tommy slowed as he passed a window. Glanced at his reflection in despair. His hair was all over the place. Well, one half of it was. The other half was neatly trimmed. If anything, it conjured up a curious image of two different people. One wild and crazed, the other prim and proper. Combine the two together and he looked like the kind of chump you found chewing on their own shoelaces behind the bins.

Tommy set off again, surprised to find that Rupert wasn't as far ahead of him as he had expected. In fact, he had come to a halt. Which meant ...

Tommy O'Strife's third rule of surveillance – if the suspect stops, you stop.

He hovered by a shop window. Used the reflection to look across the road without anybody realising. The reason for Rupert's momentary pause was all too clear. A man. Suited and booted. Stiff and unsmiling. Almost the exact opposite of Rupert, who was laughing uncontrollably whilst waving his arms about. Rein it in, son. You're not on the stage now.

Tommy leant into the window, pressed his nose against the glass. He had imagined it would give him a better view. And it did. Not of Rupert, but of a lacey bra and matching knickers. They were dark red and came in a set. Tommy stepped back and took in the entire window display. More bras, more knickers. He was stood outside a lingerie shop. One of those fancy ones. The less material they used, the higher the price. Classy as fuck. If ... *when* he got a girlfriend, he'd be back. Bring her with him. Pick what you want, darling. Preferably from the sale rail.

'Put your tongue away, pervert.'

Tommy glanced behind him. There were five women stood close by, any of whom could easily have spoken. He thought about pleading his innocence – *it's okay, I'm just following someone* – but decided against it. Instead, he beat a hasty retreat. Which reminded him.

Tommy O'Strife's fourth rule of surveillance – don't do anything to draw attention to yourself.

The book was taking shape. And, double delight, Rupert was back on the move. Still unsuspecting, still going about his everyday life, unaware that a master craftsman was tracking his every step. Tommy felt a tingle in his nether regions. God, this felt good. Exciting even. Better than coke. Sergio was right. He was fucking James Bond. No, not like that. Not man on man. Say it right. He was James Bond without the intercourse.

Whoa there, spy boy. Let's not get caught up in the drama. Concentrate. Keep your eyes on the prize.

The prize being Rupert. Not the bear, but the mole. Tommy watched as he took a left turn and disappeared from view. Cue a volley of expletives. He had broken the first rule in his own book. The publisher would go ballistic. And what would the readers think? Practice what you preach, big mouth. Shit, they were losing faith in him. He was losing faith in himself.

Tommy skipped across the road and took the same left turn as Rupert. He found himself in the entrance to a back alley. Too narrow for traffic, it was strewn with enough rubbish to ruin a landfill. Bags rather than bins, they were everywhere he looked and most places he trod. Your classic dumping ground. Out of sight, out of mind. Ignored by the council until the constant complaints triggered something on the system.

Forget the rubbish. There was no sign of Rupert anywhere.

Tommy edged forward. He could see a light in the distance where the alley opened up, but there was no way Rupert could've got there so quickly. What was he? A professional sprinter? I mean, it was a possibility ...

Tommy edged forward. He took shuffling steps rather than huge strides. What now? Go back to Sergio and get his hair finished? Yeah, that was one option.

Tommy edged forward. But to go back would be to admit defeat. He had failed. Not for the first time. Still, he was the only one in the loop and he didn't really count. He could forget about the book, though. Never mind. It was trash, anyway. Besides, who reads books in this day and age? Move with the times, you sad, old fart. Stop wallowing in the past.

Tommy stopped edging forward. Instead, he turned at the sound of stomping feet.

To his horror, there was a figure racing up behind him.

Tommy opened his mouth to speak. 'Hello—'

His sentence came to an abrupt halt as he staggered backwards. He was already unconscious as he fell into the rubbish that surrounded him, landing heavily amongst the mountain of bags. If nothing else, it was a stinking, rotting resting place for that morning's unscheduled nap.

Tommy O' Strife's fifth rule of surveillance – don't get caught on the job.

CHAPTER THIRTY-TWO

The Wild Boar Member's Only Club didn't allow women on its premises.

And yet there was one in the restroom with Clifford Goose. One who had spoken to him when he was least expecting it. One who was to blame for the last few drops of urine that splashed against his grey trousers, soaking effortlessly into the fabric.

'Bloody Nora!' Goose cried out.

The woman spoke again. 'It's Agatha, actually, but I'll let it go on this occasion.'

A furious Goose zipped up his trousers and turned around. There she was. Her back resting against one of the cubicle doors. Agatha chuffin' Pleasant.

'You did that,' he said, pointing at the wet patch on his trousers.

'Well, no, that's not strictly true now, is it?' frowned Agatha. 'I think you'll find you did it yourself. Largely because you lost control of your appendage.'

'You scared the living shit out of me!' barked Goose. 'How did you even get in here?'

'A spy never gives away her secrets.'

'You're not a spy. You're a nosey old hag who likes creeping up on innocent men.'

'Harsh.'

Goose took a breath. Tried to settle his nerves. Yes, it was harsh. And she bloody deserved it. 'You can't be here. I got a right bollocking the last time you rocked up in The Wild Boar. I had to stand before the Grand Master. I almost got my membership revoked.'

'Don't worry; I'm not staying long. Besides, I've locked the door. We won't be disturbed.'

'How did you lock the door?'

'With a key.'

'Where did you get the key from?'

'My, my, Clifford, so many questions. And here was me thinking you were desperate to get back to Councillor Martin and that other bloated weasel you've been playing footsie with.'

'Professor Eccles,' said Goose, before feeling it necessary to add. 'He's a smart arse. I've sat through breakfast fantasising about sticking my fork in his eye.'

Agatha laughed. 'I hope you don't feel the same way about me.'

'Not all the time.' Goose crossed over to the sink. Tore a paper towel from a dispenser and soaked it in water before dabbing it on his trousers. To his dismay, it only made things worse. 'So, what do you want? Let me guess. Information about Cole Burroughs—'

'And his wife and child who were murdered by a man who was way over the limit and as high as a kite. When were you going to tell me, Clifford?'

Goose wandered over to the hand dryer. Standing on tip-toes, he pressed his trousers up to the vent. 'You've done your homework,' he shouted over the sound of blowing air.

'I didn't need to,' said Agatha. 'The facts came to us. In the shape of Cole Burroughs himself.'

'You've been speaking to him?'

'Not me. One of my team. He broke into the house on Haversham Way and confessed all. She insists he wasn't a threat. Not to her, at least. But he is looking for revenge. He's going to kill Tobias Montague.'

'Ah, that's what I was worried about.' Goose turned away from the dryer. Perched on the edge of the sink. 'There were two other people in Montague's car that night. Claude Bonham and Abbie Simkin. Claude's a right posho. Him and Montague are as tight as trousers. Abbie's just a girl they picked up. Council estate upbringing, secondary school education. Pretty, though. Done a bit of modelling. They were all arrested after the crash, but the other two covered for Montague. Said he hadn't been drinking. That he didn't touch drugs. He was released soon after. No charge.'

Agatha shook her head. 'That's not how these things work—'

'They do when your father is Magnus Montague,' argued Goose. 'He's untouchable. And that means his son's untouchable, too. Daddy's been working out in Dubai for the past year, leaving Tobias home alone. He's wild. Unhinged. The police have been called to their house at least fifteen times in the past few months. Sometimes it's nothing. Noise pollution. Drunken behaviour. Other times, it's somewhat darker. Assault. Rape—'

'For pity's sake, Clifford,' cried Agatha. 'And you let this just carry on?'

'Open your ears, woman! I don't have a choice. It's above me.'

'I'm guessing Magnus Montague is a member of this club—'

'A member? He probably *owns* the fuckin' club! Christ, you're naïve.'

'And you're the Chief Constable. Do something!'

Goose drew a breath. 'What have I got? A good wage … nice house … a healthy pension waiting in the background? Big bloody deal! Montague pisses all over me. I shouldn't need to spell it out to you. Money equals power equals do what the fuck you like and to hell with the rest of them.'

'You sound scared.'

'We're all chuffin' scared!' raged Goose. 'Of something or someone. It's the way we live our lives.'

'No wonder Burroughs is so angry,' sighed Agatha. 'He's been let down by the system. He's had his whole life destroyed by Tobias Montague. And you're not prepared to do anything about it because of fear. Fear of one man. Montague's father.'

Goose shrugged. 'And it would be the same if it was me or you or anybody else involved. We're nothing. We don't matter. It's also why Burroughs is such a problem. He cropped up on our radar a few nights ago. Confronted Abbie Simkin near her home. Scared her silly. Didn't hurt her, though. He just wanted to talk.'

'And yet talking won't satisfy his need for revenge,' said Agatha. 'We need to put a stop to this before it escalates.' With that, she marched straight past the Chief Constable.

Goose breathed a sigh of relief. 'Is that it? Have you finished with me?'

'For now,' said Agatha, as she made her way towards the door. 'Some of us have got work to be getting on with.'

'Ouch! That hurts.' Goose set off after her, well aware that he had been in the restroom for far longer than was socially acceptable. 'Listen, Magnus Montague's a powerful man. If you go messing with his son, they'll be repercussions.'

'Or justice,' said Agatha, pulling open the door. 'Maybe that's what you're worried about.'

Goose was about to reply when something else caught his attention. 'I thought you said you locked this?' he said, pointing at the handle.

'I lied,' said Agatha. 'I was trying not to scare you. Looks like that ship's already sailed, though.'

CHAPTER THIRTY-THREE

Tommy began to stir.

His eyes were still closed, but his feelings had awoken. Touchy-touchy. What was that? Nails clawing at his chest ... fingers rummaging in his pockets ... a hand pulling at his trainer ... teeth unzipping his jeans ...

Whoa!

It felt nice, though. Maybe this was heaven. Laid flat on his back, surrounded by an assortment of scantily clad angels. Drink it in, Thomas. Your moment has arrived. About bloody time ...

And then the smell hit him. A violent attack on the senses, more powerful than any punch or kick, it was enough to make Tommy retch as his stomach folded in on itself. He tried to sit up, but it was too much effort. Instead, he rolled over, but it only made things worse. It was coming. He could feel it. And when it did, it exploded out of his mouth in a torrent of orange mush. A torrent that flowed relentlessly, until his insides felt as if they had escaped from his body. It left him feeling empty.

Hollow. A shell of a man.

Tommy finally sat up. Wiped his mouth first and eyes second. Wrong order. He didn't dwell on it, though, as he took in his blurry surroundings. As far as he could tell, he was sprawled out on a mattress of bin bags.

Then he remembered how he had got there.

Tommy pushed himself up. He was unsteady on his feet, swaying rhythmically from side to side. That was no surprise. He had been attacked, after all.

Attacked by Rupert.

Tommy had seen him. He was sure of it. But that was then. Things had changed. The results were in and they weren't good. Not only was Tommy seconds from falling over, but he was also seeing triple. Three men, not one. All facing him. All well within reach. Tommy looked from left to right. Focussed his gaze.

Not Rupert. Not Rupert. Not Rupert.

Bollocks.

They weren't identical either. Just three random bodies with stained clothes, greasy hair, and long, wispy beards that sprouted off in different directions. The great unwashed in low definition.

The Beards began to speak. One at a time. Not aggressive or confrontational. Observational, if anything.

'That was pretty disgusting.'

'Puking up like that.'

'You could've warned us.'

Tommy thought about apologising. Not for long, though.

It wasn't in his nature. Besides, it wasn't his fault he'd been jumped. Which reminded him. Pressing a hand against his forehead, he located the source of the pain, as well as dabbing at something wet. He studied his crimson fingers and felt the same queasy feeling in the pit of his stomach that had made him throw up only a few minutes ago. 'I'm bleeding,' he muttered under his breath.

'That you are.'

'It's practically pouring.'

'Red's your colour, though. It suits you.'

'I know it wasn't you who hit me,' mumbled Tommy. 'Any of you.'

'No way. That's not how we roll.'

'Peace and love, brother.'

'We thought you were dead, mind.'

Tommy snorted. *You thought I was dead. I* thought I was fuckin' dead. That this was heaven. That you three, you curious creatures, were women, angels, come to pleasure and …

Tommy ended the dream abruptly. Wrong time, wrong place. 'What were you doing? Why were you touching me?'

There was a lingering silence, the only noise being the incoherent mutterings of a string of excuses forming on the lips of the hairy strangers.

'Well, you know, waste not, want not.'

'Can't take any of it with you, can you?'

'Those jeans would look better on me than stuck in the bin at the morgue.'

Tommy brushed himself down. He was starting to feel a little more human. Not so dazed and confused. Less like a hangover from hell. Glancing down at his feet, he realised he was missing something, though. Just one. And one on its own was no good to anybody.

The Beard on his left was dangling it from a single finger. Casually, like he had forgotten it was even there.

'Can I have my trainer back?' Tommy paused. 'Please.'

The Beard hesitated. 'Trainer? Oh, yes, of course.' He held it out for Tommy to take. 'Like we said, if we had known you were just sleeping, we'd have left you to it.'

'We're not thieves.'

'We're just recycling. Environmentally friendly.'

Fine, thought Tommy. He wasn't going to argue the toss. They were clearly harmless. There was still one thing bothering him, though. And that certainly wasn't environmentally friendly.

'There was a smell,' he began. 'A horrible, horrible smell. Like rotting fish wrapped in dog shit. I can smell it now. It stinks.'

The Beards stepped back in horror. Accusatory glances aimed at anyone but themselves.

'That's you, that is. I told you about that leg ulcer. There are maggots crawling about in it.'

'Can't be worse than your armpits. They've not seen soap and water since the millennium.'

'Well, I think you both reek. Don't say it, though, do I? I'm too polite.'

'I'm leaving now,' said Tommy. He moved towards the men, who immediately parted to let him pass. He was already heading back along the alley when he stopped. 'I suppose I should say thanks.'

'No problem, chief.'

'Any time.'

'You know where to find us.'

Tommy reached into his pocket. His phone was still there, but nothing else. 'Sorry. I've got no cash—'

'Yep, that's true,' said one of the Beards shiftily. 'We've already looked. I mean, you had this ...' He opened his fist and revealed a handful of coins. 'One pound twenty-seven.'

'That's more than I was expecting,' said Tommy, back on the move. 'Keep it. Share it out amongst yourselves. And spend it wisely.'

See, I do care. He aimed that at all those who weren't in attendance. Agatha. Miles. Mercy. Rose and Lucas. Take note, people. Tommy O'Strife, feeding the poor and impoverished. A modern day Robin Hood. Robin Hood *and* James Bond. That was some combo.

'Who was he, anyway?'

The question stopped Tommy in his tracks. 'Who was *who*?'

'The geezer who clobbered you.'

'We saw him do it. Crept up on your blind side. Proper sneaky.'

'You been having it away with his missus or something?'

Tommy shook his head. Regretted it when a sharp pain

vibrated around his skull.

The Beards hadn't finished, though.

'He was pretty average. Nothing remarkable about him.'

'Except that massive mole on his cheek.'

'Do you reckon you might know him?'

Tommy walked away without another word. *Do you reckon you might know him?* No reckoning about it. Not now. The Beards had just confirmed what he already suspected.

I'm coming for you, Rupert. I am coming for you.

CHAPTER THIRTY-FOUR

Abbie Simkin lived on Paradise Road.

That was false advertising. Okay, so it wasn't the worst that Stainmouth had to offer, but it was hardly the most salubrious either. North of the town, it was made up of several hundred terrace houses that seemed to go on further than the eye could see. Thankfully, the Simkins lived at number eighteen. Parking was a nightmare, though, so Olaf dropped Agatha and Miles off on the street corner. He would do loops of the estate whilst they were inside before returning immediately when called upon. He was good like that.

Abbie lived with both parents and her younger brother. The brother was at school, whilst the mum was at work. The dad, Ian, was resting a bad back. He wasn't faking it, thought Agatha, as he opened the door and ushered them inside. She could see it in the way he walked back towards the sitting room. Hunched over. Wincing with every step before he collapsed onto the sofa for fear of something snapping. He was old before his time. Late thirties maybe, but with an undeniable bald spot, a protruding paunch, and the kind of hang-dog expression you only ever saw in cartoons.

'Tea? Coffee?'

Agatha said no, largely because she didn't want to put the poor man through the ordeal. Miles said no too, largely because Agatha had.

Ian called his daughter, who came running down the stairs. She stopped in the doorway and looked around. Agatha tried not to gasp when she saw her. She was stunning. And this was in joggers and no make-up. Imagine her on a night out.

Like that fateful night when Cole Burroughs had lost his wife and child.

'These people have come to speak to you about …' Ian groaned. Maybe it was his back. Or maybe it was the words buffering against his throat, refusing to break out. 'That night,' he said eventually. 'The … accident.'

Abbie froze. Glanced back up the stairs towards her bedroom. Her safe place.

'We'll be gentle,' promised Agatha. 'I understand that this has been a stressful time for all of you.'

'Unbearable.' Ian patted the sofa repeatedly until his daughter finally sat down beside him. 'It's been a living nightmare ever since she met that boy … Montague … spoilt little prick—'

'Dad.' Abbie shook her head. 'Not again.'

'We'll get on to Tobias Montague in due course,' said Agatha. 'But let's start with the other night—'

'When she was kidnapped,' finished Ian.

'Hardly,' sighed Abbie. 'He didn't drag me off, kicking and screaming. He didn't even touch me. He just wanted to talk. Ask me a few questions.'

'Bloody weirdo.' Ian smashed his fist into a cushion. 'If I was ... you know ... better ... I'd have been out there. Tracked him down. Done him some damage.'

'Dad, don't ...' Abbie rested a hand on her father's leg.

'Mr Simkin, maybe it would be better if you left us to it,' suggested Agatha. 'I can see this is distressing for you, going over old ground, but I need to know the facts. Preferably without the interruptions.'

Ian stuck his chin out. 'This is my house. You can't make me leave.'

'And neither would I wish to,' insisted Agatha. 'I'm just thinking about your daughter.'

Abbie turned towards her father and nodded. 'I'll be fine. Honestly.'

'Come on,' said Miles, standing up. 'I'll help you make that coffee you offered us before. That's a Stainmouth Town scarf on the banister, isn't it? How did they get on at the weekend?'

Agatha waited for both men to enter the kitchen. For Miles to close the door behind them. 'In your own time,' she said, smiling at the young girl.

Abbie cleared her throat. 'It was several nights ago. There's a field at the end of Paradise Road, used to be a football pitch, that leads onto the next estate. I had been to see a friend. Just talking in her bedroom. Having a laugh. I always use the field to get home.' Abbie paused. 'Never again,' she mumbled.

'I know this must be difficult,' said Agatha.

'The thing is, it shouldn't be.' Abbie tried to laugh, but it came out all wrong. Like a strangled cry. 'It wasn't that late. Half ten-ish. There are always kids hanging about in the dark. Boys giving it loads. Not horrible stuff. Just calling out. Whistling. Trying to impress me. Do you know what I mean?'

Agatha nodded.

'That doesn't bother me,' said Abbie, shrugging it off. 'I'm used to it. This was different, though. There was no one else around. The field was quiet. And then he appeared from nowhere. Right in front of me.' She shivered. 'I thought he was going to attack me. Or ... worse. But he didn't. He kept his arms by his side. Then he apologised. He was sorry for scaring me, but he wanted to talk.'

Abbie fell silent. It was a shame, thought Agatha. She was on a roll, but now she had lost her rhythm. A little prompting was required.

'How did you respond?'

'I didn't,' replied Abbie. 'I thought about running, but he seemed to read my mind. Said he wouldn't hurt me if I did, but pleaded with me not to. So, I just stood there. He wanted to know about the night the two people had died. The mother and her daughter. He wanted to know why I had lied to the police.'

Abbie stopped as the tears started to flow.

'And did you lie to the police?' asked Agatha.

Abbie nodded. 'I had no other choice. Tobias told me he

would kill me if I didn't.'

'People make that threat all the time,' said Agatha softly. 'It doesn't mean it's true.'

'Tobias is different,' Abbie insisted. 'He's done it before. Killed people. Everybody knows, but nobody speaks about it. He's executed members of rival gangs. Raped girls at parties. Tortured them. Cut them up because they won't do as he asks ...' Abbie was panting now. Struggling to breathe as the fear in her intensified.

Agatha held out her hand. 'Relax. I'm not here to judge you. I just want the facts.' She waited for Abbie to catch her breath. 'What did you say to the police?'

'I told them that Tobias hadn't been drinking or taken any drugs,' revealed Abbie. 'That the mother and her daughter had been stood in the road. That it was an accident. Claude said the same. He used to be Tobias's closest friend. I'm guessing he's not anymore.'

'And yet it wasn't an accident, was it?'

Abbie shook her head. 'We had been partying at Tobias's all day. I had just been drinking, but he had gone for it big time. Coke. Speed. Ecstasy. The lot. Vodka straight out of the bottle. He was wired. Practically frothing at the mouth. He said he wanted to go for a drive. That his dad had bought him a new car. A red Porsche. Everybody told him not to do it, but that only made him more determined. It was early evening. Six, seven. He was speeding everywhere. He didn't care. And when he turned that corner ...' Abbie held her breath. Looked towards the window. 'I can still feel the force of the collision. Tobias was howling with laughter. He didn't stop. Just carried on. We went onto another party and I slipped away unnoticed. I haven't seen him since. Only outside the police station when he threatened to kill me if I didn't lie for him.'

'And you told the man this?' asked Agatha. 'In the field?'

'Pretty much. I felt like he deserved to know.'

'What happened after that?'

'He said thank you for telling him the truth. Apologised for scaring me again. And then he was gone. He just walked away. I don't know why it freaked me out so much. He did nothing wrong. Not really.' Abbie hesitated. 'It was his wife and daughter who died, wasn't it? He didn't tell me that, but I've figured it out for myself since.'

'Yes. Yes, it was,' admitted Agatha. 'His name is Cole Burroughs. He's a good man, but he's not thinking straight. He can only see one way out of his pain and suffering, and that's by killing Tobias Montague.'

Abbie steeled herself. 'Then I hope he succeeds. If that's what he wants, then good luck to him. Tobias is evil. He won't stop hurting people. Not unless someone stops him first.'

Agatha lost herself for a moment in the girl's words. The purity of them. No grey area. She snapped out of it and stood up. Forced a smile. 'Thank you. That must have been difficult.'

'Are you the police?' asked Abbie. 'Am I in trouble?'

Agatha shook her head. 'No. To both questions.'

'Who are you then?'

Agatha was about to reply when a knock beat her to it. Abbie quickly wiped her eyes before the kitchen door slowly opened.

'Is it safe to enter?' asked Ian, poking his head around the door frame.

Agatha ushered him in. 'Of course. Thank you for your patience. We'll be on our way now.'

'Good. I mean, not good ... just ... you know ... bye.' Ian sat down beside his daughter, who rested her head on his shoulder. 'Was any of it useful? Did you get enough information to nail the bastard?'

Agatha nodded on her way out of the room. Yes, more than enough. Problem was, they weren't talking about the same bastard ...

CHAPTER THIRTY-FIVE

'You back on the coke?'

Tommy rolled his eyes. He couldn't quite decide who was pissing him off the most. Mercy with her condescending sneers and eyebrow arches, or Lucas with his ridiculous questions, purely designed to get a cheap laugh at his expense.

'I've been hit on the head,' he insisted.

'Oh, so that's why you're talking shit,' said Lucas. 'Your brains have slipped from your skull to your arsehole.'

'What brains?' chipped in Mercy. A thought crossed her mind. 'Why have you come back here?'

Here being seven Haversham Way. The surveillance house.

'Why do you think?' snapped Tommy. 'I wanted to tell you I've been attacked. And, more importantly, who by. Now, I'm not so sure why I bothered. I should've just gone back to Sergio. He'd have been more understanding.'

Lucas moved around the room for a better view of Tommy's head. 'What's with your hair, anyway? Did you only have enough money to pay for half a cut?'

'I gave all I had to some homeless dudes,' said Tommy

casually.

Mercy pulled herself away from the binoculars. Met Lucas's eye. And laughed. 'Oh, I've heard it all now.'

'It's true,' insisted Tommy. 'I swear.'

'You've lost it,' said Mercy, shaking her head.

'Now, now, let's not be hasty.' Lucas rested a hand on Tommy's shoulder. 'Allow me to repeat what you've just told us. You left here and walked into the town centre. Went to get a haircut from a lovely Italian barber who compared you to James Bond. Then you saw Rupert and followed him because, you know, that's what James Bond would do. He led you down a side street and then smacked you over the head, knocking you unconscious. You woke up thinking you were in heaven with hordes of beautiful angels desperate to get their hands on your scrawny body. Problem was, you weren't actually dead, so the angels turned to men, these ... homeless dudes, who you then gave all your money to. All one pound twenty-seven of it.' Lucas paused. 'Correct me if I'm wrong.'

'No need,' said Tommy. 'That's it, give or take. You forgot the bit when I was eye to crotch with the lingerie shop, or when I puked my guts up because of the horrendous stink, but neither of those things are key components to the story.' He stopped. Looked at the other two. 'You're going to start laughing again, aren't you?'

And they did. Louder than before. Shoulders having. Tears running down their cheeks.

Decision made. They were both pissing him off. And they

were both a pair of grade A pricks. No discussion necessary.

'Why aren't you worried about Rose?' he asked. 'Rupert's a complete lunatic. He could hurt her at any moment.'

'Oh, you care now,' sighed Mercy.

'I've always cared,' insisted Tommy. 'Of course I do.'

'I'm not buying that Rupert is a lunatic either,' said Lucas, suddenly serious. 'He's just a normal guy. A normal guy who likes Rose.'

'Then why did he hit me?'

'We *all* want to hit you,' said Mercy. 'Doesn't make us lunatics, though, does it?'

Tommy drew breath as he stared up at the ceiling. He was getting nowhere with these two. 'Where do you think Rose is now?'

'At Cockleshell farm probably,' said Lucas. 'Getting some sleep before her night shift. Like you should be.'

'Except you don't need to because you spent all last night asleep,' said Mercy. 'Do you remember that? When Cole Burroughs could've murdered you in your bed?'

'I'd rather face Cole Burroughs than Rupert,' remarked Tommy.

Mercy tutted back at him. 'Burroughs has killed people before and he wants to kill again.'

'Well, Rupert knocked me out before I had a chance to fight back,' said Tommy. 'Same difference.'

He ended the argument by storming out of the room. Down the stairs and out the back of the house. All before either of them could reply.

They were right about Rose, though. She'd be tucked up in bed by now, fast asleep before tonight. So, that was where he would go, too. No, not to her bedroom. To Cockleshell Farm. Wait for her to wake up and then tell her the truth.

Sorry, Rose, but your boyfriend is a violent nutjob.

And if she didn't believe him, he would show her the cut on his head. The dried blood that he refused to wash off. Even his wonky haircut because that was a piece of the jigsaw. Not even Rose could argue with that. And if she was upset, then he'd provide the shoulder for her to cry on. And he wouldn't even try it on, because that would be inappropriate. And people who cared didn't like to be inappropriate.

Because that was what he was.

A caring person.

Yeah, that was settled. Tommy to the rescue. Again. It was getting boring now. Why didn't someone else take the lead for a change? Still, everyone needs a role model in their life.

Just one problem.

How the fuck was he going to do all this if he couldn't even get back to Cockleshell Farm?

CHAPTER THIRTY-SIX

Rose wasn't in bed.

She wasn't even at Cockleshell Farm.

But she was sat in The Ugly Mug cafe enjoying a latte and a slice of carrot cake with the man of her dreams.

Because that was what he was. She had decided that after leaving the others at Haversham Way. She had compared him to Lucas and Miles. Not Tommy. Tommy didn't even register. But compared to the other two, Rupert had come out on top. He was kinder. Softer. Not so brash and abrasive. He had nothing to prove. There was no front there. Just a purity that she recognised in herself.

Without warning, she reached over the table and grabbed him by the hand. Squeezed it tight.

'What was that for?' he asked, smiling.

'I don't know,' said Rose. 'I just wanted to.'

Rupert laughed. 'Well, there's something I want to do for you. You might not believe this, but I'm a phenomenal cook. I can open any tin or packet, and my microwave skills are out of this world. Seriously, why don't you come round to mine tonight? No pressure; just dinner. I'll try to make it as special as I can.'

'That sounds lovely ...' Rose glanced around the cafe to buy herself some time. She had been here once before with Mercy and a local gangster called Frank DeMayo. It had ended with Mercy throwing a chair through the window. Frank was dead now. It was funny how things always seemed to work out that way.

'Earth to Rose,' said Rupert. 'So would you like to come round or—?'

'Not ... I mean, no ... I do ... of course I do ...' Rose groaned out loud.

'I'm sensing there's a *but*.'

'But I can't. I'm busy tonight. I'm working ... if you can call it that.'

Rupert rested his elbows on the table. Sighed. 'That's a shame. Tomorrow?'

'Tomorrow?' Rose shifted awkwardly in her chair. 'Still working. Probably.'

'Is this your way of letting me down gently?'

'No ... not at all ... never,' blurted out Rose. 'I'd love to come round. Honestly. I really am busy, though. I wish I wasn't.'

'You never told me what you do?'

'Didn't I?'

'Definitely not.'

'Didn't I?' repeated Rose for no apparent reason.

'No.' Rupert ran his fingers across the back of her hand.

'You know all about me. My job at the printers. The amateur dramatics—'

'I don't know your surname,' said Rose.

'Now you're just trying to avoid the question.' Rupert pretended to think. 'All I know about you is that you live in a house-share with a group of people you don't even like.'

'That's a bit harsh.'

'You said it. Not me.'

Rose nodded. Had she, though? Said such a thing? Possibly. She couldn't remember, but then she felt so relaxed when they were together it was hard for her to hold back. There was so much she wanted to tell him. So much of her life that wasn't her own, but she was desperate to share with someone. No, not someone. With him. With Rupert.

'So, what do you do?' he asked.

'Where do I begin?' shrugged Rose. 'It's ... hard to explain.'

'We've got time.'

Rose drew a breath as she contemplated her answer. What do I do? *Oh, I'm just part of a team of random strangers who nearly died – of which my own death was anything but accidental – but now I'm forced to spy on a heartbroken man who's lost his family in tragic circumstances. Is that normal enough for you, Rupert? Do you still like me?*

'It's voluntary work,' said Rose. That much was true, at least. In a roundabout way. 'I don't get paid much.' Ditto. 'I keep an eye on vulnerable people who are struggling. Check that they're okay. If I can stop something bad from happening, then that's my job done.'

Rupert pulled away. Leant back in his chair. For one awful moment, Rose feared she had said something to upset him. Thankfully, she hadn't.

'Wow,' he gasped. 'That's amazing. Such a sweet thing to do. I don't know why you're so coy about it, Rose, because that's worth shouting from the rooftops. How much better would the world be if there were more people like you in it? Suddenly I feel like such a selfish arsehole.'

'Don't,' said Rose hastily. 'You're not. And I'm not that great. And I will come round to yours. Soon. I promise. Once this case I've got has ... erm ... resolved itself.'

Which probably meant that Cole Burroughs would have to kill or be killed, thought Rose, but she tried not to dwell on it.

'Okay,' nodded Rupert. 'That's fine by me. I'm ready when you are. We're not in any—'

'Can I take these?' A waitress leant over the table, cutting Rupert off mid-sentence. He sat back and watched as she started with the side plates, choosing to balance them on her forearm before she reached for the cups.

Rose, ever the pessimist, could see what was about to happen moments before it did.

In slow motion, one of the plates slid down the waitress's arm and knocked a cup out of her hand. It landed on the corner of the table, smashing upon impact, sending remnants of cold coffee splattering against Rupert's shirt.

'Watch what you're doing, you stupid bitch!' he snapped.

The whole cafe seemed to freeze in time as the waitress fell to her knees and picked at the pieces of ceramic.

'Christ, it's really not that difficult,' spat Rupert, glaring at the girl by his feet. 'Minimum wage for a basic service and you can't even get that right.'

'Rupert ...' Rose climbed off her chair and knelt down. 'Please.'

'Don't you dare help her!' Leaning over the table, Rupert grabbed Rose by the wrist and tried to drag her up off the floor. She felt his nails dig into her skin as his grip tightened. She was about to pull away when a man wandered over and Rupert let go voluntarily.

'Is there a problem?'

Rose looked up. Not a man, but a boy. A smattering of spots and a bum fluff moustache were enough to support that theory. A white short-sleeve shirt and black trousers, only one small step from a school uniform, were extra confirmation.

'Who the hell are you?' asked Rupert bluntly.

'Darryl,' replied the boy sheepishly. 'I'm ... erm ... acting manager.'

Rupert turned his nose up in disgust. 'Well, which one is it? Are you acting, or are you the manager?'

'I'm ... um ... the manager,' decided Darryl. 'But just for today. Mags is at the hospital.'

Rupert slowly exhaled. 'Well, Darryl, I suggest you exert some managerial power and fire this ... pitiful excuse for a waitress.'

'Don't be like that,' said Rose.

Darryl peered down at the ground. Dabbed his shoe in the spilt liquid. 'It's only a cup. Not the end of the world—'

'And that's what you think, is it?' Rupert crossed his arms in defiance. 'That it's fine to smash a cup? That it's acceptable to be useless at your job?'

The waitress wiped her eyes on her sleeve as she finally stood up. 'It was an accident.'

'It was an accident,' repeated Darryl.

'Oh, that's okay then.' With a flick of his wrist, Rupert lashed out at another cup, sending it flying off the table before it smashed on the floor. 'Sorry,' he grinned. 'Accident.'

Darryl swallowed. An honest reaction of a young man out of his depth. 'Would you like me to get you another drink?' he asked, his voice hitting an all-time high.

'No.' Rupert stood up suddenly. 'Not today. Or tomorrow. Or ever. We're leaving and, trust me, we're never coming back. And don't think that word won't get out. People need to know about the sub-standard service you offer here. The lack of respect you have for your customers. With any luck, you'll be shut down by the weekend.'

And on that note, Rupert marched across the length of The Ugly Mug Cafe and exited the premises.

Rose could feel the heat from her cheeks as she used the table to pull herself up. The rest of the cafe was still silent, their attention fixed on the last remaining member of the troublesome two. 'I'm sorry,' she mumbled, avoiding eye contact with both Darryl and the waitress. 'I'll pay for any damages.'

'It's only a cup,' Darryl repeated. '*Two* cups. I break them all the time.'

Rose nodded. Smiled. And then hurried out of the cafe without another word. She didn't look back for fear of an angry glare or, worse still, a sympathetic smirk from a stranger she didn't even know and would probably never see again.

She found Rupert waiting for her outside, just around the corner. He had his back to the wall, scuffing the sole of his shoe repeatedly against the brickwork.

'I've ruined everything, haven't I?' he muttered under his breath.

Rose shook her head. 'Not at all.'

'I don't know what came over me. It just annoys me when people can't do their job properly. I don't know why. She's probably trying her best. And it *was* just a cup.'

'That's what Darryl tried to tell you.' Rose had to fight the urge to smile. 'The look on his face. Poor boy.'

'I feel bad now,' admitted Rupert. 'Maybe I should go back in and apologise—'

'No,' replied Rose hastily. 'That'll just be awkward for everyone. I'm sure they'll have got over it by now, anyway. It must happen all the time.'

Rupert stared at her for a moment. 'Thank you. You always seem to know the right things to say. I'm lucky to have you. Come on, I'll walk you to your car.'

Rupert took her hand and they set off along the pavement.

His head was down and he had gone quiet. Rose could tell that his outburst had troubled him immensely. It shouldn't have. Not really. People often reacted badly. Got angry. That was life. It wasn't unusual and it wasn't anything to worry about. It was embarrassing, yes, but Rose had spent the vast majority of her life feeling embarrassed, so this was nothing out of the ordinary. He was still the man he was before. Kind. Gentle. Caring. Nothing had changed.

She leant over and kissed him on the cheek. He smiled back at her.

He was still the man of her dreams.

Just.

CHAPTER THIRTY-SEVEN

Next on Agatha's list was Claude Bonham, the other passenger in Tobias Montague's Porsche on that fateful evening.

Bonham wasn't available, though, largely because he wasn't even in the country. Peru had been his destination of choice after investigations had come to an end, and Montague had been cleared of any wrong-doing. He needed to rest, relax and recuperate, the stresses of everything that had happened having taken their toll.

How the other half live, thought Agatha. Throw enough money at a problem and it could always be solved. Mental and physical. Still, if Bonham was elsewhere, then it was time to move on to the next on the list. The man himself. The reason they were running around town trying to figure out the cause of Cole Burroughs's rage.

Tobias Montague.

It came as no surprise to find that he lived in a big house. Or rather, his father lived in a big house. One of many, most probably. Located on the outskirts of Stainmouth, Montague

Manor was an uncomfortably large country house set deep in its own estate. Agatha ticked the features off one by one as they drove along the sprawling driveway. The beautiful stonework that complimented the stunning landscape gardens. The grand central portico and mansard roof. The vast glazed openings – also known as windows to the less pretentious – that effortlessly filled the interior of the property with natural light.

Miles seemed to read her mind as he climbed out of the Audi and took in the property. 'Must be nice to a have a few million to spare,' he muttered.

'Magnus Montague is a very rich man,' said Agatha, setting off towards the front door.

Miles followed close behind. He was about to speak when the sound of smashing glass beat him to it. At the same time, a champagne bottle came flying out of a top-floor window. Agatha barely flinched as it landed on the driveway beside them, skidding across the gravel before it came to a halt.

'Relax,' she said, shaking her head as Miles moved towards his gun. She listened carefully and heard loud music coming from beyond the broken window. 'Sounds like somebody's having a good time.'

'Remind me what one of those is again,' Miles remarked.

Agatha's gaze fell from the top floor to the front door. A man had appeared in the entrance. Small in size, with a bald head and tiny spectacles. Dressed smartly in a waistcoat and black trousers, white shirt and black tie, and, curiously, a flowery apron with a variety of red stains on it. He glanced over at the bottle, tutted, and then turned to Agatha and Miles. 'I don't suppose that's got anything to do with you two, has it?' he said sombrely. 'Or is that just wishful thinking?'

'The latter,' replied Agatha. 'Throwing bottles isn't really my thing.'

'In that case, I'd better call the glazier ... again,' sighed the man in the apron. 'Now, how can I be of assistance? You two don't look like the usual visitors we have for one of young master Montague's parties.'

'Bit early for a party,' said Miles.

'Or late. This one's been going on for over two days now. I can't be certain, but I think it might be coming to an end. There's been no more gunshots since late last night, so that's always a good sign.' The man in the apron stopped. Seemed to visibly scold himself. 'Sorry. How rude of me. My name is Pendleton. I take care of Montague Manor in the absence of its owner.'

'Magnus Montague?' said Agatha.

Pendleton nodded. 'Mr Montague works away. Dubai at this current moment in time. Taking care of the house largely involves me taking care of his son. Cooking, cleaning, general maintenance. I'm sure you get the picture.' He paused. 'You might not be here for a party, but I'm still guessing that you're here to see young master Montague. Are you the police?'

'Not quite,' said Agatha. 'But, yes, we are here because of Tobias. Would you like to see our ID?'

Pendleton shook his head. 'That won't be necessary. Young

master Montague is in his room. Would you like me to go up and prepare him for your arrival?'

Now it was Agatha's turn to shake her head. 'Sometimes the element of surprise is beneficial. I prefer to take people how I find them.'

'You won't be saying that in a minute,' frowned Pendleton. 'Young master Montague has a peculiar set of principles. Or should that be, lack of.'

'You don't get on?'

'I despise him with every inch of my being,' said Pendleton matter-of-factly. 'He's a boorish young man without an honourable bone in his body. I do, however, have the utmost respect for his father. I've worked for him for almost thirty years now and he pays well. If he wants me to babysit his son, then so be it.' Pendleton gestured towards an elegant spiralled staircase. 'Young master Montague's is the fourth room on the left. Don't say I didn't warn you.'

'I won't,' nodded Agatha, as she made her way across the marble floor towards the stairs.

'Poor bugger,' whispered Miles, once Pendleton was out of earshot. 'Somebody's not happy in his work.'

'Not everyone can have as understanding a boss as you.' Agatha stopped mid-step. Studied what had been discarded on the stair beside her. 'Knickers,' she remarked accurately.

'And there's the matching bra,' said Miles, pointing three steps further up. 'Either someone couldn't find the laundry basket—'

'Or they were desperate to get their clothes off,' finished Agatha. They turned left at the top of the staircase. Passed three closed doors before they arrived at the fourth at the end of the corridor.

Miles looked at Agatha, who nodded her approval. With that, he knocked once. He didn't need to strain to hear giggling coming from somewhere behind the door. No answer, though.

'Lead the way,' said Agatha.

Miles pulled down on the handle. Stepped inside and did a quick sweep of the room. It was large in size, with exposed beams and an eye-catching floor-to-ceiling window. The furniture was a mismatch of styles, from ornately antique to extravagantly modern. There were clothes strewn across the floor, alongside empty alcohol bottles and cigarette packets.

There was no sign of Tobias Montague, though.

Miles frowned. 'What's going on? I thought Pendleton said—'

A flurry of movement was enough to cut him off. It was followed by a loud *pop* that echoed around the room. Instantly recognisable. Unnervingly familiar.

Like the *pop* of a gunshot.

CHAPTER THIRTY-EIGHT

Claude Bonham wasn't in Peru.

That was what he had told his friends, but he had soon changed his mind. It was just too far away, too daunting on his own. Instead, he had gone to see his sister in Peterborough. Not quite as exotic, but it seemed to do the trick. Meg Bonham lived with her husband in relative modesty compared to Claude's own lavish lifestyle. An English teacher at the local secondary school, she surrounded herself with as many moth-eaten books as she could fit into their cramped yet comfortable cottage. It must've sparked something in Claude because he started to read one during his month-long stay. *Anna Karenina*. The first few chapters were okay, but then it got a little dull and repetitive in places. *Most* places, if he was being honest. Practically the entire book. Once he'd given up on literature, he turned to exercise. Running at first, before he signed up for a free trial at the local gym. He went every day, sometimes twice, the routine enough to keep him on the straight and narrow. No more drink. No more drugs. No more Tobias Montague.

All three would be hard to avoid now he was back in Stainmouth, however.

He had been home for two days. First day, he had followed his own example and joined the gym at the leisure centre. A year's membership paid in full. It would be worth every penny if it kept him out of trouble. He had even gone that night. A cardio session, a few weights. Nothing too strenuous. There, he had got talking to some of the other guys. A fireman. A window cleaner. A couple of students. They were friendly, encouraging. Just normal people living normal lives.

The second day he had got up early and gone first thing. The temptations of old were prickling at his conscience. Calling out to him. Pleading with him to stray. Exercise would focus his mind, though. If he kept himself busy, he could keep the past at bay. And yet there was one big problem looming on the horizon. Nobody can work out all day, however hard they tried.

And that was why he messaged Lolly.

She was an on-off girlfriend who leant heavily on the side of off. She was pretty. She was posh. That would do for now. As far as he knew, she hadn't missed him whilst he was away. Probably hadn't even realised he had gone. She was like that. Not exactly air-headed; just consumed by her own existence. Still, at least she wasn't overly possessive. She didn't nag. She just wanted to have a good time all the time, thankfully without the aid of stimulants. That was fine by Claude. Especially after everything that had happened.

His message had been short and sweet.

Fancy a spot of lunch?

Lolly had replied within seconds, unsurprising for someone who had their phone permanently glued to their hand.

Sure thing, babes. Jean-Pierre's. On you.

So, that was that. It was a date. Claude had booked a slot at Jean-Pierre's Brasserie for two people. Where it went after that was anybody's guess.

First, he had to get there, though. Claude had left the gym late after showering. The walk to the restaurant was close on fifteen minutes and he had given himself less than twelve. It didn't do to keep Lolly waiting. She got easily distracted. Before you knew it, she'd be in a different establishment with a different man.

Eleven minutes later and it was panic over. He could see Lolly up ahead. Leant up against some metal railings outside the entrance to Jean-Pierre's, she was wearing a short skirt that almost reached her waist and a fitted blazer that did little to contain her ample cleavage. What admiring glances she got, however, she barely acknowledged. Instead, she focussed on her phone. Or rather, her phone was focussed on her as she repeatedly clicked away. Those same photos, filtered and edited, would be on social media later in the day, along with some inane hash tag.

Living my best life. You gotta' make it happen. Girls just wanna' have fun.

Heaven help her if she ever met Tobias Montague, thought Claude. He took fun to a new level. Where it was no longer enjoyable. Where it destroyed lives and left scars that were so deep they would never heal.

Claude increased his pace. Had Lolly seen him coming? Maybe. Probably not. He thought about running, but decided against it. He didn't want to look like a little kid, all giddy and excited. He was a man now. Or as good as.

That didn't stop him from picking up speed, though. He couldn't help himself. Longer strides, but not quite so obvious. There were cars parked up on the roadside, but he barely saw them, his eyes fixed on the girl against the railings.

That all changed, however, when the passenger side door of one car in particular flew open and the driver leant over to talk to him. It was a woman. She was wearing a pair of sunglasses despite the obvious lack of sun, and a headscarf that covered much of her face. It was the latter that made it impossible for Claude to hear what she was saying.

Bending forward, he ducked inside the car. 'Sorry, I couldn't quite make out ...'

His sentence came to an abrupt halt as the driver removed her headscarf.

And that was when Claude Bonham realised that all was not quite how it seemed inside the bright yellow Honda Civic.

CHAPTER THIRTY-NINE

Miles moved swiftly.

With one stride, he stepped in front of Agatha. At the same time, his right hand reached for his gun. He was in the moment. Focussed on the facts.

Neither of them had been shot. Neither of them was hurt.

But if that was a gun, where was the gunman?

Stop. Facts only.

There was no gunman because there was no gun. The noise they had heard wasn't a gunshot, nor was it an explosion of any kind. It was loud, though. Unnaturally so.

Miles's eyes darted around the room. He stopped at a luxurious four-poster bed. Curtains had been drawn to cover all four sides, but he could still make out movement behind it. He edged towards it, his gun at arm's length. He stopped when a head appeared. A girl. Blonde. Just the right side of legal. One head turned to two. Two turned to three. And three turned to four. Two of each sex.

And then a fifth. Another young man. Fashionably unkempt hair. Wild eyes and sharp cheekbones. His right hand clutched tightly around the neck of a Champagne bottle, the opening of which explained the loud *pop* that had greeted Agatha and Miles's arrival.

The young man took a drink before he spoke. 'That was quick. Don't mind us. You just get on with fixing that window.'

Miles returned his gun to his pocket. 'You must have me mistaken for someone else.'

'We're here to see Tobias Montague,' added Agatha, drawing level with her number two.

The young man stared at them both, blank-faced and bewildered, before the bravado returned. 'Is this a joke? Did Pendleton send you? Bet he did. He's a fuckin' madman. Well, I'm not complaining. Don't just stand there. Get your kit off. There's room for two more.'

Agatha raised an eyebrow. 'Trust me, neither of us will be removing our clothes. You must be Tobias ...'

'The one and only.' Tobias Montague took another gulp from the bottle. Burped. 'If you're not here to join the fun, then I'd rather you buggered off forthwith. You know where the door is.'

Miles took a step forward. A second was sure to follow when Agatha put a hand on his shoulder.

'This is important,' she began. 'You can get back to whatever it is you're doing after we've gone. It shouldn't take long. I'd rather we spoke in private, though.'

'Whatever it is, I didn't do it,' smirked Tobias. 'And even if I did, I wouldn't tell you two. The police don't hold any sway in this house. You do know who my father is, don't you?'

'We're not the police,' remarked Agatha. She had said that so much recently it was becoming her catchphrase. 'Nor are we here to accuse or lay blame. We're here to ... help.'

'Intriguing.' Tobias wriggled about behind the curtain. 'Fine. Let's hear what you have to say.'

'In private ...' repeated Agatha.

Tobias rolled his eyes. 'You heard the woman,' he barked. 'Wait outside. I've got a spot of business to attend to with these two stiffs.'

Right on cue, the curtains moved and the four heads climbed out of the bed. Four heads attached to four naked bodies. Hands in all the appropriate places, they hurried out of the room whilst giggling uncontrollably.

Agatha waited for the door to close behind them before she spoke. 'Thank you. This is a sensitive issue that I'd rather not discuss in public. You're in danger—'

'I'm in danger?' Without warning, Tobias reached under his pillow and produced a gun. It was an antique Colt Single Action Army revolver. He pointed it at Agatha and closed one eye. Fixed the target in his sights. 'Looks like the tables have turned, ma'am,' he began, his voice mimicking those from an old western. 'Youse the one in danger now. Yee-haw!'

Miles held his nerve. Resisted the urge to pull out his own gun and take aim. 'Have you got a licence for that?' he asked calmly.

'I don't need a licence,' laughed Tobias. 'Do you know who

I am?'

'You're an arrogant little shit,' snapped Miles. 'An arrogant little shit who should think about putting that gun away before somebody gets hurt.'

With that, Tobias threw the curtains to one side. Like the others, he was completely naked. 'Put what away?' he asked, feigning innocence as he leapt up onto the mattress. Eyes fixed on Agatha, he started to gyrate. 'Do you like this? Do you think I'm sexy?'

Agatha pulled a face. 'No offence, but I prefer Rod Stewart.'

'I don't get it,' shrugged Tobias, still gyrating as he moved closer to the edge of the bed.

'A bit before your time,' Agatha sighed. 'Now, why don't you do us all a favour and put some clothes on? Then we can talk. And then we can leave. And then everybody's happy. It's that simple.'

'Suit yourself.' Tobias hopped off the bed. Glared at both Agatha and Miles on his way across the room. 'You're not my type anyway,' he said, picking a dressing gown up off the floor. 'Neither of you are. You're police, whatever you say. I can smell it on you. Well, you're wasting your time. One phone call to my father and you'll both be out of a job in seconds.' Tobias placed the gun down on a dressing table. Reached for another bottle of Champagne. 'Go on. Remind me. What have I done now?'

'Killed a mother and her daughter,' said Miles bluntly. 'You ran them down and refused to stop.'

'Is that it?' Tobias tried to take a drink, but the bottle was empty, so he tossed it across the room. 'Bollocks. Where's Pendleton when you need him? The way things are going, that silly old fucker would be more use to me dead than alive.'

'Did you feel the same about Charlotte and Sophie Burroughs?' asked Miles.

Tobias pulled a face. 'Who?'

'The mother and daughter ...' said Agatha.

'Are you people still going on about that?' Tobias snatched the Colt from the dressing table and walked up to Miles. Poked him in the chest with the nozzle. 'It was an accident. They were in the road—'

'You keep telling yourself that,' said Miles.

Tobias stuck his bottom lip out. 'I'm the victim. It's been very traumatic. Now, I'm no expert on the subject, but it's poor parenting, if you ask me. Letting your kid wander straight into traffic—'

'It was a hit and run.' Miles leant forward. Touched foreheads with the younger man. 'That makes you a murderer in my eyes.'

Tobias held his gun steady. 'Once a murderer, always a murderer. I could kill you if I wanted. Right here, right now. Nobody would ever know.'

'Except me,' said Agatha.

Tobias spun away, his dressing gown flailing behind him. 'And what are you going to do, grandma? Hit me with your Zimmer frame?'

'No, I'd put a bullet between your eyes,' said Agatha coldly. She let that hang there for a few seconds before she smiled.

'That's not the reason for our visit, though. We came with a warning. A man has threatened to kill you. The husband and father of the two people involved in the ... *accident*. His name is Cole Burroughs.'

'Is it really?' A distracted Tobias looked around the room before passing the Colt to Miles. 'Take care of that, will you, big boy? It's time for my mid-afternoon pick-me-up.'

Agatha watched as the young man wandered over to a chest-of-drawers. Crouching down, he emptied a small packet of white powder over the surface. 'I don't think that's advisable,' she began. 'You need to clear your head and pay attention. Cole Burroughs won't just go away—'

'Oh, yeah, blah, blah, blah.' Tobias rolled up a twenty-pound note and pressed it against the powder. Leaning forward, he took a huge snort before lifting his head. 'He wants to kill me, does he? Well, join the fuckin' queue. One more won't make a difference.' He stood up. Gestured towards the door. 'You can go now. It's been nice meeting you, but please don't call again. Oh, and you can keep that gun,' he said, patting Miles on the bum on his way past. 'I've got plenty more where that came from.'

Opening the door, Agatha was surprised to find the four naked bodies huddled together on the landing.

'Tell my guests they can come back in,' shouted Tobias, as he flung off his dressing gown and dived back into bed. 'I'm ready and waiting.'

The four bodies heard for themselves and scurried back into

the room. Miles closed the door behind them and then walked silently alongside Agatha as they made their way towards the staircase.

'What are you thinking?' she asked, eventually.

'I'm wondering how big that queue is to kill him,' replied Miles. 'I wouldn't want to lose my place.'

'You're angry. I get that—'

'And you're not?'

'No, I'm angry. But I'm also confused.'

'About?'

'The law ... what's right and wrong ...'

Miles nodded. 'Your head says one thing, but your heart says another.'

'No. Funnily enough, my head and heart both say the same thing,' said Agatha, as they reached the foot of the staircase.

As if by magic, Pendleton appeared in the hallway and opened the front door. At the same time, the house was filled with music. It was coming from upstairs. Blaring out of powerful speakers.

'And how was young master Montague?' asked Pendleton, a wry smile etched across his face.

'Utterly obnoxious,' replied Agatha.

Pendleton nodded as if that were the correct answer. 'I did try to warn you.'

'And we tried to warn him,' said Miles. 'We believe that someone is coming here to kill him. We don't know when, but it might be soon.'

Pendleton raised an eyebrow. 'That is good news, sir. I'll be sure to make myself scarce when the joyous moment arrives.'

Agatha smiled at that as she left the house. She heard the door close behind them soon after. Turning to Miles, she was all set to speak when her phone began to vibrate. Reaching inside her handbag, she grabbed at the offending article and studied the screen. It was the Chief Constable.

'Hello, Clifford … okay … yes, that is unexpected … I'll be right over …'

She ended the call abruptly. Slipped her phone back inside her handbag and sighed.

'Bad news?' asked Miles, reading her expression.

'Possibly,' replied Agatha, somewhat vaguely. 'There's been a change of plan. Looks like Claude Bonham is back in Stainmouth, after all. Problem is, he's been kidnapped.'

CHAPTER FORTY

Tommy jumped up from the sofa at the sound of the front door.

Racing out of the sitting room, he found Rose on the doorstep. Still upright. Still in one piece. Nothing broken. Nothing bandaged. No cuts or bruises. No scars. Not on the outside, anyway.

'Where have you been?' he cried.

Rose stared at him, confused. 'Pardon?'

'Where have you been?' repeated Tommy. 'I've been worried sick.'

'Sorry ... dad.' Rose placed the car keys in the tray by the door. 'What time is it? Five o'clock?'

'Quarter-past. It's dark. I've been pulling my hair out here.'

Rose took that literally. 'So I can see.'

'Ignore that,' said Tommy, waving a hand dismissively at his half haircut. 'Long story. Safe to say it ended badly.' He switched his attention to the cut on his forehead. At the dry blood in particular, which he refused to wash off. 'Someone attacked me. Even managed to knock me out.'

A stunned Rose stepped forward for a closer look. 'Really?

That's terrible. I just thought it was tomato ketchup and you'd missed your mouth whilst eating. Are you okay?'

'I'll survive.' Tommy held out a hand. Not to push her away, but as a warning. 'There's something I need to tell you. You're not going to like it, but it's the truth. It was Rupert.'

'What was Rupert?'

'Who knocked me out. He jumped me in the middle of nowhere. Nailed me good and proper.'

Rose shook her head. 'That's not ... it can't be ... why would he do that?'

'Because he's a fuckin' maniac,' blurted out Tommy. 'Believe me, Rose. I'm not messing about. Old mole face was gunning for me. And if it's me today, it could be you tomorrow. I don't want you to get hurt.'

Rose's head was still shaking as she pushed past Tommy on her way towards the stairs. 'Rupert isn't like that. I know what you're trying to do—'

'I'm watching out for you,' insisted Tommy, scampering after her. 'I've just told you that.'

'And I'm not listening,' shot back Rose. 'It's all lies. I don't know why ... maybe Agatha put you up to it ... maybe she didn't ... I don't care either way. But I want it to end. I mean it, Tommy. I'm with Rupert—'

'You're with him?' Tommy screwed up his face. 'That's escalated quickly. Yesterday you were just friends.'

Rose stopped mid-step. 'It's none of your business what we are,' she snapped. 'It's nobody's business. Only ours. What makes you think you have the right to interfere?'

'It's not interfering,' Tommy argued. 'It's ... caring.'

'Rubbish. You don't care about anybody but yourself.' Rose rested her hands on the banister. Closed her eyes and took a deep breath. This time, she didn't shout or scream. 'Don't talk to me. Not now. Not later. I don't want to hear another word from you. And I won't let you ruin things for me.'

Tommy threw up his hands as Rose bounded up the stairs. 'Oh, come on. It's not like that. I'm not trying to ... ah, bollocks!'

The expletive came as a result of Rose closing the door to her bedroom. She wasn't listening, but then she probably never had been. Not really.

Love does that to you, thought Tommy, as he took a slow walk back to the sitting room and collapsed onto the sofa. It makes you blind. And stupid. And that was what Rose was now.

She was blindly, stupidly in love with a psycho.

And there was nothing he, or anybody else for that matter, could do about it.

CHAPTER FORTY-ONE

Miles called Mercy on their way to the police station.

'What's up?'

'I was about to ask you the same thing,' said Miles. 'Why aren't you watching Cole Burroughs?'

'I am. I can see him now. Well, the back of his head, at least. He's in his sitting room. He's barely moved all afternoon.'

'That's all I needed to know.' Miles hung up abruptly. Turned to Agatha, who was sat beside him. 'Did you hear that?'

'Pretty much,' she said. 'It would've made more sense if they had let him slip, though. If Cole Burroughs didn't kidnap Claude Bonham, then who did?'

Olaf turned the Audi into the station car park. Hesitated for a moment before Agatha told him to park in the spot reserved for the Chief Constable.

'He won't mind,' she insisted. 'Largely because he won't even know.'

With that, the two of them exited the car and made their way towards the station entrance. They were greeted by the duty officer, Sergeant Biggerstaff, who smiled, yawned and then stuck up a hand, blocking their way. 'Nothing to see here, folks.'

'We'd like to talk to Lolly ... erm ... Lorelei Ford-Ballard,' said Miles.

'You'll be lucky,' snorted Biggerstaff. 'She's been hysterical ever since she got here. Crying her eyes out non-stop. Reckons her boyfriend has been kidnapped.'

'And how likely do you think that is?' asked Agatha. 'How often do young men get kidnapped in Stainmouth?'

Biggerstaff stroked his chin, deep in thought. 'Is this one of those trick questions? You know the kind. Where the answer's either really high or really low. Something like fourteen thousand ... or minus six. Oh, I can't even guess.' He paused. 'Go on. How many?'

'I've no idea,' sighed Agatha. 'It was a rhetorical question.'

'Ah, one of those crafty bleeders, was it?' nodded Biggerstaff. 'I'll take your word for it. No, if it was anybody else I'd have my doubts, but Miss Ford-Ballard is pretty insistent. She says Mr Bonham was on his way to the restaurant when he went missing. She had him in her sights one minute, and then he just vanished without a trace. There was something about a yellow car, but it was hard to decipher through the constant wailing.'

'I still think we should talk to her,' said Agatha.

'Come closer.' Biggerstaff beckoned them both towards him. 'Listen carefully. Can you hear that?'

That was the sound of a woman sobbing her heart out in another part of the station. The sobbing was interspersed with the occasional cry of anguish and random scream.

'Now, I'm not going to stop you going in there,' began Biggerstaff. 'That's above my pay grade. But I will ask you this. What do you think she's going to tell you in that state? Because I'd imagine not very much.'

Agatha and Miles exchanged glances. He had a point. A good point. One that it was hard to disagree with.

'If anything changes, I want to be the first to know,' Agatha demanded. 'There's barely any evidence to suggest that Claude Bonham has actually been kidnapped. He might have just changed his mind. Gone off with somebody else. Another friend. Or girlfriend.'

'There's a female officer in there with Miss Ford-Ballard even as we speak,' said Biggerstaff. 'She'll hopefully calm down at some point and we can question her further.'

Agatha had heard enough. Without another word, she headed out of the station and back towards the Audi.

'What now?' asked Miles.

Agatha pulled open the car door. 'I say we call it a day. Go back to the Nightingale and recharge our batteries. The others know where to find us. We're just a phone call away.'

'And tomorrow?'

'Tomorrow we start again,' said Agatha, climbing onto the back seat. 'You never know, Cole Burroughs could always decide that killing Tobias Montague isn't top of his wish list, whilst Claude Bonham declares himself safe and well. Stranger things have happened.'

'Not in this lifetime,' muttered Miles, sliding in beside her.

'Better that than the alternative, I suppose. Everybody ends up dead and we get the blame.'

Agatha turned towards the window as Olaf reversed the Audi out of the Chief Constable's parking spot. It was funny that Miles should say that because that was her worst fear.

Dead bodies seemed to follow her around with an unerring regularity.

Please, not again.

CHAPTER FORTY-TWO

The changeover from day shift to night shift passed relatively smoothly.

Rose drove herself and Tommy from Cockleshell Farm to the house on Haversham Way at slightly below the speed limit. As was the norm, Tommy tried to fill the air with mindless babble, but got nothing in return from his companion. It infuriated him how she didn't believe a word he said, but so be it. He wasn't going to argue his case. She was too involved for that. Rupert could've chopped Tommy's head off with an axe and Rose would still say it was Tommy's fault for getting too close to the blade.

Back at the townhouse, they found Mercy and Lucas on the verge of some kind of boredom paralysis. Through a series of groans and grumbles, it didn't take them long to run through the events of the day. Or rather, lack of. Cole Burroughs hadn't left the house once. He'd had one visitor, though. A woman. Wrapped up for winter in a headscarf that covered much of her face, it had only been a fleeting visit. In and out in less than half-an-hour.

And that was that. There was nothing to say and no need for small talk. Back on the move, Mercy and Lucas were out of the surveillance room and down the stairs a moment later.

See you in twelve hours. We've got a whole evening to look forward to. Don't want to waste another second of it staring blankly through someone else's window.

A weary Tommy slumped down on the recliner and tried to get comfortable. He was shattered, but he couldn't go to sleep. Not yet, anyway. With any luck, Rose would drop off first and he could follow her lead. She would never know. So, what could he do in the meantime to occupy his mind?

Bugger all, that's what.

He was stuck in an empty house with a deluded woman and a pair of binoculars. If nothing interesting happened across the road, this was going to be the longest twelve hours of his life.

***

But something did happen.

And it didn't take twelve hours.

Forty-five minutes into their shift, a bright yellow Honda Civic pulled up outside number eight and a woman emerged from inside. Rose recognised the headscarf from Mercy's report and called Tommy over. She didn't want to speak to him; she just needed the confirmation.

'Strange,' he muttered from over her shoulder. 'Why would she come back for a second time?'

Tommy left it there. No need for any cheap innuendo. Rose would probably react badly. On second thoughts, there was no *probably* about it.

Like last time, the woman left after thirty minutes and Rose logged it. That was where the excitement ended, though, and she soon went back to staring at the house across the road. The house with its curtains closed. The house that, one by one, the lights went out, plunging it into darkness.

***

It was later that evening when Rose first started to question her life choices.

Or rather, one choice in particular. Her afternoon date with Rupert. It had seemed like a good idea at the time. Now, however, she was rueing those lost hours of sleep as her eyes started to droop and her head rested against the binoculars. Tommy had nodded off a while ago. She knew he would do, especially when he kept on insisting he wouldn't. That was always a telltale sign. He had even tried to run up and down the stairs to stave it off, but that was only a temporary solution. The moment he had sat back down to catch his breath, his eyes had closed and he had fallen into a deep slumber. His snoring was the only thing that reminded Rose that he was still alive.

And now she was heading the same way. Out for the count. See you in the morning. The point had come when she could fight it no longer. She had already started to hallucinate. At that very moment, she could see Cole Burroughs stood in the road outside, waving up at the window, urging her to join him. It felt so real that she pulled away from the binoculars. Rubbed furiously at her eyeballs until they began to sting. Then she looked again.

It *was* real. He was real. Burroughs was out there. No doubt about it.

Without thinking, Rose stood up and crept slowly across the room. Careful not to be heard, she set off down the stairs. Carried on through the house until she reached the back door. For a moment, she hesitated.

What was she doing?

She did it, anyway. Unlocking the door, she stepped outside and made her way around to the front of the house. Cole Burroughs was still there, in the middle of the road, waiting for her.

'I was wondering if you might show up,' he said quietly. 'And here you are.'

'How did you know it was me in the window?' asked Rose.

Cole shook his head. 'I didn't. It was a lucky guess. If it had been one of your ... *friends*, I'd have gone back inside. It was only you I wanted.'

That sentence alone was enough to make Rose lose her nerve.

'There's something I'd like to show you.' Cole pointed along the road. 'We have to walk there, but it shouldn't take long.'

Rose glanced back at the house. Suddenly, she wished she had woken Tommy and told him what she was doing.

'I can see that you're on edge,' said Cole. 'That's understandable. I've already promised that I won't hurt you, but I guess words don't always mean much. I trust you, though, Rose. And I'd like to ask your advice about something.' He turned and set off down the street. 'I'm going, anyway,' he said matter-of-factly. 'It's up to you whether or not you tag along.'

CHAPTER FORTY-THREE

Don't do it.

I mean, that was obvious. The kind of thing you'd learn at school. Don't talk to strangers. And whatever you do, don't follow them into the unknown in the middle of the night.

Rose watched as Cole Burroughs made his way out of Haversham Way. She couldn't just let him leave. He had threatened to kill Tobias Montague. Maybe he was going to do that now. Could she stop him?

No, not physically. Maybe there was another way, though. He listened to her, after all. He had said that himself. They weren't friends, but maybe she was the closest thing he had to an ally.

Rose set off after him. Cole must've heard her footsteps, noticed when she appeared by his side, but chose not to say anything. Instead, he walked in silence.

'Where are we going?' asked Rose.

'The cemetery,' Cole revealed. 'I want to show you something. Maybe you can help me come to a decision.'

Rose carried on walking. Tried to convince herself that his

reply wasn't as creepy as it sounded. 'I want to trust you,' she said, putting emphasis on the *want*.

'Good,' nodded Cole.

It was as vague an answer as you could possibly get. The doubts had kicked in, but it was too late for Rose to change her mind. All she could do now was cross her fingers and hope for the best.

'You had a visitor today.' Rose tried to make it sound casual, but it came out like an accusation.

Not that Cole seemed to notice. 'That's right.'

'It was a woman.'

'Yes, it was.'

Rose drew a breath. 'Sorry ... I don't know why I said that. We shouldn't be watching you. It's wrong.'

'I understand,' said Cole. He left it at that. Rose could tell that he didn't want to talk. She didn't either. Not really. But then she hated the silence even more. It spooked her. And the thought of going into the cemetery only made things worse.

That was a thought, however, that was fast turning into reality.

Like the previous evening, the main gates at St. Benedict's were chained up. Unfortunately, that wasn't the only way to get in.

Without a word being passed between them, they entered through the side gate and set off along the path. It seemed to get darker with every step, so dark, in fact, that Rose could barely see where she was going. Not that it mattered. With Cole leading the way, she simply followed close behind. Silent and obedient. There was a question that needed to be answered, though.

'What do you want to show me?' she asked warily.

'You'll see,' replied Cole. 'We're nearly there.'

The wooden bench under the over-hanging tree was up ahead. It surprised Rose when they ducked underneath the branches and carried on walking. The path continued, with more gravestones on either side of them. It didn't go on forever, though. They had almost reached the other end of the cemetery. There was an exit there. Maybe that's where they were heading. But that didn't make sense.

It made even less sense when Cole steered them to his right and they stopped at a small, wooden shed.

'I stumbled across this one day by accident,' he began. 'I managed to break in without damaging the lock. It's a gardener's shed, rammed full of tools and bits of equipment. I thought at the time it might come in handy. And it has.'

Cole removed a sharp implement from his pocket and started to unpick the lock. The door swung open soon after. It was enough to make Rose step back. She thought about turning to run, something that Cole must've sensed because the next time he spoke, they were words of reassurance.

'This isn't a trap. I wouldn't do that to you. I feel like we have a ... bond.'

Rose held her ground, rooted to the spot. 'I do, too ... I think. I just don't want you to do something you later regret.'

'It's funny you should say that ...' Cole made his way into

the shed. He emerged a moment later, but now he wasn't alone. There was a man by his feet. On his hands and knees. Blindfolded and gagged.

Rose could barely draw breath. 'What's going on?'

'I've not kidnapped him, if that's what you're thinking,' insisted Cole.

'And yet you've got him held prisoner inside this shed.' Rose stared at the man in disbelief. 'Who is he?'

'His name is Claude Bonham,' Cole revealed. 'He was in the car with Montague when he killed my family. I grabbed him this afternoon. Straight off the street. Nobody saw. I just wanted to know the truth. What really happened that night. Not what he told the police.'

'And he told you?'

Cole nodded. 'Bonham confirmed what I already knew. Montague murdered Charlotte and Sophie in cold blood before continuing with the rest of his evening. Their lives ... they meant nothing to him after he had run them down. There has to be some kind of payback.'

'And what's that got to do with Claude Bonham?' asked Rose, fearing the worst.

'That's where you come in,' said Cole. 'The anger ... the hatred I feel towards Montague has blurred my moral compass. Part of me wants Bonham to suffer, too. Revenge by association. And the other part of me—'

'Wants to let him go,' blurted out Rose. 'Please tell me that's what you're thinking.'

'Yes, that was an option,' Cole admitted. 'I'm guessing you'd prefer it if I did that, right?'

Rose could feel her heart rate rising. Things were getting out of hand. If she wasn't careful, this little walk in the dark with Cole would lead to her being an accessory to murder. 'Just let him go and we can forget about it,' she pleaded. 'You've done nothing wrong. Not really.' Rose stopped. Looked down at the man on his hands and knees. 'He can hear everything we're saying, can't he?'

Claude Bonham lifted his head and nodded.

Then Cole nodded, too. 'He won't say anything. He knows what the alternative is. What would happen to him if he went to the police.' Crouching down, Cole removed the gag from the other man's mouth. 'You're a lucky boy,' he said calmly. 'My friend here is clearly a better person than I am. You have her to thank for your release.'

'I won't tell anyone,' whimpered Claude. 'This can end here.'

Cole lifted his prisoner up off the ground. Whispered in his ear. 'I'm going to remove the blindfold now. Once I've done that, you can go. We're in St. Benedict's cemetery. That's all you need to know. I'm sure you can make your way home from here. I have no more issues with you. Stay away from Montague, and you won't see me again. I promise.'

True to his word, Cole removed the blindfold before guiding his prisoner out of the shed. Claude wobbled for a moment, unsteady on his feet, before his eyes adjusted. Then he was off, stumbling slightly as he hurried along the path towards the exit.

Rose breathed a sigh of relief as he disappeared into the darkness. If nothing else, she had enabled him to escape unharmed. At best, she had saved a life.

'Thank you,' said Cole, as he closed the door and locked up the shed. 'I don't think he deserved to be punished. Not in the big scheme of things. Maybe he was just unlucky. Like me. Like Charlotte and Sophie. Maybe we're all victims of Montague.'

'You need to get back to Haversham Way.' Rose tried to speak with authority, but her voice was trembling. 'If the police come and ask about Claude Bonham, you can tell them you've been in all night. I'll back you up. As long as you go home now and don't do anything else.'

Cole shook his head. 'You still don't get it, do you? I don't care about the police. I'm going to kill Montague, whatever happens. There's no coming back from this.' He let his gaze rest on Rose. 'You look cold. I'll walk you back before you freeze to death.'

Side by side, silent but for their footsteps, they set off along the path. By the time they had reached the side gate, there was no sign of Claude Bonham. Thank goodness for that, thought Rose. If he had any sense, he would go into hiding and not come out until all this was over.

'You're a good person,' said Cole, out of the blue.

'I've heard that before,' groaned Rose. 'Is that the same as being nice? Boring? Inoffensive?'

'Not in the slightest,' insisted Cole. 'Whatever happens, however this ends, I'll see that no harm comes to you.'

Rose felt a wave of relief as she saw the sign for Haversham Way. She stopped when she reached number seven. Felt the need to whisper. 'When are you going to do it? You know ... the thing you have to do ... the killing thing?'

'Soon,' said Cole. 'The time has come. No more excuses.'

'Not tonight, though?'

'Not tonight.' With that, Cole crossed the road between the houses. Found his key in his pocket and slotted it into the lock.

'Goodnight,' said Rose, as loud as she dare.

'Goodnight.' Cole hesitated. Gave it a moment and then glanced over his shoulder. Rose was making her way towards the back of the house. A few seconds later, she had vanished from view.

Pulling the key out of the lock, Cole stuck it back in his pocket and moved away from his door.

Not tonight, he had told Rose. And he was telling the truth. He had no intention of killing Tobias Montague before the night was over.

No, first he had a spot of business to attend to. Someone was about to get an unexpected visitor.

Destination The Nightingale Hotel.

CHAPTER FORTY-FOUR

Agatha couldn't really complain.

She was staying at The Nightingale, the only five-star hotel in Stainmouth. She had one of the best suites. More than adequate for a long stay. And the food there was exceptional.

So why did she find it so hard to sleep?

It wasn't the bed, or the noise, or any other random excuse people plucked from thin air to explain away their insomnia. It was just her. Or rather, her mind. The way it ticked. The way it turned. The way it ran with a thought, and squashed it and squeezed it until it exploded into countless other thoughts that each did the exact same thing.

At the core of that evening's mind battle was one basic question.

What was the difference between right and wrong?

Cole Burroughs wanted to kill Tobias Montague for murdering his wife and child. Good. Go ahead. Be my guest. If it was her, she would feel the same. At least, that was what her heart said. Revenge or justice, it didn't really matter which term you used, it was the same thing. And why not? Who was she to stop him?

But was it right? Or did it go against everything she stood for? *They* stood for.

Because she had sat with Miles in the hotel bar until nearly midnight discussing that very topic. Unlike her, he had no doubt in his mind. One meeting with Montague told him everything he needed to know. He was a spoilt little rich kid who had crossed the line. Where money bought others power, it had given him an unswerving sense of self-importance, an indestructible arrogance that bordered on insanity. Take his father out of the equation and he wouldn't be missed. His friends were just leeches, clinging on to someone else's lavish lifestyle before they grew up and moved on. If Montague was to die tomorrow, then so be it. Miles wouldn't lose a minutes sleep.

Which was quite ironic because, on that note, he finished the last of his drink, wished Agatha goodnight, and then went up to his room to do just that.

Don't take it to bed with you. Put it to the back of your mind. Keep it locked up until the morning.

Agatha had been told that throughout her career by other colleagues in her line of work. It was easier said than done, though. And, besides, it was gone two now. It *was* the morning.

Rolling over in bed, she reached for the telephone and considered calling room service. Maybe a night cap would help her drop off. A brandy or whiskey. Or something not so sharp. A hot chocolate perhaps. Or one of those vile malt drinks that she always imagined old people sipping in their pyjamas, their false teeth nestled in a glass of water beside them. Well, that was what she was now, wasn't she? Whether she liked it or not, she was getting older. They'd be pensioning her off soon. Kicking her out the door before she stank the place out.

That day was edging closer. Just not today.

Agatha removed her hand from the telephone and climbed out of bed. It was dark in the room, so she padded slowly across the carpet on her way to the bathroom. Once there, she flicked the switch. Her initial reaction was to squint as the bathroom was illuminated by a powerful spotlight. Shuffling over to the sink, she waited for her eyes to adjust before she poured herself a glass of water.

Cheaper than room service and you didn't have to wait for it.

She sipped from the glass whilst staring at her reflection. Leaning forward, she pressed her nose up to the mirror. Looked deep into her own eyes. She wasn't old; she was mature. Big difference. And she was still capable. Not part of the Horlicks crew yet. Not for a few more years, at least.

Placing the glass down by the sink, she turned off the light and left the bathroom. She had prepared herself for the sudden descent into darkness.

What she hadn't expected, however, was to step into a partially lit room. The glow was coming from a lamp on the bedside table. It threw light over the armchair beside it.

The armchair that was currently occupied by a shadowy figure dressed all in black.

CHAPTER FORTY-FIVE

Miles sat up in bed.

Only seconds earlier, he had found himself immersed in a particularly intense dream. In it, he had been walking up the driveway at Montague Manor when a steady stream of champagne bottles had come flying out of the window, heading straight towards him. Before any of them could hit their target, Pendleton, the housekeeper-cum-dogsbody, had appeared from nowhere in a yellow car and driven him to safety. Miles had woken shortly after that. And stayed awake. With his brain up and running, it wasn't the dream that bothered him, but one particular detail.

The yellow car.

On two occasions that day, a yellow car had been spotted at Haversham Way, its driver the mysterious woman in a headscarf.

Lolly, the girlfriend of Claude Bonham, had then mentioned a yellow car between sobs when he had supposedly been abducted.

Coincidence? Perhaps. But how common were yellow cars?

Miles reached for his phone. It was gone two, but his mind

was racing now. As were his fingers as he tapped at the screen.

What percentage of cars are yellow in Stainmouth?

He waited impatiently for the results. When they came, it was a huge disappointment. Just car dealerships around the town. Maybe the search was too narrow. Too niche.

He tried again. Expanded it.

What percentage of cars are yellow in the UK?

Ah, that was better. The results were still varied, but the consensus seemed to be the same. Yellow cars accounted for less than one per cent of those on the road.

That was all he needed to know.

Scrambling out of bed, Miles climbed into his trousers and grabbed a jumper from a pile. He was halfway out the door when he remembered his shoes. Or lack of. Ducking back inside, he found them in the wardrobe and pulled them on.

The Nightingale was deathly quiet as he crept along the corridor. Agatha's room was another floor up, on the other side of the hotel. A slight upgrade on his own, but he wasn't complaining. She was the boss, after all. She had earned it.

He passed through a door marked *Fire Exit* and took to the stairs. He was practically running now, keen to fill Agatha in on what he had uncovered.

Two yellow cars spotted on the same day. Possibly the same vehicle.

What did it mean? That the woman who had called upon Burroughs had then gone and kidnapped Claude Bonham? If Agatha thought that was likely, then they would have to act.

Burroughs would have to be brought in for questioning. Forced to reveal the identity of his visitor. Maybe he would plead ignorance. It wasn't beyond the realms of reality that he had told her what to do and how to do it.

Staircase complete, Miles pushed through another door and found himself in a wider, brighter, more elegantly furnished corridor. A better class of floor with a better class of room for a better class of customer. Turning to his right, he hurried towards Agatha's door. When he got there, he lifted his hand and ...

What was he doing?

It was the middle of the night, for pity's sake.

He could picture Agatha now. Her disapproving frown as she opened the door in her dressing gown and peered outside. And what would she say?

Let's leave this until the morning. We can talk about it then. When I've got my eyes open.

Maybe he could message her. Again, what was the point? She wouldn't read it until she woke up.

The yellow cars were important, he was sure of it. But were they *that* important?

He had come to a decision. One that, if he was being honest, he could easily have made several minutes ago from the comfort of his bed.

No late night disruption.

No call or text message.

This could keep. And it wasn't as if he had to wait a long time, either. Less than five hours and he could tell Agatha in person. Face to face. When she was wide awake, showered and dressed, after a good night's sleep.

Mind made up, Miles crept back along the corridor. He breathed a sigh of relief with every passing step. He had been a split-second from knocking, from causing an unnecessary commotion, before common sense had taken over.

Tomorrow, over breakfast, they would get to the bottom of things.

CHAPTER FORTY-SIX

Agatha wasn't convinced that she would make it to breakfast.

She had always suspected that something like this would happen.

That somebody would come to kill her.

And here he was. Emphasis on *he*. The shadowy figure in the armchair was a man. His hood was up so she couldn't quite make out his features, but it was his build that gave him away. Broad shoulders and thick arms. Sat with his legs spread wide open in a way that women rarely ever do.

All manner of thoughts darted around Agatha's brain, most of which were linked to survival. Could she make it to the exit? Probably, but opening the door would undoubtedly slow her down. What about a weapon? There was nothing behind her in the bathroom, barring her toothbrush and makeup bag. She could always whip him with a towel. Splash him in the face with water.

That was the panic talking ...

'How did you get in?' asked Agatha. Partly to buy her some time, partly because she was genuinely interested.

'That'd be telling,' said the man, his voice barely audible despite the silence in the room.

'The door's locked from the inside, and there's no balcony or fire exit on the other side of the window.' Agatha stopped herself. She was rambling. Nerves probably. Time to face up to the inevitable. 'We both know why you're here, so please make it quick.'

'Make what quick?'

Agatha cleared her throat. Did she really have to spell it out? 'If you're going to kill me—'

'I'm not here to kill you,' said the man calmly. 'I'm here to talk.'

Agatha allowed herself to breathe. Talking she could deal with, even at two in the morning. And then it dawned on her. There was only one person who would be here, in her hotel room, at this time of night. Who could get in without being detected.

'Cole Burroughs,' she said under her breath.

The man nodded. 'And you must be Agatha Pleasant. At least, I hope you are.'

Agatha returned the nod. 'Yes, it would be a little awkward if you had broken into the wrong room, wouldn't it? How did you find me?'

'You can find anyone if you try hard enough,' said Cole. 'And I *really* wanted to find you.'

Agatha shivered. Not from fear. Well, not much. But mainly from the cold. It was chilly stood there in the bathroom doorway, in nothing but a nightie. Cold and exposing.

Cole seemed to pick up on this. 'Would you like to get dressed? I can look the other way. I'm not here to humiliate you.' With that, he lowered his head. Studied the carpet.

Moving to her right, Agatha removed her dressing gown from the hook on the door and threw it over her shoulders. Another step and she found what she was really looking for. Hidden at the top of the wardrobe, she quickly removed it and checked for bullets. It was loaded.

When Cole lifted his head, there was a gun pointing straight at him. 'Sneaky,' he said.

'Says the man who somehow crept into my room in the middle of the night,' replied Agatha.

'I came here unarmed, though. I just want to talk.'

'And we can still do that. But I'll be the one asking the questions. Was it you who kidnapped Claude Bonham?'

Cole weighed up his answer. 'I *borrowed* him. And now I've given him back. Safe and sound. You've got Rose to thank for that.'

'Rose?' Agatha felt her grip tighten on the gun. 'If you've hurt her—'

'I would never do that,' insisted Cole. 'She told me to release Bonham unharmed, so I did. I trust her. She's honest. She's also the reason I'm here.'

'Go on,' said Agatha.

'I'm going after Tobias Montague,' Cole began. 'That seems to be common knowledge, right? I'm not sure when, but it'll be soon. I can feel it. There's a pressure inside me ... it's built up so much that I have to release it. My only worry is that you'll send your team to try to stop me. That's where Rose comes in. I don't want her getting caught in the crossfire. If anything was to happen to her, I'd never forgive myself.'

Agatha shook her head. 'I don't get it. You talk about killing Montague and caring for Rose in the same breath. That's not normal.'

'Normal isn't really an option anymore,' said Cole. 'Let's focus on the facts. Rose is an innocent and I've grown to like her. Montague is a murderer who deserves to die. It's that simple.'

'Right and wrong,' muttered Agatha under her breath. 'That's something I've been struggling with recently. It's such a fine line between the two.'

'It's not that difficult,' said Cole. 'Promise you'll keep Rose out of my way, and I promise that no one else will get hurt. Only Montague. I also promise that I'll leave now without causing a scene—'

'Read the room,' said Agatha, interrupting him. 'Only one of us is holding a gun. You're not in control anymore. What's to stop me from ringing the police? They'd lock you up on my word. Not forever, but maybe long enough for us to get Montague to safety.'

If Cole was concerned, then he didn't show it. 'Do what you want. You're only prolonging the inevitable, though. The rage inside of me will grow and grow until I eventually find

Montague and end his life. I won't stop. I have to do it. Do you understand that?'

Agatha took a moment. 'I'm sorry for your loss. Truly, I am. But I can't just let you walk out of here and kill another man. It's wrong. Lawfully. Morally. Ethically. It goes against everything I stand for ... that I believe in. You need help. I can see that. You're a good man. Rose says so and, like you, I trust her. But there are professionals who deal with this kind of thing.'

'I don't need to see a shrink,' said Cole.

Agatha moved across the room towards the desk. Picked up her phone. 'It doesn't have to be like that. I'm going to call someone. A friend of mine—'

She had barely glanced at the screen when the lights went out, plunging her into darkness. Gun steady, she tried to focus. She could hear movement, but it was shifting away from her, not edging closer. She was still staring blindly into space when the door to her room opened suddenly and Cole Burroughs disappeared outside. Raising the gun, she aimed it at the opening. For a split-second, she had a clear shot. Something told her not to pull the trigger, though. In a hotel like this, the repercussions would be immense. As for Cole, he didn't deserve to, at worst, die, or, at best, suffer a flesh wound. He was disturbed, yes, but he wasn't completely unhinged.

The door closed with a dull *thud*.

Agatha fumbled around in the gloom until she found the light switch. Sitting down on the edge of her bed, she placed the gun by her side whilst she waited for her eyes to adjust. As for her phone, suddenly it was surplus to requirements. She had no wish to call the police anymore. Cole had been and gone and hadn't harmed a hair on her head. What was he guilty of? Breaking and entering? Big deal. The police wouldn't be rushing around for that.

Laying her head on the pillow, Agatha gazed up at the ceiling. Sleeping was off the agenda. If it had been difficult before, it was practically impossible now. Still, at least she had an answer for the question that had been bugging her all evening. Cole knew it too, but then he had his own personal grief to show him the way. To guide him by the hand and expose him to the light.

There was no right and wrong. There was only staying alive and dropping down dead.

Soon to be the difference between Cole Burroughs and Tobias Montague if the former got his wish.

CHAPTER FORTY-SEVEN

The next day started with a screech of brakes and the repetitive blast of a car horn.

Rose lifted her head off her shoulder. She must've dropped off. Fallen asleep on the job. For how long, though, was anybody's guess. Minutes? Hours? She had no idea. But the commotion outside had woken her up.

What time was it?

She found her phone in her lap. Stared at the screen. Just after six. Morning then. Early morning. Still dark.

Moving the binoculars to one side, she made a gap in the blinds with her fingers and peeked outside. A red Porsche had pulled up outside the home of Cole Burroughs. Two men had climbed out of the vehicle. One had stood back, whilst the other took the lead. Curiously, the more confident of the two was wearing a cowboy hat and a thick sheepskin jacket. Swaggering up to the house, he clenched his fist and pounded on the door with as much force as he could muster.

'Wakey, wakey,' he shouted out.

Rose turned back into the room. Tommy was fast asleep on

the recliner behind her. She looked around for something to throw at him and settled upon an empty water bottle. Grabbing it with one hand, she tossed it without taking aim. Incredibly, it hit its target and bounced off his head.

Right on cue, Tommy's eyes opened. 'Weird,' he muttered. 'Could've sworn something just—'

'Get over here now,' demanded Rose.

The urgency of her voice was enough to make Tommy push himself up off the recliner and shuffle over to the window. 'What is it? Don't tell me you were missing my company—'

'I won't,' said Rose, shifting to one side.

Crouching down, Tommy peered through the blind. Tried to focus. 'Looks like it's kicking off out there. Who are they?'

'I don't know. Not for sure. Could be Tobias Montague, I suppose.'

'Could it? What makes you think that?'

'The Porsche.' A light went on in a top floor room as Rose spoke. Next thing she knew, the curtains opened and Cole Burroughs appeared in the window. Staring down at the road below, he crossed his arms.

'Ah, there he is,' cheered the man in the sheepskin jacket. 'I'll get straight to the point. Rumour has it you want to kill me. Well, go on then. Do your worst. I'm waiting.'

Rose glanced at Tommy, who nodded back at her. It *was* Tobias Montague. No doubt about it.

'Seems to me that somebody might be a little scared,' smirked Montague. 'It's easy shooting your mind off behind my back, but not so easy when we're face to face, eh?'

Cole didn't move from the window. The rest of Haversham Way was awake now, though. Lights on. Curtains twitching. Front doors opening just an inch.

Montague hadn't finished, though. 'If anything, you owe me an apology. I'm an innocent man. I've never killed anyone. Not intentionally, anyway, but accidents do happen. Especially when people lose concentration.' Montague shrugged his shoulders. 'Why do you think they wandered into the road like that? Such a shame. So careless. So ... sad.'

With that, Cole vanished from view. Moments later, the front door opened, and he appeared in the entrance.

'You've got a lovely house,' said Montague, grinning from ear to ear. 'You must get lonely in there, though. All alone, but for your thoughts. Quite bleak, really. Probably why you go around threatening to kill people.'

The sight of Cole visibly tensing up was enough to spur Rose into action. Pushing past Tommy, she had almost reached the door when she felt a hand on her arm. 'Whoa! You're not going out there.'

'Let go of me,' cried Rose, trying to remove Tommy's fingers one by one. 'I need to help.'

'It's not your fight,' said Tommy, tightening his grip. 'Just stop and listen. The police are on their way now.'

That much was true. Rose could hear sirens in the distance. Relaxing a little, she waited for Tommy to finally release her before she made her way back towards the window. By the time she had got there, Montague was back in the Porsche, albeit leant out of the driver's side window.

'Come for me,' he shouted out. He mimed a gun with his fingers. Pretended to pull the trigger. 'Today. I dare you.'

With that, he ducked back inside the Porsche and reversed out of Haversham Way. Cole watched for a while before he lowered his head and disappeared back into the house.

Across the road, Rose slowly exhaled. The moment had passed. For now.

Her problems, however, had only just begun.

CHAPTER FORTY-EIGHT

Less than an hour after Tobias Montague had sped away in the Porsche, they reconvened at the townhouse on Haversham Way.

They being Agatha, Miles and the Nearly Dearly Departed Club. All six of them squeezed together in the surveillance room. Unsurprisingly, everybody tried to speak at the same time. Agatha stopped that immediately. There was a pecking order that she was at the head of. She waited for silence and then filled them in about her late-night visit from Cole Burroughs. About how protective he was of Rose. Which prompted Rose to tell everybody about her trip to the cemetery and the subsequent release of Claude Bonham. Throw in the unexpected early morning arrival of a hate-filled, drug-fuelled Tobias Montague and there was only one possible conclusion.

'You get up to all sorts whilst we're asleep, don't you?' said Mercy.

'Yeah, what do you reckon, Tommy?' grinned Lucas. 'Rose gets up to all sorts whilst you're asleep, doesn't she?'

'Not funny,' replied Tommy. 'I wasn't asleep all night. Tell them, Rose. I wasn't, was I?'

'No, not *all* night,' Rose had to admit.

'You were awake for a few minutes,' said Lucas.

Tommy pulled a face. 'Me and Rose shouldn't have to listen to this—'

'No, she shouldn't, should she?' agreed Lucas. 'I'll just talk to you, instead.'

'All joking aside, neither Miss Carrington-Finch nor Mr O'Strife were exactly paying attention when Burroughs slipped out to visit me at The Nightingale,' said Agatha drily.

The room fell silent. Sometimes it was impossible to argue with the truth.

'Thankfully, nothing came of it,' continued Agatha. 'That moment has passed, and I'm still alive. Like Miss Carrington-Finch has insisted from the outset, I don't think Burroughs is a threat. Not to us, anyway. Tobias Montague might not be quite so fortunate, however.'

'So, what now?' asked Lucas. 'Burroughs is after Montague, and Montague is practically urging him on.'

'Come and have a go if you think you're hard enough,' chipped-in Tommy.

'And Burroughs *is* hard enough,' said Lucas. 'At some point, he's going to make his move. What are we supposed to do?'

'What we've always done,' replied Agatha. 'Miss Mee and Mr Thorne, you're on the day shift, so stay here and keep an eye on Burroughs. Follow him if he leaves the house. Miss Carrington-Finch and Mr O'Strife, go back to Cockleshell Farm and get some sleep. It's been another eventful night and neither of you are any use if you can't stay awake.'

Lucas raised a hand. 'We could end this right now. Burroughs is hardly innocent, is he? Breaking and entering ... kidnapping ... threats to kill. Get the police to arrest him and we've removed the problem.'

'*Temporarily* removed the problem,' said Agatha, correcting him. 'Burroughs has already told us that there's only one way that this will end. Tobias Montague has to die. And you can lock Burroughs up for days ... months ... years even, but it won't make a difference. He'll still do it.'

'I think he's going to try today,' muttered Rose under her breath.

And that was greeted with the kind of silence that suggested nobody disagreed.

After a series of weary goodbyes and half-arsed encouragement, the other four left Mercy and Lucas to get on with the job in hand. The job of watching Cole Burroughs as he either moved around the house like a man desperately in need of a distraction, or sat in front of the television, staring vacantly at the flashing images that played out before him.

Free for the rest of the day, Tommy bounded down the stairs at a frantic pace, whilst Rose took the safer option of one at a time. Miles waited until the other two were out of earshot before he spoke in a hushed tone. 'Why are we doing this?'

'Doing what?' shrugged Agatha.

'Still watching Cole Burroughs. He's already proven that it's a waste of time. All we're doing is putting our people in danger.'

'*Our* people.' Agatha tried not to smile. 'I didn't know you were so fond of them.'

'You know what I mean.'

'Yes, I do. But I also know that we've got our hands tied. The Chief Constable's practically pulling my strings at the moment. There's always room for a little leeway, though. What would you suggest we do?'

Miles took a second to pick his words carefully. 'I think we should go back to Montague Manor. That's where Burroughs will go if... *when* he decides to strike. That's got to be better than running around Stainmouth like a pair of headless chickens.' He paused. 'You don't have to agree—'

'But I do.'

'You do?' Miles perked up a little. 'You think it's a good plan?'

'Not particularly,' said Agatha bluntly. 'But it's all we've got. And having something is often better than having nothing at all.'

'And on that note ...' frowned Miles, as he opened the back door and stepped out into the garden. 'Time to put this not particularly good plan of mine into action.'

CHAPTER FORTY-NINE

Déjà vu.

That was Mercy's first thought when the day sparked into life and she spotted something out of the ordinary.

It was the same *something* as yesterday. A bright yellow Honda Civic. At approximately half-past nine, it pulled up outside the home of Cole Burroughs.

'She's back,' called out Mercy, as the door opened and Headscarf Lady emerged from the vehicle.

Lucas wandered over to the window. Screwed up his face as the new arrival walked into the house without knocking. 'Bit early for sexy time. Not that I can remember what that—'

'Yeah, too much information.' Mercy watched as the front door closed and Headscarf Lady disappeared from view. Picking up her phone, she started the stopwatch. 'I wonder how long it'll take today ...'

***

Twenty-nine minutes.

Mercy was still glued to the binoculars when the door opened and Headscarf Lady hurried back out to the Honda. Head down, collar up, she climbed into the car and started the engine. Before Mercy had time to think, she was on the move.

'That was quick,' remarked Lucas. 'Just a fleeting visit. In and out, shake it all about.' The look on Mercy's face suggested she wasn't overly fond of that comment. Time to shift the conversation. 'Can you see Burroughs?'

'Not at the ... got him!' Mercy strained for a better view. 'He's just sat in the sitting room. I can see the back of his head. He's watching TV.'

'Seems pretty relaxed for a man who keeps threatening to kill someone,' said Lucas. 'Still, as long as he's in the house, he can't get up to any mischief, can he?'

'I guess not,' agreed Mercy. But maybe that was just too black and white. Something didn't quite sit right. She couldn't explain what, but she had a feeling that, one way or another, all would be resolved in the not-too-distant future.

Preferably before she died of boredom.

CHAPTER FIFTY

Rose was awoken by an incoming message.

She rolled over in bed and picked up her phone. Stared at the screen. She feared the worst – also known as Tommy – but there was no need.

It was Rupert.

Are you free? There's something I'd like to show you xx

Her heart fluttered as she read it over and over again. Was she free? Well, she wasn't exactly doing anything. Only sleeping. Not anymore, though. Glancing at the clock, she realised it was just after twelve. Barely midday. She had been asleep for about three hours. Not enough to live off, but, hopefully, this wouldn't last for long. *This* being her current situation. She regretted thinking like that when she considered the consequences. For this to end, Cole Burroughs would have to kill – or at least attempt to kill – Tobias Montague.

Rose chewed on her lip. There were several ways to reply to the message. Yes, no or maybe. As usual, she veered towards the latter. Some vaguely coherent sentences that made no sense, but would provide an adequate excuse, for now if not forever.

I'd love to ... more than anything ... but I can't ... not today ... because I might be doing something else ... even though I'm not at the moment ... tomorrow would be better ... or the day after ... definitely ... maybe ... possibly ... don't forget about me, will you?

Rose was fully awake now. Eyes wide, brain spinning. There was no need to deny herself. If she wanted to go, then she should go.

And she did want to go.

With that in mind, she tapped out a message.

Yes, I'm free. Give me half-an-hour and I'll be ready. She paused. Took a moment to think before adding *xx*.

She hit the send button. And then waited. She wondered how long it would take for him to reply.

Seconds ...

That's brilliant. Can't wait. Tell me where you live and I'll come and pick you up xx

This time, Rose didn't delay. She gave him the address for Cockleshell Farm and then leapt out of bed. Grabbing her towel, she dashed through to the bathroom. Thirty minutes was nothing. Eighteen hundred seconds, to be precise.

Eighteen hundred seconds to look her best for Rupert. Or, at the very least, make herself presentable.

The countdown had begun.

CHAPTER FIFTY-ONE

Olaf eased the Audi to a halt at the gates to Montague Manor.

Still as grand. Still as impressive. Still as unnecessarily large for one man's son and his butler. No wonder Tobias Montague filled it with partygoers and parasites, thought Agatha, as she climbed out of the car. It was such a waste of space otherwise.

Unlike yesterday, the gates were closed. There was even a guard there. Not exactly suited and booted, more scruffy jeans and a bomber jacket. Hired help from an unscrupulous source. He was armed to the teeth, though, which made him potentially dangerous if prodded and poked.

'Who are you?' he growled.

Agatha chose not to answer that. 'We're here to see Tobias Montague.'

'To check that he's still alive,' added Miles. 'Be a shame if he wasn't.'

The guard puffed out his chest. 'Tobias ain't seeing no one.'

'But he's in there, yes?' said Agatha, pointing towards the house.

'What's it got to do with you?' The guard's eyes narrowed.

'Who are you? The pigs?'

'No, we're not the ... *pigs*,' sighed Agatha. 'We're concerned bystanders. Tobias is in great danger. There's a threat to kill him. A genuine threat.'

'Yeah, we know,' nodded the guard. 'That's why we're here. Not that Tobias is scared.' He lifted his weapon – a sawn-off shotgun – and grinned. 'And I certainly ain't.'

'You know you can't just shoot somebody in cold blood, right?' said Miles.

The grin switched to a laugh. 'I'm out shooting pheasants, mate. If an intruder gets caught in my line of fire, then that's just unfortunate.'

Agatha looked around the grounds of the house. 'And how many more of you are there out there shooting pheasants?'

'Enough.' The guard leant forward. Lowered his voice. 'Whatever the law says, if this man dares to come here, he won't get out alive.'

'What's your name?' asked Agatha.

The guard smirked. 'Mickey Mouse.'

'Well, Mr Mouse,' began Agatha, barely batting an eyelid, 'let me fill you in with some of the finer details that might have escaped your attention. The man in question, the man who supposedly won't get out of here alive, is called Cole Burroughs. He's a trained professional. He's faster than you, stronger than you, smarter than you. Practically unstoppable. Unstoppable *and* unstable. He's lost his mind with grief. He won't rest until the job is done. Whereas your motivation is a few extra pounds and small town machismo, he's fuelled by pain. Do you understand me? You can't stop someone with nothing to lose.'

'Ah, fuck off.' The guard turned away. Leant against the gate as he looked back towards the house.

Miles took a step forward before Agatha placed a hand across his chest and led him back towards the Audi.

'There's no helping some people,' she said. 'We've warned him of the consequences. There's nothing more we can do. If Montague wants to fight fire with fire, then so be it. We, however, will not be getting burnt. No, I suggest we head back to Haversham Way and reassess the situation.'

Olaf waited for them to get comfortable in the back of the car before he started the engine and turned the Audi around. They were on the move a moment later. In silence. Agatha had nothing to say, whilst Miles felt too angry to vent his frustrations. Angry about the man on the gates. Angry at himself for not teaching him some manners. A quick jab would've done the trick. Knocked a bit of sense into him. He couldn't say that to Agatha, though. She wouldn't approve. Which explained why Miles kept his lips sealed and his eyes fixed on his surroundings as he gazed out of the window. They were deep in the countryside, the trees and bushes just a blur as the Audi sped past. He tried to focus, but all he could see was green.

Green ... and yellow.

Miles slammed his hand on the driver's headrest. 'Stop!'

Olaf reacted instinctively, pressing down on the brakes with enough force to bring them to a sudden halt. All three of them jerked forward in their seats, but not enough to cause whiplash.

'What's the matter?' asked Agatha, clearly shaken up.

'Back there.' Miles gestured over his shoulder. 'I thought I saw ...'

Without another word, he pulled open the door and clambered out of the Audi. He got his bearings and began to jog back the way they had come. He slowed down after about twenty metres. Looked around. Maybe it was nothing. Just his imagination. What was he? Sixty? Seventy per cent sure he had seen it? Parked up off the roadside, it was the colour that had grabbed his attention ...

'Gotcha'!' Miles hurried towards a row of hedges that separated the road from an open field. There was a gap between them, probably used by a farmer to squeeze a tractor through. Miles noticed the tyre tracks beneath his feet were fresh as he followed their route. Turning to his left, he felt his pulse quicken. There it was. Hidden from view. Almost.

A bright yellow Honda Civic.

'What is it?' called out Agatha from the side of the road.

Miles ignored her as he removed his gun and gave the Honda a quick once over. There was no one inside. He tried the doors, but they were all locked. Lifted the bonnet and felt the heat rise from the engine.

'Miles, what's going on?' asked Agatha, as she appeared from behind the hedge.

'This car has been at Cole Burroughs's house three times in the last two days,' he said, making his way towards her. 'Claude

Bonham's girlfriend mentioned it as well. I wanted to tell you last night, but I got distracted. I think ... no, I'm certain ... we need to get back to Montague Manor. Now.'

Agatha nodded in agreement as the two of them rushed back to the Audi. She had no reason to doubt Miles's judgement. It had never failed him before.

'Back to the house please, Olaf,' she said, strapping on her seat belt. 'No need to adhere to the speed limit.'

Olaf grunted, a sure sign that he knew what was required of him. Starting the engine, he performed a smart u-turn in the middle of the road and then accelerated hard as they shot off back along the country lane.

'You think Cole Burroughs is here now?' she said, gripping the seat beneath her.

'I'd be amazed if he's not,' replied Miles. The Audi swung sharply to their left and he fell sideways. Used Agatha's shoulder to steady himself. 'Sorry.'

She waved it away. Not with her hands because she didn't want to let go, but with a shake of her head. 'How has he done it? How does he keep on doing it? Why is Cole Burroughs so much smarter than we are?'

Miles blew out in frustration. 'It's like you told our pheasant shooting friend. Burroughs has got nothing to lose. He's prepared to put his own life on the line to avenge those he's lost.'

Olaf stamped down on the brakes, sending the Audi skidding to a halt outside the gates to Montague Manor. Now they were wide open and there was no sign of the guard.

Miles was the first out of the vehicle. 'Where's Mickey Mouse?'

'He can't be far,' said Agatha. 'We've only been gone a few minutes. Unless he's heeded our advice, of course. Maybe he's seen sense. Left them to it. Or maybe ... not.'

She nodded towards a small group of trees not far from where they were stood. There was a leg poking out from behind the trunk of one tree in particular. Agatha noticed Miles had, once again, removed his gun as they set off towards it. They stumbled upon a different gun several steps later. The sawn-off variety. Identical to the one that had been pointed at them by the guard.

The same guard that they found slumped against the trunk. His legs were wide apart, his hands were in his lap and his head had drooped so far forward that his chin was resting on his chest.

Miles crouched down beside him. Checked for a pulse in all the usual places.

'Is he dead?' asked Agatha.

'No, just out cold,' replied Miles. 'Burroughs did this. He must've. He could've killed him, but he chose to spare his life.' Miles stood up. Looked back towards the house. 'I'm guessing Tobias Montague won't be so lucky,' he remarked under his breath.

CHAPTER FIFTY-TWO

Agatha wasn't convinced.

Not entirely.

Not yet.

And she had to be one hundred per cent certain before she acted.

There was one way to find out for sure, though.

'Call Mercy and Lucas,' she said.

Miles handed his gun to Agatha before removing his phone and tapping at the screen. Agatha weighed it up in her hands. The Glock was bigger and heavier than her own weapon. Could she shoot somebody with it if the need arose? Perhaps. She had done it in the past, but times had changed.

Scrolling through his contacts, Miles stopped at Lucas. Not for any particular reason, except it came first alphabetically.

Lucas answered almost immediately. 'Hello.'

'Cole Burroughs,' said Miles. 'Can you see him?'

'Can I see him?' Lucas yawned. 'Course I can. The back of his head is all I've been looking at for the past few hours.'

'So, he's there? In his house?'

'Yeah, I just said that. He's watching TV even as we speak.' Lucas took a moment to fiddle with the binoculars. 'Let me see. It's one of those property programs. Do up a dump and sell it for profit—'

'Get Mercy,' demanded Miles.

'Mercy? Why? What's wrong?'

'Just get her.'

Lucas moved the phone away from his ear before he called out. 'Mercy, it's for you. It's Miles. He seems to have lost his manners.'

Mercy was in the other bedroom, halfway through a strenuous work-out. Press-ups. Sit-ups. Burpees. Star jumps. Rinse and repeat until the strength deserted her and she lost the will to live. Or she just got interrupted. Either way, she jumped to her feet and jogged through to Lucas with her hand outstretched so she could take the phone.

'What's up?' she asked, trying to conceal how much she was struggling to breathe.

'Can you see Cole Burroughs?' snapped Miles.

'Is that all? Couldn't you have asked Lucas?'

'I already have. He said yes. What are you saying?'

Mercy nudged Lucas to one side so she could look through the binoculars. 'The same. Yeah, I can see Burroughs. He's in his sitting room, watching one of those dreary antique shows—'

'It's not,' argued Lucas, nudging her back to regain supremacy. 'It's doing up dumps—'

Mercy dropped her shoulder and barged him into the wall.

'That's not a dump – it's a shop. He's holding up a rusty teapot—'

'It's a watering can. Are you blind? Hold on. They're not even indoors. It's someone's bloody garden—'

'Shut up and listen,' said Miles tersely. 'I need you to do something and be quick about it. Go and knock on Cole Burroughs's door. If he doesn't answer, find another way to get in. This is important. You have to see him with your own eyes.'

'If we knock on his door, then he'll know we're here,' said Mercy.

'He already knows you're there,' replied Miles. 'He's always known. Things are coming to a head and we just want to be certain. Go now.'

Miles ended the call.

That was the cue for Mercy to stand up and walk towards the door. 'Did you hear that?'

'Unfortunately so,' said Lucas, chasing after her. 'I don't like it, though. Burroughs is a borderline psycho. Just because he's got a soft spot for Rose doesn't mean he won't turn nasty with us. The last thing I want to do is wind him up by hammering on his door.'

'I'll do it then,' said Mercy, as she headed out the back door and swept around the side of the house. Moments later, she appeared on Haversham Way. Yeah, she would do it. Her heart was already racing from her workout, so why not turn things up a notch? Besides, this was exciting. An adrenaline rush. Better than sitting there with your eyes pressed up to those damn binoculars, listening to Lucas moan about the weather, or his toenails, or Tommy, or whatever else entered his head and passed his lips because he was even more bored than she was …

No, this was fun. And if they got out of it unharmed, then congratulations. Job done.

Mercy skipped across the road, her eyes glued on number eight's sitting room window. Cole Burroughs was still there. He hadn't moved. He didn't know they were coming for him.

Mercy pounded on the door with her fist.

He did now.

'Oh, yeah, because that won't annoy him, will it?' muttered Lucas, coming up behind her.

Mercy shifted to her right and peered through the window. The head was still yet to move. Surely it couldn't be fake. Like a shop mannequin. Or hairdresser's training head.

Mercy knocked again. Not on the door this time, but on the window. Impossible to ignore.

The head moved. Only slightly, but it had definitely moved.

And yet Cole Burroughs still refused to stand up or even acknowledge their existence.

'You should try shouting through the letterbox,' said Lucas.

'Thanks for your contribution,' muttered Mercy. It was a good idea, though. And she probably would've done it if Lucas hadn't suggested it.

That was all forgotten when Cole Burroughs shifted positions. Without warning, his head fell forward, his shoulders hunched. Suddenly, he was rocking back and forth on the sofa.

Mercy was no longer looking at a man staring at the television. She was watching a man break down uncontrollably.

'You need to open this door,' she said, her mouth pressed against the window. 'Please. We need to talk to you.'

She was about to speak again when Cole Burroughs stood up and walked out of the sitting room.

Mercy backed away. 'He's coming,' she said, her heart beating fast.

'Great,' sighed Lucas. 'I'm overjoyed.'

The door opened. Not all the way, but enough for Mercy to see a head of long, straggly hair and a thick beard hidden behind two hands.

'I'm sorry ... I didn't want to do it ... I had no choice.'

Mercy edged forward. 'What have you done?'

'Careful,' warned Lucas.

The hands fell away, revealing the face for the first time.

It was enough to bring Mercy to a halt. She couldn't believe her eyes. Didn't know what to say.

'Shit!' cried Lucas, conveying her thoughts in a single word. 'Shit ... shit ... shit!'

CHAPTER FIFTY-THREE

'It's not Cole Burroughs.'

'What?'

'It's not Cole Burroughs,' repeated Mercy. She practically shouted at the phone so Miles could make out every word. 'The man we've been watching on and off for the past few days is his brother, Douglas Burroughs. Dougie to his friends and family. He promised Cole at the funeral of his wife and daughter that he would do anything he asked. And this was it. Dougie's been covering for Cole whilst he goes walkabout. He's been posing as Headscarf Lady, our mystery visitor in the yellow Honda Civic. When Dougie went into the house, they swapped clothes so they could switch places. One in, one out. It also explains why Dougie has grown his hair and beard. From a distance, the two brothers look identical.'

'Where is he now?' asked Miles.

'Sat in the kitchen with Lucas,' revealed Mercy. 'He's in bits. He didn't want to do any of this, but what choice did he have? It was all Cole's idea. I believe that.'

'That doesn't mean he's innocent,' said Miles.

'And it doesn't mean he's guilty,' argued Mercy. 'Not really. All he's done is dress up as a woman and then hang around his brother's house. Hardly the crime of the century, is it?'

'That's one way of looking at it,' sighed Miles. 'So, if Dougie's at Haversham Way, where's Cole?'

'You tell me,' shrugged Mercy.

Miles decided not to. 'Right, I've got to go. Just stay with this cross-dressing brother and don't let him out of your sight. He's going to have some explaining to do once all this is over.'

A disgruntled Miles ended the call before Mercy could protest.

'So, you were right about Cole Burroughs,' said Agatha, casting an eye over the grounds of Montague Manor. 'He's here now. He's probably picking off Tobias's guards even as we speak.'

Miles nodded. 'What do you want me to do?'

'I don't want you to go after him if that's what you mean,' said Agatha. 'Besides, I think there might be a better option than going in all guns blazing. A softer approach, so to speak.'

'Which is?'

'Rose,' replied Agatha. 'We need her here. She's our only hope.'

CHAPTER FIFTY-FOUR

There were three of them.

A blonde, a brunette and a redhead. Absolute stunners. Like models. Not skinny, though. Lumps and bumps in all the right places. There was one on his left, one on his right, and another behind him. Stroking his leg. Unbuttoning his shirt. Kissing his neck. This was next level. The stuff of dreams.

Where were they? Somewhere warm, cosy. Cockleshell Farm. At that very moment, the four of them were sprawled out across the sofa.

Enter number five.

The door opened and Proud Mary ruined the moment. What was she doing here? Okay, so it was her house, but give a man a bit of privacy. Oh, that seemed to do the trick. She had gone. Good. He returned his focus to the blonde. Recoiled in horror. Suddenly, she had a beard. His head turned towards the brunette in slow motion. She had a beard, too. As did the redhead behind him.

Three beards.

No, *the* three Beards. And just like that, he was back in the alley where Rupert had lamped him. He was screaming, but nobody was listening. Instead, one of the Beards puckered his lips, partly revealing a set of blackened teeth as he leant in for a kiss.

A repetitive ringing sound tried its hardest to interrupt the terror of the moment. Got to get that. Let me go. But the Beards refused to oblige. Hovering over him, they had their mouths agape and tongues out. He turned his face away, only to find himself nose to powder with the biggest mound of cocaine in living history. It was piled so high that it disappeared into the dreary Stainmouth sky and beyond. Like Jack and the Beanstalk. An edgier version. Not for kids.

Hold on a minute ...

This wasn't a dream. This wasn't even a nightmare. This was just fuckin' weird.

Tommy woke with a start. He looked around, relieved to find that it was over. The Beards had gone. Thank God. As had the blonde, the brunette and the redhead. Shame. And the cocaine? That had vanished, too. Double shame. He could've made a mint out of that. It would've set him up for life. Several lifetimes.

And yet ...what was that noise? That ringing? It was still there, refusing to fade away.

Rolling over, Tommy slapped his hand down on the bedside table, missing his phone by a matter of inches. He tried again and made contact. The ringing didn't stop, though. It just carried on. How rude.

So, if it wasn't his alarm ...

Tommy snatched at the phone. Took the call. 'What?'

'Get Rose. I've been trying to call her, but she's not answering. I need to speak to her.'

Tommy groaned. It was Miles. Also known as Millie. Also known as Pleasant Agatha's pet dickhead. 'Why?'

'Didn't you hear me? This isn't a joke. Get her. Now.'

'You want her, you get her!'

'I'm trying to. That's the whole point. But, like I said, she's not answering. Which left me with no choice but to call you—'

'Chill out. I've only just woken up.'

'Just get her.'

Tommy raised his arms above his head. Kept stretching until he felt his spine crack. 'What time is it?'

'Get ... her.'

'I was having a proper mental dream. Must be all those night shifts I've been doing. They've scrambled my brain.'

Miles took a breath. 'Tommy, please. This is really important.'

'Don't beg, Millie. You're better than that.' Tommy forced himself out of bed before Miles could say another word. He considered putting some clothes on before quickly deciding against it, partly because Miles had been such an insistent prick, but also because it would give Rose a little thrill. Tommy in his boxer shorts was a treat for one and all. Man, woman and even several animals. He certainly had more to offer than Rupert, the sneaky, mole-faced fuckwit.

Tommy marched across the landing. Rose's door was closed, so he knocked. Better that than just burst in unannounced. Hey, he wanted to give her a thrill, not a heart attack.

There was no answer.

'Rose,' he said, crouching down by the keyhole. 'It's Miles. No, it's Tommy ... obviously ... but Miles is on the phone. *My* phone. Reckons he's been trying to call you ... pity's sake, are you even in there, or am I talking to myself? Right, I hope you're decent because I'm coming in ...'

He pushed down on the handle and entered Rose's room. It was spotlessly clean and unnaturally tidy. And minus the one thing he was looking for. The woman herself. That didn't stop him from taking a few more steps inside, though.

Tommy was about to ruffle the duvet covers when a shrill voice almost made him jump out of his last remaining piece of clothing.

'What are you doing in here, Thomas?'

Spinning around, Tommy resisted the urge to swear at the sight of his landlady. 'I was ... erm ... looking for Rose,' he said sheepishly.

A sceptical Proud Mary studied him intently. 'With just your underwear on? You haven't forgotten my house rules, have you? I don't like those sort of ... shenanigans going on under my roof.'

'Chance would be a fine thing,' muttered Tommy under his breath. His next sentence was out loud. 'It's all innocent. I was fast asleep. I still should be. But then this happened.' He held up his phone. 'It's Millie ... Miles. He wants to talk to Rose. Told me to come and get her.'

'Well, you're wasting your time,' said Proud Mary. 'She went out about half-an-hour ago. A young man came to pick her up. He seemed pleasant enough.'

'A young man?' Tommy's eyes narrowed. 'Did he have a big fuck off ... I mean, *unusually large* mole on his cheek?'

'I can't remember,' shrugged Proud Mary. 'Wait. Yes. Yes, he did. He smiled when Rose came down the stairs and it seemed to creep up his face. Rose was smiling, too. I've never seen her like that before. I thought they made a nice couple as they walked towards his car.'

Tommy lifted the phone to his ear. 'You still there? Did you hear that?'

'Yes,' replied Miles. 'You need to find her. We think Cole Burroughs is about to make his move and Rose might be able to talk him out of it.'

Tommy smiled at Proud Mary as he shuffled past her on his way back to his room. 'I was hoping to get a few more hours sleep if I'm being honest,' he sighed.

'What's wrong with you?' snapped Miles. 'Don't you care about anybody but yourself?'

Tommy stopped dead in his tracks. There it was again. That word. *Care*. It had haunted him these past few days. *Care for*. *Care about*. *Don't care*. He couldn't explain why it bothered him so much, but it did. It struck a nerve. Sliced it in half and stamped all over it.

'Sleep can wait, I suppose,' he said. 'Where is she?'

'I don't know, but I'll find out,' said Miles. 'Put some clothes on and get ready. It pains me to say it, but we're relying on you. For once in your sorry life, you might just be able to do some good.'

CHAPTER FIFTY-FIVE

'Where are we?'

Rose took in her surroundings as Rupert eased his car to a complete standstill. He drove a rundown Vauxhall Astra that made them both laugh as it coughed and spluttered its way through the streets of Stainmouth. Rupert apologised from time to time, but Rose could tell that it didn't bother him. That was one of the things she liked most about him. He wasn't a show-off. He had never tried to impress her by being flash or ostentatious. So he drove a clapped-out banger? Big deal. It was the man inside that mattered. Not his means of transport.

'We're not going in there, if that's what you're thinking.' Rupert pointed at a pub across the car park. The Mucky Duck. 'It's a vile place. I wouldn't wish an hour in there on my worst enemy.' He rested a hand on Rose's shoulder. 'I especially wouldn't wish it on you.'

'Pleased to hear it,' smiled Rose. 'The thing is, there's nowhere else to—'

Rupert hushed her with a single finger before turning his attention towards the side of the pub. There was an iron stairway there, leading to a top floor door. 'Up there,' he said. 'That's where we're going. You know I do amateur dramatics, right? Well, I thought you'd like to see where we rehearse. I mean, it's not exactly the most glamorous location for a date ...'

Rose raised an eyebrow. 'So, this is a date, is it?'

'Why not?' shrugged Rupert. 'Are you hungry? I've got some bits in the back of the car. We can have an indoor picnic. Come on. Let's go.'

Rupert climbed out of the Astra and moved around to the boot. He grabbed a box and then slammed it shut. 'It's so cold out here,' he said. Taking her by the hand, he hurried across the car park. 'Can't wait to get inside.'

The two of them skipped up the steps at the side of the pub. When they reached the top, Rupert produced a key from his pocket.

'I borrowed this from Bingo,' he said, slotting the key into the lock. 'Or rather, I took it without him realising.'

'Bingo?' frowned Rose.

'Montgomery Wingston,' explained Rupert, pushing open the door. 'He's the chairman of the Stainmouth Amateur Dramatics Society. He does everything for us. He won't mind me showing you around, though.'

Rose stepped inside. The room was square in shape, with a scuffed wooden floor, drapes along every wall, and tripod floor lamps in each corner. There were rails of clothing, costumes mostly, and a small stage at one end.

'Take a seat,' said Rupert, gesturing towards a battered

leather sofa. 'Would you like a drink? I've got some wine.'

'I don't really drink,' admitted Rose, as she sat down.

'Suit yourself.' Rupert removed a bottle and a stack of plastic beakers from the box he had taken from the car. 'I'm having some. Hope that's not a problem.'

'Not at all.' Rose thought about it. 'Go on then. If you are, I will.'

A smiling Rupert unscrewed the bottle and poured a generous measure of wine into two of the beakers. 'There you go,' he said, handing one to Rose. He sat down beside her on the sofa. 'This is nice, isn't it?'

Rose nodded. Rupert was staring at her, so she took a sip of wine. Swallowed without tasting it. 'What play are you performing?' she asked, looking over at the stage.

'It doesn't matter,' said Rupert. He glanced at his watch, agitated. 'Have a drink. This is nice, isn't it?'

'You've already said that,' laughed Rose. She did as he suggested, though, and took another sip. 'What else have you got in that box?'

'What box?' Rupert was barely listening. If anything, he suddenly seemed on edge. 'Oh, yes, *that* box. Not much, really. I'll take a look in a moment.'

'Let me.' Rose was about to stand when a knock at the door beat her to it. 'Who's that?' she asked warily.

Rupert was already up and off the sofa. 'I'm not sure. It'll be nothing to worry about, though. Just try to relax.'

'I am relaxed,' insisted Rose. 'I just thought ... why don't you ignore them?'

'No, I don't think so.' Shaking his head, Rupert marched across the room. 'It'd be rude of me not to see who wants to join our little party, wouldn't it?'

CHAPTER FIFTY-SIX

The way Miles saw it, they had two choices.

They could either go back to The Nightingale and use the tracking equipment in his room to find Rose, or not. It was that simple. No grey areas to get tangled up in.

Agatha, however, proposed a third option. An option that involved them going their separate ways. 'Olaf will drive you to the hotel, whilst I stay here,' she said matter-of-factly.

Here being Montague Manor.

'Stay here and do what?' frowned Miles.

'I'll keep an eye on things,' Agatha explained. 'As soon as you've located Miss Carrington-Finch, you can inform Mr O'Strife, who can pick her up. You can come straight back here after you've passed on the info. It shouldn't take long.'

Miles weighed it up. Less than ten minutes to get from Montague Manor to the hotel. Even less time in his room if the internet played nicely. And then the same ten minutes on his return drive. If the traffic lights were on his side, he could be back here within twenty-five minutes, give or take. Especially if Olaf put his foot down.

'We're wasting time,' said Agatha, breaking his train of thought.

'I'm just worried that this'll be all over by the time I get back,' confessed Miles.

'I very much doubt it. Burroughs will have to work his way through Tobias's pheasant shooters before he reaches the man himself. This could go on for hours.'

'Should I call for backup?'

'And have hordes of local bobbies crashing in unannounced?' Agatha shook her head. 'That's the worst possible outcome. The casualties will be immense. No, I think we can solve this my way.' She paused. '*Our* way. That's if we act quickly.'

Miles took the hint. 'Okay. Just ... you know ... don't do anything stupid, will you? Not for the sake of someone like Tobias Montague. He's not worth it.'

Agatha tried not to smile. 'Thank you for your concern, Miles, but I'm perfectly capable of taking care of myself. Now, go. I'll be fine.'

With that, Miles turned towards the Audi. Shuffling onto the passenger seat, he spoke to Olaf before closing the door. Moments later, they were back on the move.

Agatha watched them go. She waited until they were out of sight before she made a move of her own. The police weren't the only ones she wanted nowhere near a gunfight. There was Miles, too. He had a family back in London. She had a duty of care. And it wasn't as if she really needed Rose to save the day, either. That was just an excuse to get rid of Miles. No, let her have her afternoon with her new boyfriend, however shady he may be.

Passing through the open gate, Agatha started the long walk towards Montague Manor. Towards Tobias Montague. Towards Cole Burroughs. Towards the impending spectre of death that hung over them both.

With any luck, Miles would be right.

With any luck, it would all be over by the time he returned.

CHAPTER FIFTY-SEVEN

Rupert opened the door to the rehearsal space.

He didn't speak. Instead, he stepped to one side so two men could enter the room. They were both dressed in dark suits, but that was the only thing they had in common. Like polar opposites, one was heavy and bald, whilst the other was stick-thin with a thick head of fluffy hair. Both seemed on edge, though. Shuffling feet and twitchy fingers. Eye contact at a minimum.

Rose stood up from the sofa. Wobbled slightly as she did so.

'Sit back down,' said Rupert hastily. 'It's fine. Have another drink.'

Rose did as he suggested. At the same time, she watched the bald man hand Rupert a brown envelope that he pushed into the back pocket of his trousers.

She was still staring at them when her eyes began to glaze over. She tried to focus, but it was all just a blur.

'Are you okay?' Somehow, Rupert had appeared by her side. Just like that. As if by magic.

'I … I don't know.' The words rolled awkwardly off Rose's

tongue. More a slur than a sentence. 'What's wrong with me?'

'There's nothing wrong with you,' smiled Rupert, stroking her hair. 'You're perfect in every way.'

Rose could feel herself disappearing into the sofa. Placing her hands by her side, she tried to push herself up. They had barely taken her weight before they gave way and she toppled backwards. Moving quickly, Rupert grabbed her around the waist. Lowered her gently back down onto the sofa.

'Take it easy,' he said, his voice fading in and out. 'Relax.'

But Rose was relaxed. Too relaxed, if anything. In the last few minutes, she had started to lose the feeling in her body, almost as if it didn't belong to her. Without warning, her grip failed and she dropped the beaker. She barely noticed as it landed by her feet.

'Butter fingers,' said Rupert. Pushing the beaker across the floor, he mopped up the spillage with a costume that was hung close by. 'How much have you had to drink?'

'Not much,' mumbled Rose. 'I don't think so.'

'I was joking.' Kneeling by her side, Rupert ran his fingers over her leg. 'Just lie back and close your eyes. Don't fight it. You might even enjoy it.'

Rose took a moment to process his words. Then another to form her own. 'Enjoy what?'

'Enjoy us,' said Rupert. 'You and me. Me and you. Together at last. No pressure, though, my darling. You just have to follow my cues. The spotlight, as ever, will be on me. The leading man. It's a role I was born to play.' He took Rose by the hand.

Squeezed with too much force. 'Don't ruin things for me, will you? I could've chosen anyone, but I chose you. You should be thanking me. *This* is how you can thank me.'

Rose tried to shake her head, but her neck muscles weren't willing to oblige. 'No ... this isn't ... I just want to go home,' she spluttered. She looked across the room. She couldn't see the men, not clearly, but she could make out their outlines. They were closer now. 'Why are they here?'

'They're our audience,' explained Rupert. 'They've paid for the privilege. Paid a lot. They obviously recognise talent when they see it.'

Rose's head was spinning. What was happening to her? What was *about* to happen to her? 'I'm not feeling very well. I think I've been poisoned.'

Rupert looked deep into her eyes. 'You've not been poisoned,' he said softly. 'I put something in your drink, that's all. It relaxes the limbs, blurs the senses. It'll make things easier. These gentlemen want to see a show and I don't want to disappoint.'

With that, Rupert stood up and unzipped his trousers.

Rose, eyes glazed over, head lolling from side to side, watched them fall to the floorboards.

Then she screamed.

CHAPTER FIFTY-EIGHT

Tommy put the phone down on Miles.

He had everything he needed. An address for Rose. The Mucky Duck pub. He had never been there before, but Miles had given him pretty clear directions. No problem for a man of his calibre.

Tommy started the Mini's engine and pulled away from the kerb. He had already driven into Stainmouth. It was a lucky guess but, for once, luck had been on his side. The pub was only a few minutes away from his current location.

As expected, he found it easily. Turning into the car park, he drove into the first space he saw. There were only three other cars in there. Not exactly a bumper afternoon crowd.

Climbing out of the Mini, he locked up, stuck the keys in his pocket, and strolled over to the pub's entrance. He wandered in without breaking stride. Took in his surroundings. Years of experience had taught him how to spot a shithole when he saw one. And this was a shithole par excellence. At first glance, it was a bleak establishment that had decayed badly over time. At second glance, it was a bleak establishment that had decayed badly over time and only seemed to serve men. About ten of them were gathered around one large table in the corner of the room. Skins and tatts and beer bellies in abundance. Bitterness rising on the Stainmouth front.

'What can I get you?' asked a man behind the bar. He was big, bald and barrel-bodied. If he didn't play darts and eat pork scratchings then he was missing his calling.

'I'm good,' said Tommy. 'I'm actually looking for a friend of mine. Don't think she's here, though.'

'No, don't reckon she is,' agreed the barman. 'Doesn't mean you can't have a drink and find some new friends, though.'

'Okay.' Tommy pulled a face. 'Sounds a bit odd if you ask me.'

'Nothing odd about like-minded people coming together in a bid to make this town great again.' The barman held out his hand. 'I'm Barry, the landlord. I run the S.O.S Society from here. Save Our Stainmouth. If we all join forces, surely we can find a way to wipe out the foreign invaders. The uninvited scum that walk our streets and steal our—'

'Yeah, listen, mate, I'm in a bit of a hurry.' Tommy ignored the out-stretched hand as he edged towards the exit. 'See you later.'

Not.

He ducked outside and closed the door behind him before anyone in the pub could protest. He had no wish to get into a conversation like that, and no intention of ever going back. Not now. Not ever.

And yet if Rose wasn't in The Mucky Duck, then where the

hell was she?

None the wiser, Tommy was all set to head back towards the Mini when he heard a muffled cry coming from somewhere above his head. He looked around and saw a set of stairs running up the side of the building. They led all the way to a door at the top of the pub. The cry – if that's what it was – was coming from behind the door. Probably. Tommy wasn't exactly convinced. And those stairs were steep. Not to mention slippery. Was it worth it? Or was all that just an excuse because he couldn't be arsed?

He had come this far. Surely it was better to check every possible lead.

Head down, Tommy took to the stairs. His plan was simple. Get to the top. Realise there was nothing up there. Come back down again. No time wasted. Well, seconds at most, but he could live with that. Then he'd have to ring Miles.

Wrong directions, Millie. Can't find her anywhere. Get your facts straight next time.

Tommy reached the top step. He could hear talking coming from behind the door. Lifting his hand, he was about to knock when …

What if it really was Rose? What if she was in trouble?

Crouching down, he peered through the keyhole. He had to squint, but eventually he could see what was inside.

He stood up soon after, the image seared in his brain. He had seen some strange shit in his life, but this was right up there.

He knew what he had to do.

Now he just had to do it.

CHAPTER FIFTY-NINE

Agatha kept her eyes open and her senses on red alert as she hurried across the garden.

She was still some distance from the house when she spotted another of Tobias Montague's pheasant shooters. She refused to slow, but took in as much as she could on her way past. Laid flat on his back, this man had been dealt with accordingly and then left to sleep it off. Agatha just hoped that's all it was. That he was asleep. And that Cole Burroughs hadn't seen red and killed him.

The sound of a gunshot ringing out around the grounds of Montague Manor was enough to make her run for cover. Ducking down behind a bush, she was fairly certain that the shots weren't aimed at her. She eventually found the gunman on the roof, his back to Agatha as he fired repeatedly at a particular spot in the garden. That was all the reassurance she needed to set off again. Her pace had slowed, though, and there was no way of picking it back up. It made her a moving target if the gunman turned and half-fancied the practice. A *slow*-moving target. Like a snail without the protection of its shell.

'This way!'

Agatha scoured the grounds. The voice was coming from Montague Manor itself. From a man stood by a discreet side door at one end of the palatial property. Scampering across the grass, it was only when she got closer that Agatha realised it was Pendleton, the Montague's housekeeper. At the last moment, he slipped back into the house and held the door open so Agatha could follow him inside.

'That was somewhat distressing,' said Pendleton matter-of-factly. At the same time, he slammed the door shut behind her. 'You haven't been hit, have you?'

'Fortunately not.' Agatha looked around as she caught her breath. They were in a small laundry room. Two washing machines and a tumble dryer had been pushed up against one wall, whilst an ironing board occupied much of the floor space. 'Thank you,' she said, resting a hand on the butler's shoulder.

'There's no need for that,' said Pendleton, dismissing her gratitude. 'I couldn't just leave you out there, could I? Not with ... *them*. It seems as if we have something of a shoot-out going on in the garden.'

'Indeed you do,' nodded Agatha. 'I did try to warn Tobias that a man was coming to kill him.'

'Perhaps things would've gone a little smoother without the warning,' Pendelton muttered. 'Nevertheless, I think I know a way I can get you out of here—'

'I'm not going anywhere,' insisted Agatha.

Pendleton raised an eyebrow. 'I had a bad feeling you might

say that.'

'Am I really that predictable?' Agatha squeezed past the ironing board before opening a door that led deeper into the house. 'Now, are you going to take me to Tobias, or do I have to find my own way there?'

CHAPTER SIXTY

It wasn't a scream.

Not really. Not in the conventional sense of the word. No, it was more of a strangled yelp that got caught in her throat before coming to an abrupt halt. Rose knew that no one would ever hear it. They had barely heard it in the room, if she was being honest.

It was loud enough to make Rupert kneel down and place a hand over her mouth, though.

'Don't do that,' he said. 'I'd rather not hurt you, but I will if you persist in such childish behaviour. We're both adults and we both like each other. Just give in to your feelings, Rose.'

Rupert stood up and took off his jumper. He was completely naked. Not that Rose was aware, her eyes fixed on the ceiling. She barely felt his touch as he lifted her foot and removed, first, her shoe and then her sock. He did the same with the other foot. Then he moved up her legs and started to unbutton her trousers.

'I don't want to,' mumbled Rose. As far as she could tell, she was pushing him away. In reality, her hands were simply patting him gently.

The two men in dark suits had moved closer to the sofa. A front row view of the main event.

'Are you warm enough?' asked Rupert. 'Do you want another drink?'

Rose couldn't believe her ears. He was so well-mannered. So calm and relaxed. And yet it was all an act. How could he do this to her? He was the one. The love she had been waiting for.

Rupert slowly lowered her trousers over her hips and past her knees.

The two men leant forward. They were barely breathing as they stared through unblinking eyes at the scene before them.

Rose was still. Not through choice, but the drugs had fully kicked in now. Rupert was looming over her, but all she could see was a blurry outline of a man. The ordeal was about to begin. Soon it would be over, though. At least she could cling on to that.

Rose closed her eyes as Rupert slipped his fingers into her knickers.

And then opened them a moment later as the door crashed open and a bellowing voice echoed around the rehearsal room.

'Greetings, motherfuckers. Sorry I'm late.'

CHAPTER SIXTY-ONE

A big set of balls can only get you so far.

There always comes a point when people see through the bravado, the bluster, the bullshit. Sometimes, you've got little more than a few seconds. If you're lucky, you can get away with it for days. Weeks. Months. Never an entire lifetime, though. The *point* always comes before that.

Just not now, thought Tommy. Any time but now.

Stood in the doorway, he took in the room as fast as his eyes would allow. There were rails of brightly coloured clothing everywhere he looked, most of which seemed unsuitable for everyday use, a small stage at the far end, and a large box full of props and equipment right in front of it. That was all detail, though. None of it really mattered.

Tommy was only concerned with the bodies.

There was four of them in total. The two closest to him he had never seen before. One fat, one thin. Pick a name. Any name. Jelly Man and Rat Boy. Yeah, that'd do. And behind them, Rupert and Rose. The unlikely couple. He focussed on the latter. Something wasn't right. The light had gone out in her eyes and her face had fallen to one side. He had seen that look many times before. Never in broad daylight, though, in some kind of makeshift theatre, but in bars and clubs, in the early hours when most sane folk had given up the ghost and drifted off to bed.

Rose was lost in another dimension. More commonly known as off her head. Completely spangled.

And Rupert ... he was stark-bollock naked.

Combine the two together and the day had taken a strange turn for Tommy O'Strife. Strange enough for him to bellow at the top of his voice, 'greetings, motherfuckers. Sorry I'm late'

He puffed out his chest, gritted his teeth and raised his fists. Wow, that was convincing. Who wouldn't be intimidated by such a powerful show of strength?

Well, just about everybody who had ever been born. No, don't think like that. Stick to the positives. He was a rock-hard warrior. Violence came easy. If anything, he enjoyed it. Unless he was getting his own forehead bounced off the floorboards, of course. Nobody enjoyed that.

Tommy let his eyes settle on Rupert. Knelt down between Rose's legs, he had turned quickly when the door had swung open. Relaxed when he saw it was Tommy. *Only* Tommy. No threat. No worry. Just a minor interference. He confirmed all of this when he did the one thing that ignited Tommy's fuse.

He smiled.

Without thinking, Tommy bounded across the room with Rupert set firmly in his sights. What he hadn't bargained on, however, was Jelly Man. He shifted at the same time as Tommy, his vast frame lumbering towards the exit. They were all set for a head-on collision when Tommy did the unexpected and threw a flying head-butt. Good in theory, but poorly executed, he got it all wrong and hit Jelly Man fair and square in the chest. Tommy wobbled, whilst Jelly Man went one step further. Staggering backwards, he lost his balance and crashed into a rack of clothes that collapsed under the man's extreme weight. Jelly Man went down with it and landed in a heap amongst the colourful costumes.

Tommy kept his footing. Readjusted. Spinning around, he found himself face to face with Rat Boy. He didn't fancy it. Anyone could see that. Tommy was proven correct when the thin man turned his back and cowered behind his hands. Tommy swung anyway, his fist connecting with the back of Rat Boy's head. He yelped out loud and dropped to his knees, leaving Tommy free to rush past. Those two were nothing more than an apéritif, though. Now it was time for the main course.

Rupert finally stood up. Placed his hands on his hips and frowned. 'You shouldn't be here. Get out!'

Tommy ignored him. Focussed on Rose instead. Laid out across the sofa, her eyes had glazed over whilst her body flopped unnaturally. 'What have you done to her?' Tommy spat.

'Nothing,' shrugged Rupert. 'I didn't force her to come here. And now I'd like you to—'

His sentence was cut short when Tommy punched him in the face. He fell a moment later, hitting the floorboards a moment after that. His head was spinning as he tried to sit up. He had barely made it when Tommy grabbed him around the throat and hauled him to his feet.

'What have you done to her?' he repeated.

'It was just a pill,' spluttered Rupert. 'I put it in her drink ... to loosen her up a little.' He steadied himself. There was something he had to say. 'She wanted to do it. I know she did. But she couldn't let go. I had to help her. She didn't know how to give herself to me—'

Tommy slapped him hard across the face before he could spout any more bile. Threw him back down onto the floorboards before switching his attention to Rose. Crouching down, he tried not to look as he pulled up her knickers and then her trousers. She seemed to be staring straight at him, but he doubted she could see properly.

Rose on drugs. Any other time that might have been funny.

This time, however, it was anything but.

Positioning both hands under her arms, Tommy lifted her to her feet. He glanced over his shoulder, relieved to see that both Jelly Man and Rat Boy had done a runner. Tommy wasn't entirely sure why they were there to begin with, but he could probably fathom a guess. What sort of sicko watches a barely comatose woman being raped by a twisted pervert? And Tommy thought his morals were pretty low. For fuck's sake, he was like Mother Theresa compared to these degenerates.

'What's ... happening?' groaned Rose, as her legs gave way beneath her.

'I've got you now,' said Tommy, supporting her weight as they shuffled towards the exit. 'You'll be okay.'

Rose sighed. 'Will I?'

Tommy left the question hanging. Experiences like this left scars that sometimes never healed. Who was he to tell Rose how she would feel in the future? Maybe she was scarred already by the past.

'They'll be others,' called out Rupert. He was sat on the floor, legs spread, powerless to stop the flow of blood that dripped from his nose onto the wooden boards. 'Rose isn't anything special. She's just one of many sad, lonely women desperate for love. Looking for ... *the one*. If anything, I'm doing them a favour. And then they return that favour when the moment arises. You ruined that today, although Rose had already tried her best before that. So, yes, take her if you want. It won't stop me, though. I'll just do it again with some other pitiful whore.'

Tommy stopped in the doorway. Careful not to drop her, he leant Rose up against the wall before marching back into the room.

'Oh, I suppose you're going to hit me again,' sneered Rupert. 'That's all your kind understand, isn't it? You're just a common—'

His sentence ended abruptly with a wide-eyed, open-mouthed gasp as Tommy strode forward and hit him where it hurts.

A broken nose was satisfying, but a vicious stamp to the testicles was the ultimate coup de grâce.

Tommy had seen and said enough. No more witty retorts or biting remarks. No more fists or feet. Just get out of there before the tide turned and he found himself outnumbered by the returning Jelly Man and Rat Boy. Collecting Rose by the door, he carried her out into the open. He could hear Rupert sobbing uncontrollably, but it gave him precious little joy. Instead, he made his way down the stairs with Rose by his side.

'You're safe now,' he whispered. 'It's over.'

'Thank you,' mumbled Rose. She felt a blast of cold air against her face. The shock of it was enough to clear her head. Focus her mind. 'I want to go back to Cockleshell Farm. I need to lay down ...'

'Yeah, about that ...' Tommy tried to pick his words carefully as he led her towards the Mini. 'There's something I've got to tell you.'

Rose understood immediately. 'It's Cole Burroughs, isn't it?'

Tommy nodded. 'How did you guess? It's happening, Rose. He's on the rampage. And, according to Miles, you're the only one who can stop him.'

CHAPTER SIXTY-TWO

Agatha followed Pendleton through the bowels of Montague Manor.

He knew every nook and cranny of the house. Every crack and crevice. They passed through narrow corridors that seemed untouched by foot. Secret tunnels and hidden staircases that avoided both guests and intruders. That was the whole point, after all. Whether it be an acquaintance of Tobias Montague, or the man on a mission, Cole Burroughs, they had no wish to bump into anybody if they could help it. And Pendleton *could* help it.

It didn't take long for them to emerge on the same landing as Tobias's bedroom. Agatha had expected to see another pheasant shooter standing guard, but there was no one in sight. Cautiously, they crept up to the door. Pendleton got there first and knocked, only to be greeted with silence from inside the room.

'Maybe young Master Montague is dead already,' he said, straight-faced.

Agatha didn't reply. She couldn't explain why, but something felt wrong. Without warning, she pulled Pendleton to one side and pressed him against the wall. He was about to object when a flurry of rapid gunfire beat him to it, peppering the door with bullet holes.

'Die!' screamed a voice from inside the room.

Pendleton waited for the gunfire to fade before he dared to call out. 'No, stop this. It's me ... may I come in?'

The door swung open. It wasn't Montague, but another pheasant shooter. A heavy set man with dark eyes and a pock-marked face. The way he carried his rifle suggested it wasn't the first time he had wielded such a weapon.

He turned away so Agatha and Pendleton could enter the room. Tobias Montague was over to their left. Dressed in a pair of skinny jeans and an over-sized sweatshirt, he was rocking from side to side, unsteady on his feet. Nerves perhaps. Drink and drugs almost certainly. 'What the fuck do you want?' he slurred.

'You have a visitor,' said Pendleton.

Montague's eyes shifted over to Agatha. He wobbled as he tried to focus. 'Where are they?'

'Where are *who*?' replied Agatha.

'The cavalry. Don't tell me you've come alone. There's a lunatic trying to get into my house.'

'I did try to warn you.'

'Well, you didn't try very hard, did you?' Montague shot back. 'I want protection. The police. The army. I'll tell my father.'

Agatha shook her head. 'It's too late for any of that now.'

'Well, if I die, you die.' Marching forward, Montague produced a pistol from his waistband and pressed it against Agatha's temple. 'Keep talking shit and maybe you'll die first.'

'Or maybe nobody has to die at all,' said Agatha, as calmly as she could. 'That has to be the best outcome. For this to come to a peaceful conclusion and we all walk out of here alive.'

'No, the best outcome would be for you to shut your fuckin' mouth and get on your knees,' ordered Montague, waving the gun around. 'Both of you.'

Agatha and Pendleton did as he demanded. She felt the vibrations of her phone on her way down. She couldn't answer it for fear of a violent reaction from Montague, but she could guess who was calling.

Miles.

He must've returned to the house. Wondered where she was. He had told her not to do anything stupid. Could this be considered stupid? No point answering that.

Montague moved towards the side of the window. Peeked outside without showing himself. 'This is insane. Wait 'til my father hears about this. You'll be sacked, Pendleton. Mark my words. You're supposed to be looking after me.'

'I think the days of you having your bottom wiped, young Master Montague, are long gone,' remarked Pendleton drily. 'And, for your information, I quit. Any respect I have for your father is unfortunately over-shadowed by the utter contempt I have for you.'

Montague spun back into the room. Rolling the pistol around his fingers, he was about to whip the old man across the face when a knock at the door stopped him mid-swing. For a moment, the room fell silent.

'Who is it?' asked Montague, his voice straining.

The reply came instantly. 'The man who's going to kill you. Can I come in?'

CHAPTER SIXTY-THREE

By the time Tommy and Rose had arrived at Montague Manor, there was another car and two men waiting at the gates.

An Audi and Olaf and Miles.

The former hadn't moved from the driver's seat, whilst the latter was stood beside the bonnet, looking over the grounds of the vast country house, surveying the scene. He turned when he heard the Mini. Frowned at the two of them as they climbed out of the vehicle.

'Is she okay?' he asked. The *she* being Rose. The same Rose who could barely stand up by herself. Who, with Tommy by her side, walked in slow, shuffling footsteps with her head down and gaze fixed to the floor.

'I'm fine,' she muttered.

'She's not,' argued Tommy. 'She's been drugged. Rupert was going to stick one up her whilst she was half asleep. Guy's a snake.'

'That's not true,' said Rose weakly. 'He wouldn't do that. I don't know ... maybe it was a misunderstanding.'

Tommy snorted. 'That was no misunderstanding; that was

planned. You'd have been all over the internet by tonight if he'd gone through with it—'

'We can sort this out later.' Miles rested a hand on Rose's shoulder. Removed it just as quickly when she shuddered at his touch. 'And we *will* sort it out,' he insisted. 'I promise. But this has to take priority.'

Rose nodded wearily.

'From one psycho to another,' said Tommy. 'Where's Burroughs?'

'Your guess is as good as mine.' Miles gestured towards Montague Manor. 'We think he's somewhere in there.'

'We?' Tommy looked around. There was someone missing. 'Where's Pleasant Agatha?'

'I left her here,' said Miles, pointing at the ground beneath his feet. 'I've tried to call her, but she's not picking up.'

Tommy flinched at the sound of a gunshot. Tried to pretend he hadn't as he peered over at the house. 'You don't think she's—'

'Yes, that's exactly what I think,' replied Miles, meeting the question head-on. 'Maybe this was what she wanted all along. I'm going to follow her in—'

'*We're* going to follow her in.' Tommy turned back towards the Mini. 'We've come this far, after all. Might as well see it through. It's not as if we haven't seen worse.'

Miles nodded in agreement. Moving over to the Audi, he tapped on Olaf's window until the driver lowered it.

'Wait here and keep an eye out for Miss Pleasant.' Miles

hesitated. 'Please.'

Olaf's only response was a solitary grunt before he pressed the switch and the window started to rise. Satisfied, Miles hurried back towards the Mini. By the time he had got there, Tommy had slid Rose onto the back seat.

'I'll drive,' said Miles, holding out his hand for the keys.

'Yeah, good joke,' grinned Tommy. 'I'd rather let Rose loose at the wheel and she can barely see straight.'

Miles wanted to argue, but knew that time was of the essence. Instead, he entered through the passenger side and strapped on his belt.

'Don't you trust me?' asked Tommy, as he joined the other two in the car.

'What do you think?' muttered Miles.

Tommy took that as his cue to start the engine. The Mini stalled for a moment before it shot forward. Passing through the gates, they began to pick up speed. Tommy let the vehicle drift slightly from the gravel path to the garden whilst he took in his surroundings. 'Fancy living here. You could have a different bedroom for each day of the week. Imagine the parties. The women who would ... what the bloody hell was that?'

Miles had heard it, too. A loud *ping*, it sounded as if something solid had bounced off the Mini's roof. A second later and a similar something struck the windscreen and a large crack appeared in the top corner.

'Fuck this for a game of soldiers.' Tommy stamped down harder and the Mini sped up.

The sudden acceleration was enough to shake Rose into life. 'What's going on?' she mumbled. 'Why are you driving so fast?'

'Needs must,' said Tommy.

'What does that mean?' asked Rose.

Another *ping* off the car's bonnet seemed to answer her question.

'We're under attack,' said Miles, holding on tight. 'Somebody's shooting at us.'

CHAPTER SIXTY-FOUR

Being shot at doesn't always have to be a negative thing.

Seconds earlier, Rose had been a bleary-eyed, limp-limbed husk of a woman. Then the bullets had rebounded off the roof of the Mini and she had been transformed. A combination of shock and fear had focussed her mind and realigned her senses. Suddenly, staying alive took priority over everything.

Took priority over Rupert and what he had done to her.

At that very moment, Rose wasn't even sure that she wanted to live. But she was certain that she didn't want to die. Not here. Not like this. When it happened, she wanted it to be on her own terms.

Just survive then. That would do for now.

Miles seemed to think along the same lines. 'Stop!'

The Mini veered to one side as Tommy turned to look at him. 'What?'

'Stop!' repeated Miles. 'Now! Before we crash!'

Tommy stamped down on the brakes, sending the Mini skidding along the gravel before it eventually shuddered to a halt in the garden.

'Get out,' yelled Miles.

They did as he asked. Ducking down, Rose pulled open her door and crawled out onto the grass. Tommy did the same, leaving the door open so Miles could clamber over his seat and join them outside. With the gunman on the other side of the vehicle, the Mini provided a barrier from the gunfire.

'He's on the roof,' said Miles. He kept his head low as the bullets struck the car's bodywork. 'Don't look. Not unless you want to get your brains splattered across the driveway.'

'What do you suggest we do, then?' frowned Tommy. 'We're like sitting ducks out here.'

'I'll cover you,' said Miles. 'I'll take a few shots at our trigger-happy friend up there and scare him off. At the same time, the two of you can make a run for the house.'

'Rose can't run,' insisted Tommy. 'Have you seen the state of her?'

'I'm fine,' said Rose. She wasn't. Not really. Nobody else needed to know that, though. 'I can do it.'

'Somebody's back in the land of living,' said Tommy, raising an eyebrow. 'A minute ago, you were completely off your head.'

Rose waved it away. 'That was then. This is now.'

Satisfied with her response, Miles removed his gun from his inside pocket. 'Get ready. Start running when I start shooting.' With that, he leant over the bonnet, took aim, and fired at the man on the roof. It was just a warning shot and flew safely over his head. The man didn't know that, though, and ducked for cover. 'Go!' shouted Miles.

So they did. Scrambling to their feet, they set off together. Heads down, fists pumping. Tommy knew that if he turned back he would undoubtedly slow, but he did it regardless. He needn't have worried. Rose was keeping pace, which was a massive weight lifted. He hadn't believed her when she said that she was fine. What Rupert had done to her ... had *almost* done to her ... would haunt her for a long time. The horror of her ordeal would probably resurface later on that day, when all this was over. Better to keep a low profile when it did, thought Tommy. That sort of shit was way out of his comfort zone.

For the time being at least, Rose was running on adrenaline. But then they both were.

Don't think. Don't feel. Just move.

His stride lengthening, Tommy was the first to reach the entrance to Montague Manor. Yanking down on the handle, he felt a surge of relief as the door opened immediately. Stepping inside, he waited for Rose to run straight past him before he closed it behind them.

'I think I've burst a lung.' Tommy bent over so he could catch his breath. It was several seconds before he felt well enough to lift his head and look around. 'Wow! This place is pretty special.'

Which was probably the biggest understatement of the day.

Without another word being passed between them, they did a quick sweep of the ground floor, ducking in and out of every room in search of Agatha or Cole Burroughs. Tommy hesitated in the last room they came to. He had spotted something that needed closer inspection. A leather holdall, it was just sat there on an antique sideboard. Uncared for and neglected. And certainly not needed, judging by the size of the house. Because it was what was inside of the holdall that really piqued Tommy's interest. He checked Rose wasn't watching and then tip-toed towards it. The closer look was enough to make his heart pump a little faster. Then a lot faster.

Slow down, buddy. Stay cool.

Opening the holdall, he peeked inside. It was full of money. Drugs money at a guess. All used notes rolled up into neat little bundles. Tommy picked one up. Studied it. Then stuffed it down the front of his jeans. He did the same again, but this time didn't bother to study it.

'What are you doing?' asked Rose, appearing in the doorway.

Stood with his back to her, Tommy took a moment to rearrange himself before he turned around. 'Nothing ... not really ... I thought I saw something, that's all. I was wrong.'

He hurried past her as quickly as he could. As soon as he was out in the hallway, he could hear noises coming from the next floor up.

'After you,' said Tommy, gesturing up the stairs. 'Age before beauty.'

Rose ignored that as she took to the first step. Less easy to ignore was what followed next. The sound of gunshots. Three in total. Coming from the floor above, at the front of the house.

Rose took a step back. 'No, after *you*. It's only fair.'

'So, we're still going up there?' frowned Tommy.

'You said it outside,' shrugged Rose, pushing him gently in

the back. 'We've come this far. Let's try to finish what we've started for a change.'

CHAPTER SIXTY-FIVE

Tobias Montague raised his pistol and fired wildly at the door.

The bullets struck in random places, but all hit their target. A moment later, there was a cry of anguish, followed by a dull *thud* as something heavy slumped against the door outside.

'Got him!' cheered Montague, hopping up and down on the spot. 'I got him!'

Rushing forward, he pulled open the door. As he did so, a body fell face-forward into the room. It was enough to make Montague jump back in horror. He blinked once ... twice ... three times before his bloodshot eyes and drug-addled mind both came to the same conclusion.

'I know this guy,' he mumbled. 'He works for my father. He's on my side.' A pause. 'He isn't Cole Burroughs.'

'He's not dead either,' remarked Agatha, examining the man from her kneeling position. 'He's still breathing and there's no sign of any blood, even though he's just been shot. *Supposedly* shot—'

'What the hell do you know?' spat Montague. 'Just shut your mouth so I can think.'

He moved swiftly towards the door. He was all set to close it when it flew back in his face, sending him staggering back into the room. If he thought he could stay on his feet, he was sadly deluded. Instead, he lost his balance and hit the ground hard. By the time he had recovered enough to push himself up, it was too late.

There was a figure in the doorway, blocking out the light from the landing.

A dark shadow hell-bent on revenge.

Hand shaking, Montague closed his eyes and fired off several shots. When he looked again, the shadow was upon him. A vicious kick sent the pistol flying out of his hand. Then he was being hauled up onto his feet. Slammed against the enormous window.

'Remember me?' hissed Cole Burroughs in his ear.

Montague tried to wriggle free, but it was all to no avail. Burroughs had already twisted his arm behind his back. If he moved, he would break it. If he didn't move, he would probably break it, anyway. Or worse.

Worse arrived in the form of a curved blade. In slow motion, it flashed across Montague's face before it eventually came to rest against his neck.

'You know why I'm here,' said Cole calmly. 'You know what I'm going to do. And you know you can't stop me.'

'And I know that's probably not your best course of action,' began Agatha. She tried to speak with authority as she climbed to her feet, but there was an uncertainty to her voice. Fear of the unpredictable.

'You two leave,' ordered Cole, his eyes fixed on Agatha and Pendleton. He turned towards the other man in the room. 'And you as well. There's no reason for any of you to be here.'

The pheasant shooter with the pock-marked face dropped his gun and hurried out of the room. He was the only one, though.

'We're here to stop a murder,' said Agatha, standing her ground.

'It's not murder – it's justice,' insisted Cole. 'I can succeed where the law failed. Tell me that's wrong. Go on. Tell me I'm a killer ... a murderer.'

'I'm not going to judge you,' said Agatha. 'I'm trying to find a way out of this without anybody having to die.'

Cole shook his head. 'We've had this conversation. Nobody can help me now.'

'Maybe I can.'

Cole looked towards the door. Two more people had entered the room. A man and a woman. He recognised them both immediately. Liked one more than the other. Wished that the same one was anywhere but Montague Manor.

'What are you doing here?' he asked through gritted teeth.

Rose edged in front of Tommy. Swallowed before she spoke. 'I'm here for you,' she said. 'I want to save your life.'

CHAPTER SIXTY-SIX

Cole Burroughs glared at Agatha.

'I told you not to bring her here,' he said angrily. 'I don't want her involved.'

'It was *you* who involved me in the first place,' said Rose, speaking for herself as she shuffled deeper into the room. Her head was still spinning, but she knew what she had to say. 'You involved me when you broke into the house in the middle of the night. When you took me to the cemetery. You didn't have to do that. I think you wanted me involved. That was your plan all along.'

Cole shook his head. 'It wasn't ... I didn't. You're a good person. You shouldn't be anywhere near me.'

'It's not too late to stop.' Rose took another step. There was less than a metre between them now. 'If you want me to come and save you, then you only have to ask. This isn't you, Cole. You're not a murderer.'

'No, but *he* is.' Cole pressed the knife against Montague's neck until it drew blood. 'And that's why he deserves to die.'

Rose took another step. They were well within touching

distance now. 'Maybe you're right. He did a wicked thing that went unpunished. He took two lives, two innocent lives, and he's about to take a third. Yours. If you kill him now, your life will be over. What would they think about that? Charlotte and Sophie? Would it make them happy?'

'Don't talk about them!' snapped Cole. 'Not here. Not in front of him.'

'Why not?' said Rose. 'Because it's too soon? If I shouldn't be here, then neither should you. We could leave now, together. Nobody will stop us.'

'But then he'll walk free.' Cole shook his head. 'It'll destroy me. I can't just let him go.'

'And if you kill him, will that make things better? We both know the answer to that. It won't fill the void. The hurt will persist until enough time passes and it slowly starts to ease.' Rose held out her hand. 'Why don't you give me the knife? We can find peace another way.'

Cole blinked away the tears. All of a sudden, he looked beaten. As if the pain and sorrow had ripped the life out of him.

Without warning, he moved the knife away from Montague's throat and offered it to Rose. 'Take it. Please.'

Rose reached out. Her fingers were about to touch the handle when Montague got there first. Wriggling free of Cole's grasp, he snatched the knife and then spun around. He had both of them in his sights now. Like a man possessed, he went straight on the attack, swiping the knife wildly from left to right. Cole swerved to one side, and it narrowly missed his chest.

Rose wasn't so quick, though.

The blade was about to slice into her shoulder when Cole stepped in front of her. Shielding his face, he winced as it cut into his forearm and the blood began to flow.

Then he made his move.

Montague was all set to strike again when Cole threw himself at the other man. The force of the collision was enough to knock the knife out of Montague's hand before his feet left the ground. Flying through the air, he crashed into the window behind him. It smashed upon impact and he began to fall. As a last gasp reaction, he clung onto Cole, his hand clamped tight around his wrist. It wasn't the support he was looking for, though.

Suddenly, Cole was falling, too.

They were both falling.

Out of the window and over the edge.

Out and over.

Over and out.

CHAPTER SIXTY-SEVEN

Rose couldn't just stand back and watch.

This was a day for letting go, not giving up.

Without a thought for her own safety, she lunged forward and made a grab for the disappearing Cole Burroughs. Her hand found his hand and he stopped falling. For now. Just a temporary fix to an ever-escalating problem, though. Truth be told, the three of them in a line made for a precarious balancing act. If Rose was at one end, then Tobias Montague was at the other, hanging out of the window, clinging on desperately to Cole's other arm. Cole himself was teetering on the brink, half in, half out, his last ounces of strength preventing him from going all the way over the edge.

The difference in weight, not to mention gravity, meant there was only one way this was going to end, though.

Before she could dig her heels in, Rose began to slide across the floor. Closer to the window. Closer to her own death.

Cole, sensing the danger, reacted accordingly. Kicking out, he caught Montague full in the face with the sole of his shoe. The pain was so acute, so unexpected, that Montague loosened his grip. And once it had loosened, he had little choice but to let go.

He landed not far from the front door in a crumpled heap. A puzzle of dishevelled limbs that refused to stir. A life snuffed out in the blink of an eye.

With Tobias Montague no longer part of the problem, the pressure on Rose diminished. One less person equated to half as much weight. She was still sliding, but at a slower rate. Yes, she was still going to fall, but at least she had time to think about it.

Cole held her gaze as he struggled to keep his footing. 'You know what you have to do.'

'I can't.' Rose shook her head. 'I won't ...'

'Please,' said Cole. 'I'm begging you. There's only one way this should end.'

And that, for Rose, was when it all suddenly made sense. It wasn't a stubborn demand; it was a heartfelt plea that came from a place of absolute despair. Cole Burroughs had nothing left to live for. He had repeated that over and over again. Who was she to ignore him? How dare she be the one who got to pick and choose if he lived or died?

'It's time to let go,' Cole whispered.

So that was what Rose did.

She let her head rule her heart.

And let go.

CHAPTER SIXTY-EIGHT

The emergency services came and went as the day drew to a weary close.

There were questions to be answered. Awkward questions that refused to go away. Agatha kept her cool, though, her calm demeanour and obvious authority enough to appease the boys in blue, if only for the time being. In the long term, she was confident that the Chief Constable would clear things up. They were only acting on his orders, after all, albeit unsuccessfully. Things could've been worse, of course. A lot worse. If anything, it was a relief the paramedics only had two bodies to deal with, not two dozen.

Two *dead* bodies.

Cole Burroughs and Tobias Montague.

The latter's pheasant shooters had woken in due course with battered heads and bruised egos, before scuttling off to whichever pub, club or hellhole they regularly frequented. Lucky for them that Cole was such a skilled operator, thought Agatha. That he had the ability to disable and disarm without too much fuss or frenzy. But then he only had eyes for one, didn't he? The goons were just an unavoidable inconvenience, whilst Montague had murdered his wife and daughter. Big difference.

It was dark by the time Pendleton walked her to the door. He watched as an ambulance departed the scene before he drew breath and passed judgement. 'It's been quite a day, hasn't it?'

'That's one way of putting it,' sighed Agatha. 'What now? For you, I mean. Do you think you'll carry on working here?'

Pendleton shook his head as he looked out across the grounds. 'I can't see it somehow. Magnus Montague asked me to take care of his son in his absence. His son's now dead. The buck has to stop somewhere. Someone always has to take the blame.'

'That's not your fault,' said Agatha.

Pendleton shrugged. 'Maybe it's a sign. I nearly died back there. We both did. I'm too old for drugs and guns and naked bodies and all-night parties. I'd rather settle down with a good book and a hot water bottle these days.' He gave Agatha a moment to think. 'Surely you feel the same. There has to be a point when enough is enough.'

'You're only as old as the team who works under you,' Agatha remarked. 'And I've got a pretty young team.'

She gently touched his arm and then turned towards the door, keen to avoid another round of probing questions. Pendleton's words had hit a nerve. If she carried on the way she was going, she would be dead before retirement. That was a fact. Tobias Montague had come close to pulling the trigger on her before he had toppled out of the window. Maybe Cole Burroughs had considered something similar in her hotel room.

'You okay?'

She looked up and saw Miles on the driveway. 'Just about,' she replied. 'Sometimes it's best not to dwell on your own thoughts, though. Why don't you tell me something to cheer me up? Something positive?'

'At least the Mini is still in working order,' said Miles. 'The windscreen will be an easy fix. The bullet holes maybe not so.' He gestured back towards the house. 'I heard what Pendleton was saying. That someone has to take the blame. It got me thinking. Is this our fault? We could've pulled Cole Burroughs off the street at any time. Taken him hostage if needs be. All this would never have happened.'

'Hindsight,' said Agatha, dismissing it with a casual wave of her hand. 'Burroughs had done nothing wrong. Nothing we could arrest him for.'

'He broke into the house on Haversham Way. Kidnapped Claude Bonham. We could've held him for a few days just for those two things alone—'

'And then he would've come out and killed Montague anyway,' shrugged Agatha. 'It was just a matter of time. The wheels were in motion long before we arrived on the scene. After everything that had happened, Burroughs was an unstoppable force. We were trying to prevent the inevitable—'

'Which we failed to do.'

'Because it was inevitable,' countered Agatha. 'It's not all bad news, though.' She pointed at the gates that separated Montague Manor from the rest of the world. The Audi was parked there, Olaf stood rigid by the driver's door, staring into the middle distance. Rose was slightly behind him, hunched over, head in hands, whilst Tommy proceeded to pace up and down, kicking his heels as he waited impatiently. 'We're all still here,' said Agatha. 'No casualties our end. Maybe we should count our blessings. Sometimes that's as good as it gets in our line of work.'

They were close to the gates now. In a matter of seconds, they would be safely ensconced in the Audi. Heading, first, to Cockleshell Farm, and then on to The Nightingale Hotel, the events at Montague Manor a thing of the past.

Miles, however, hadn't quite finished. Without warning, he stepped across Agatha, forcing her to slow down. 'Can I ask you something?' He lowered his voice for fear of being overheard. Considered his words carefully. 'Don't get offended, but ... is this what you wanted all along? For both Burroughs and Montague to die? For a clean slate?'

'What do you think, Miles?' replied Agatha, swerving around him as she dodged the question. Answer me that. What do you think?'

CHAPTER SIXTY-NINE
THE FOLLOWING DAY

Olaf eased the Audi to a gentle halt.

He had parked up outside eleven Jefferson Meadows. On the face of it, a perfectly normal, impressively average house to the west of Stainmouth.

In reality, it was the home of a criminal.

'His name is Rupert Knight,' said Agatha from the back seat. 'He's only been out of prison a few months. He's got a history of accusations that eventually led to a string of convictions. Inappropriate behaviour that turned to rape and sexual assault. I guess that's why he never told you his surname.'

Rose nodded. Was she listening? Not really. Was she even there? In body perhaps, but her mind was somewhere else entirely. Somewhere darker. Somewhere that scared the life out of her.

'I'm sorry,' continued Agatha. 'I should have done more. My attention was focussed on Cole Burroughs and I let Knight become a ... sub plot. I let you down. It won't happen again.' Agatha hesitated. Drew breath. 'Oh, here we go. Maybe this can go some way to reassuring you.'

Right on cue, two police cars pulled up on the opposite side of the road. At once, three officers bundled out of each vehicle and bounded up the short path that led to the front door of number eleven. A series of rapid-fire knocks followed. When nobody answered, a battering ram was produced, and the door was knocked clean off its hinges. No messing about, thought Agatha. Less than a minute later and Rupert was being dragged towards the nearest vehicle. He was trying to resist arrest, despite the cuts and bruises he had suffered at the hands of Tommy. Despite the fact that one testicle was now lodged somewhere it shouldn't be, and would probably need to be surgically removed.

The arrest had taken less than three minutes from start to finish. Clean, efficient. Maybe Clifford Goose had given them strict instructions. Warned them there would be spectators.

Agatha waited for the sirens to fade before she spoke again. 'Knight will be placed in remand before he's sentenced. He's a threat to women. I can't imagine he'll be walking the streets any time soon.' She paused. 'I hope that's provided some kind of ... closure.'

Rose nodded again. She hadn't watched any of it. It meant nothing to her.

'You did well yesterday,' remarked Agatha, keen to change the subject. 'With Cole Burroughs, I mean. This life ... it's not all punch-ups and shoot-outs. Sometimes you need a softer side. That's where you differ from the others. You've got the human touch. Burroughs warmed to you. You appealed to his better nature and it almost worked.'

'Almost,' mumbled Rose.

'Some things are out of our control,' sighed Agatha. 'It's the way of the world, I'm afraid. Just keep being you. Never change. That's all I ask ... ah, that is frustrating.' She reached into her handbag at the sound of a persistent buzzing. Removing her phone, she studied the screen. 'Frustrating ... yet predictable. Do you mind? I should probably take this ...'

Agatha didn't wait for Rose to reply. Instead, she opened the car door and stepped outside. Took a weary breath and prepared herself for the inevitable grilling. 'Good morning, Clifford. Keeping well, are we?'

The Chief Constable responded with a noise like a startled cow. 'Shit's about to hit the fan,' he blurted out.

'Not the greeting I was expecting—'

'Magnus Montague is coming back to Stainmouth for his son's funeral,' barked Goose. 'He's raging, as you'd expect. Heads will roll.'

'Surely not your head?'

'Who chuffin' knows? Cole Burroughs was hardly a shock, was he? He was on our radar. He even told us what he was going to do. If Montague gets wind of that, he'll go bananas.'

'Aren't you forgetting something, Clifford? His son was far from an innocent victim. He was a murderer.'

'Not in the eyes of the law.'

Agatha groaned. 'Perhaps not, but certainly in the eyes of

every right-minded person on the planet. Do I really need to remind you, Clifford? This whole case stinks of corruption, and all because you and your cronies at the Wild Boar are too scared to stand up to a man with a ton of money. I thought you were better than that. Behind all the bluster, I thought you were a man of dignity.'

Goose hesitated. 'Have you finished? For pity's sake, woman, you don't half go on when you've got a bee in your beret—'

'Bonnet,' sighed Agatha.

'What's that?'

'Doesn't matter.'

'Well, as long as you know which side your bread's buttered, that's all,' said Goose. 'Stick close to me and we can bat this thing away together. Tight as arseholes, we need to be. Best bosom buddies.' Goose stopped. That particular combination of phrases had got him thinking. 'What are you doing this very minute?'

Agatha's defences shot up immediately. 'Why?'

'I'm outside the Sanctuary of Serenity,' said Goose. 'I've got an appointment with Gunther. You remember Gunther, don't you? Built like a brick shit house, but with hands like an angel's eyebrows. I thought you could come along for the ride. See what all the fuss is about. We could get to know each other a little better whilst Gunther rubs the pair of us up the right way—'

'No, thank you, Clifford. Goodbye.' Agatha ended the call abruptly. Shuddered at the thought of where the conversation had been heading. 'Drive please, Olaf,' she said, climbing back into the car. 'Let's leave this moment of our lives – and that phone call – well and truly in the past, shall we?'

Olaf did as she asked, much to Agatha's relief. She turned towards the window as the Audi moved away from the kerb. If only she could switch off and watch the world go by. Unfortunately, a rather unpleasant image of Goose slipping out of his tiny towel had ingrained itself in her mind. That would certainly take some shifting. Three or more drinks and a good night's sleep at the very least.

Rose, meanwhile, had switched off long ago. An unthinking, unblinking entity. What did the future hold for her? She didn't know. She didn't care. Maybe nothing. Not if Rose had her way.

Cole Burroughs had begged her to let go, to free him from his misery.

All she had to do now was free herself.

CHAPTER SEVENTY

Tommy drove the Mini through the streets of Stainmouth at a speed that, only a few short months ago, would've made his toes curl.

Twenty miles per hour tops. Nice and steady. No need to rush. If he drove too fast, he could easily scare them off. Send them scurrying back into the shadows. Out of sight, out of mind. That was how society liked it, after all. If you can't see them, they don't exist. Not my problem.

Tommy had already spotted several lookalikes. Close, but not close enough. They could always have moved on to pastures new, of course. Somewhere more glamorous. Maybe Stainmouth had lost its appeal, although Tommy doubted whether it had that much to begin with. It was hardly the most desirable of places if you operated at the top end. If you wallowed around at the bottom, it was probably hell on earth.

So, yeah, maybe they had gone.

Or maybe they hadn't.

They *definitely* hadn't.

Tommy spied the beards before he noticed the men

themselves. Bushier than ever, they seemed to move separately from their respective bodies as they walked as one, huddled together, heads down and shoulders hunched. Your bog standard pedestrian scrambled to safety at the sight of them, avoided eye contact just in case.

In case what?

In case you caught *it*. It was contagious, after all. Everybody knew that. One lingering look too long, one touch too many, and you were doomed. Before you knew it, you'd be sleeping under a cardboard box. Drinking lighter fuel for breakfast. Fighting over discarded roll-ups.

No, it's not that I've got anything against them, but if the chance arose, yes, I would rather they didn't exist.

Regardless of his own faults, Tommy couldn't care less about any of that bullshit. He had been down on his luck in the past. And up. Up and down on the same day. Hour. Minute even. It wasn't about what you are, but who you are. A dick is still a dick whether you're dressed in a silk tie or a bin bag. No point arguing with that. The logic of a true visionary.

Despite his snail-like pace, Tommy hit the brakes too hard before parking up in the first available spot. He was out of the Mini a moment later. Smiled at the bullet holes that marked the car's bodywork. Agatha had promised to get it booked in for repairs, but Tommy was in no rush. The bullet holes gave him an edge. A fabricated back story created for the general public.

You don't mess with someone who's been shot at and lived to tell the tale. They were invincible. Indestructible.

They were Tommy fuckin' O'Strife, baby.

He locked the car and skipped across the road, dodging in between the traffic. Yeah, he was invincible, but that didn't mean it wouldn't hurt if someone clipped him. Once he was safely across, he ducked down a side street. He could see them in the distance. The last thing he wanted was to lose them now.

'Hey!'

The Beards jumped as the word bounced off the walls, echoing around them. Their natural fears kicked in and they thought about running. The fear subsided when they recognised the familiar face that was rushing up behind them, though.

'Hello there, fella'.'

'You look better than the last time we saw you.'

'Did you ever find your man? The one who clobbered you?'

'What do you reckon?' grinned Tommy. 'Let's just say that he won't be riding a bicycle in the foreseeable future.'

The Beards nodded amongst themselves. Shifted awkwardly from foot to foot.

'Is there something we can do for you?'

'It's been a while since we did much for anybody, in all honesty.'

'First time for everything.'

'I came here to give you this.' Tommy reached into his pocket. Removed the two thick bundles of banknotes he had stolen from Montague Manor. For a moment, he froze. Then the moment passed and he handed the bundles to the Beard in the middle. 'Share this out. Do what you like with it. Food ... drink ... drugs. Whatever takes your fancy.'

The middle Beard held it up. Stared at it in disbelief. 'No, no, we can't.'

'There's too much ... way too much.'

'There must be hundreds there.'

'Thousands,' said Tommy, correcting him. 'I started counting, but got bored. That could change your lives. I don't know ... maybe you don't want them changing. Like I said, it's yours. Spend it how you like.'

The Beards were warming to the idea.

'I don't know what to say.'

'This is ... unbelievable.'

'Don't you need it yourself?'

Tommy laughed. It was either that or cry. Of course he needed it. Needed *and* wanted it. He could do all sorts with that kind of cash. Some of it illegal, all of it enjoyable, none of it particularly healthy. 'Nah, you have it,' he replied through gritted teeth. 'I'm feeling generous.'

He turned to leave without another word. Better that than stare longingly at the money. The money that could change his own life.

Did it need changing, though? Was a life at Cockleshell Farm with the rest of the inmates really so bad?

No. Probably not. It was bearable. Just.

He started to walk. He could hear voices coming after him and the patter of excited feet.

'You're a lifesaver, my friend.'

'A real diamond. One of the best.'

'A true guardian angel.'

Tommy nodded and smiled and smiled and nodded, but refused to slow his step. He got back to the Mini and started the engine. Moving away from the kerb, the last thing he saw was the three Beards waving him off. Their facial hair disguised it, but they seemed happy. Ecstatic even.

It gave Tommy a warm glow.

That's for you, Agatha. And Mercy. Lucas. Rose. Even Miles, the over-privileged ponce. There was no denying it now. The proof was there for all to see and hear. Etched onto the faces of three hairy strangers who were down on their luck. Spoken by their joyous tongues. Say it loud and say it clear. Shout it out for all to hear.

Tommy O'Strife cared.

He had always cared.

He would always care.

Until the day he died, no pun intended.

CHAPTER SEVENTY-ONE

Violence erupted in the Mucky Duck public house at precisely two minutes past ten.

There was no warning. No knock at the door. No *come on in and introduce yourselves*.

Just a sudden explosion of sound and movement.

They surged through the doors like a scourge of rats. Rats in tracksuits and balaclavas. Armed to the teeth. Baseball bats and golf clubs mainly. Used to inflict damage at the earliest opportunity on mind, body and furniture.

Barry Blackstock, the landlord, was behind the bar. *His* bar. How dare they? Didn't they know who they were dealing with?

Ten minutes ago, he had been chairing the weekly meeting of the S.O.S Society. Save Our Stainmouth. It was a hard sell amongst the local community, but then not everyone was invited, anyway. Certainly not those that didn't belong. Whose faces didn't fit. Still, despite the lack of promotion, it had been a fairly strong turn-out. Thirteen. All men, but then women were harder to convince. If only he could get more followers on their side. More possible punters through the door.

Not like this, though.

'Get out of here!' cried Barry. He reached for a metal scaffolding pole he kept hidden under the bar. It had been sawn in half for ease of use. The perfect weapon for close combat.

At the same time, all thirteen members of the S.O.S Society jumped to their feet, clenched their fists or grabbed a pint glass, and got ready to engage in battle. To fight for the pub. For Stainmouth.

Fuck that, thought Barry. Let them smash the place up. He could claim it back on the insurance. Probably make a profit.

Head down, he hurried across the length of the bar until he made it to the other side. There was a door there. A door that led into a small courtyard at the back of the property. Barry rummaged about for the key. He found it as a bar stool hit the wall beside him. He kept his nerve and slotted the key into the hole. Turned until it clicked. Fingers shaking, he pulled down on the handle and squeezed through the opening. Closed the door gently behind him and locked it. Better to keep them all trapped inside than out there with him. He flinched at the sound of smashing glass. Bloody animals. They deserved everything that was coming to them.

Turning away from the door, Barry looked around the courtyard. He hadn't been out there for a week or two, but nothing much had changed. There were a few extra barrels and the odd crate scattered about, but that was all. If push came to shove, there was a gate that led out into the car park, but that was a last resort. With any luck, the fight would end quickly and the S.O.S Society would come out on top.

And if they didn't, well, so be it. Not his fault.

Barry sat down on an empty barrel, caught his breath. Surely that was the first rule of being a good leader. Know when you're outnumbered. Flee gracefully.

Live to fight another day.

He jumped as something moved in one corner of the courtyard. Most of the rats were inside, destroying his pub, but maybe one had scurried out into the open. He stood up. This was more like it. One on one. And he had a metal pole. A metal pole that he placed behind his back, ready to unleash when the time was right.

'We meet again.'

Barry watched as a figure stepped out of the shadows. Not a rat. Not even a kid. A woman. Young. Black.

'Who the fuck are you?'

'I'd rather not tell you my name,' replied Mercy. 'Don't want you passing it onto the police once I've beaten the shit out of you.'

Barry gestured towards the pub. 'Are they with you? Those thugs?'

Mercy shook her head. 'Not really. They're just hired help. I needed them to cause a disturbance. I had a feeling you might come running for cover if things got ugly inside.'

'Things are pretty ugly out here, too,' sneered Barry. He focussed on her face. 'You look familiar. And not in a good way. Have we met before?'

'Just the once,' said Mercy. 'You left a lasting impression on me, though. If I remember correctly, you said any time, any place. Well, here I am. *This* time. *This* place.'

Barry looked her up and down. Smirked. 'Get real. There's nothing on you.'

'And you're a big man, but you're in bad shape. With me it's a full-time job.' Mercy kept her face still. Tried not to smile. Nice line that. From an old film, but she couldn't remember which one.

'Oh, listen to you. Silly little bitch.' Barry turned his head towards the pub at the sound of an anguished cry. Mercy followed his gaze. It was the distraction he was hoping for.

Lunging forward, Barry brought the pole out from behind his back and swung it with all his might. He had Mercy's head in his sights, and would've connected if she hadn't ducked at the last moment.

He steadied himself and came again.

By now, Mercy had backed away. Re-positioned herself in the centre of the courtyard.

Barry swung and Mercy swerved to her left. As the pole passed her face, she leant into her attacker. He tried to swing again, but she was too close. Close enough to strike.

Barry doubled up as two blows hit him in the centre of his stomach. The breath caught and his body froze. He wanted to fight back, but that was impossible. Instead, he had to watch in despair as the woman's fist struck him under the chin. He dropped the pole and hit the ground soon after.

Mercy stood over him whilst he lay there, flat on his back, powerless to retaliate. 'The police will be here soon. They'll find a load of racist propaganda in the pub. Posters. Leaflets. Stickers. You'll be closed down. Prosecuted—'

'Bullshit,' cried Barry, spitting blood. 'I don't keep that sort of stuff on show.'

'You do now,' said Mercy. 'That's what those naughty boys and girls are doing even as we speak. Flyering the Mucky Duck. Enjoy your time in prison. I'll be waiting when you come out if you want to go again.'

Barry was still writhing around in agony, silently gasping, as Mercy passed through the gate. Without slowing, she made her way across the car park. She could hear movement behind her as the gang of youths from Rocketway Heights came running out of the pub. They were shouting, laughing. All still in one piece by the look of things. Mercy made a note to thank Agatha. She had called in a favour with crime boss, Zara Carmichael. Carmichael had provided the youths, and the youths had delivered.

Mercy picked up her speed at the sound of sirens. She didn't want to get caught up with the others.

She thought about Lucas as she started to run. What he had said to her back at Haversham Way.

You've got an anger issue.

He was wrong. Of course he was. Yes, she got angry, but it wasn't an issue. It was only an issue if it was a concern. A problem.

For Mercy, it was liberating. A release. That was the way it had been back in her boxing days. The way it would always be.

And the likes of Barry Blackstock did well to remember that.

CHAPTER SEVENTY-TWO
THE BEGINNING

Cole Burroughs didn't know what time it was.

Or what day. Week. Month. Year. Or where he was. Or how he had got there.

But he was alive.

He shouldn't have been, but he was.

He had been awake for several minutes now. The first minute he had spent trying to move. Bad idea. Largely because he couldn't. Not that there was anything holding him down. No straps or restraints. It was just the sheer effort it took. He simply didn't have the strength.

The next minute passed whilst he took in his surroundings. He was laid on his back, probably on a bed of some kind, in the centre of a square room. White walls and ceiling. Bright lights shining down on him. No windows. Practically empty, except for a selection of medical implements displayed on a small portable table.

A minute later, the door opened.

'Ah, you're awake.'

The voice edged closer until a friendly face appeared above the bed, blocking out the light. It was a man dressed in a long white overcoat. Late-twenties perhaps. Maybe younger. Smiling like he'd won the lottery.

'My name is Doctor Cheung. I'm here to take care of you.'

Cole cleared his throat. 'Am I in hospital?'

Doctor Cheung considered his answer. 'You're in a facility for those in need.'

'I don't want to be here.'

'It won't be forever. With any luck, you'll be fit and raring to go in no time. Isn't that what we all want?'

Cole didn't answer. Instead, he grabbed Cheung by the arm. Or, at least, tried to. In reality, his grip was weak, and the doctor removed his fingers like he was picking fluff off his jacket.

'You're still very fragile,' began Cheung, 'which is a shame because you have a visitor. I don't think you're ready, but she's very persistent. She also pays my wages, which makes it difficult for me to object to her demands. Just lay there and listen to what she has to say. I'll be back once she's gone to give you a more thorough examination.'

Doctor Cheung left the room without another word. In the blink of an eye, he was replaced by another. Almost an exact opposite, in fact. A woman. Early-sixties. Not smiling.

'Good afternoon, Mr Burroughs. It's nice to see you again.'

Cole closed his eyes. He knew it would be her. Who else could it be? 'I thought I was dead,' he croaked. 'I *wanted* to be dead.'

Agatha gently shook her head. 'It wasn't your time, I'm afraid. You're still here. And now you're stuck with me.'

'What about Tobias Montague?'

'Oh, he's dead,' replied Agatha casually. 'Unlike you, it wasn't quite worth the effort to keep him alive.'

Cole heard her words, processed them, but felt nothing. He tried to sit up, but soon gave in when the effort became too much. 'You're wasting your time,' he groaned. 'I'm no use to anybody.'

'No, not at the moment you're not,' agreed Agatha, 'but time is a wonderful healer. Your death would have been a tragic loss—'

Cole cut her off with a rasping bark. 'And who do you think's going to miss me? I've got nobody. You should've left me to die!'

'You're too good a man to just let slip away.'

'A good man?' Cole laughed. 'I'm no better than Montague.'

'You're good at what you do,' explained Agatha. 'You're a skilled professional. You perform at an elite level. Which is why I have a proposition for you. I want you to come and work for me. When you're ready. Not just physically, either. Mentally ready. I want you at your best.'

'I'm never going back to Stainmouth.'

'Who said anything about Stainmouth? Trust me, I'd rather not be there myself, but I'm somewhat anchored. No, I was thinking you could stretch your wings a little further afield. London perhaps. Or beyond.' Agatha leant forward until her hands were resting on the mattress. Stared at him with such intensity that he had little option but to look her in the eye. 'I'm not suggesting that this could ever replace your family,' she began, 'but it will give you a purpose. A meaning to your life. Don't waste that opportunity. Just run with it and see where it takes you. If nothing else, think it over. I'm not in any hurry.'

Cole took a breath. Winced as a sharp pain flared up in his chest, 'Do I have a choice?'

'Do any of us have a choice?' replied Agatha. 'But I'll ask you this. What's your alternative?'

'I could take my own life,' muttered Cole under his breath. 'The moment you leave the room. Or when I'm feeling better. I could end it once and for all. Draw a line under this empty existence. What would you do about that? What could you do to stop me?'

Agatha held up her hands. 'Nothing. But I wonder what Charlotte would make of that. Was that the kind of man she married? Weak? Selfish? And Sophie—'

'Don't,' said Cole. 'Please.'

'Then I won't.' Agatha glanced at her watch. 'Ah, I've got to go. Duty calls. You rest up and recover, and then we'll talk again. But I'll warn you now; I'm insufferably stubborn. You're a valuable asset to me alive. Practically priceless. I'd hate for you to waste those skills you've so finely crafted. Dead, however, you're just another corpse on a slab. Gone forever and soon to be forgotten. Think about it, Mr Burroughs. That's all I ask.'

With that, Agatha made her way towards the door. She didn't look back, didn't falter in her step. That wasn't her way. She wasn't playing games.

Her fingers were resting on the handle when Cole called out to her. 'Okay. I'm in.'

Agatha turned slowly. 'I'm sorry ...'

'I'm in,' repeated Cole. 'It appears that somebody, somewhere, doesn't want me to die, so, yeah, maybe I can do something. Something worthwhile. I don't know ... your words ... they seem to have ... connected.'

'I think they call that your conscience.' Marching across the room, Agatha stopped at the bed and rested a hand on her patient's shoulder. Smiled for the first time that day. 'You've made the right choice, Mr Burroughs,' she said. 'Welcome to the Nearly Dearly Departed Club. I look forward to working with you.'

NOTE TO READER

The end. I hope you enjoyed reading it. I certainly enjoyed writing it, so much so that I'm desperate to dive into book four in the series, which should be out by late summer '24. If only I had faster fingers ...

Feel free to leave a review on Amazon if leaving reviews on Amazon is your kind of thing. It's not easy for a new author so please be kind. Four or five stars would be nice. If you're drifting towards one or two stars then close your eyes, take a breath and try to erase everything I've written from your memory. Don't worry; Cole Burroughs won't appear in your bedroom in the middle of the night. And, even if he did, he'd only want to talk.

Big thanks to Stuart Bache for the cover. The best in the business. Excellent work as usual.

Stay safe and look after each other.

Until the next time ...

OTHER BOOKS IN THE SERIES

THE NEARLY DEARLY DEPARTED CLUB (BOOK 1)

Meet the Nearly Dearly Departed Club. Four random strangers with one thing in common. They're all dead. Deceased and departed. No longer with us.

Or maybe not …

Teenager Benji Hammerton has gone quiet. Worryingly so. Fearing the worst, his parents turn to the one person who might be able to help – Agatha Pleasant, an ageing secret agent who operates largely in the shadows, unburdened by rules and regulations. As luck would have it, Agatha has a batch of new recruits at her disposal. Untapped potential desperately in need of work experience.

Enter the Nearly Dearly Departed Club.

Their search takes them to Stainmouth, a grim Northern town with little to offer except bitter winds and a toxic atmosphere. With a life hanging in the balance, they hunt tirelessly for the missing boy. They make friends along the way, but also enemies. The kind of enemies who think nothing of taking a life if the need arises. As tensions mount, and the risks start to outweigh the rewards, the team question their involvement. Their purpose. Their future. Is any of it really worth dying for?

Especially when you're dead already ...

LOST SOULS FOREVER (BOOK 2)

For better or worse, the Nearly Dearly Departed Club are back ... and this time it's a matter of life and death.

Or rather, stay alive long enough to protect the dead. That's the plan, at least. But then what do they say about best laid plans?

There's been a death at HM Prison Stainmouth. The corpse in question is one Impetus Stokes, criminal mastermind, found dead in his cell from an overdose. For no obvious reason, Agatha Pleasant's team of squabbling misfits are assigned the task of collecting his coffin, sitting on it for a few days before handing it over to the necessary authorities. It makes no sense whatsoever, but then why break the habit of a lifetime?
Besides, how hard can it be to watch over a coffin?
Very hard, as it happens. Practically impossible. Especially when the dead refuse to stay dead.

Something that the Nearly Dearly Departed Club are only too aware of themselves.

Printed in Great Britain
by Amazon